By Dean Murray

Forsaken

Dean Murray

Forsaken is a work of fiction. Names, characters, places and incidents are the products of the author's imagination or are used fictitiously. Any resemblance to actual events, locales, or persons, living or dead, is entirely coincidental.

Published by Fir'shan Publishing

ISBN 978-1-9393633-5-0

www.FirshanPublishing.com

First Edition

For the Alec or Adri that lives inside each of us

Chapter 1

Alec Graves
Graves Estate
Sanctuary, Utah

The blank canvas staring at me hadn't changed in weeks. I still went through the motions, still came here regularly and mixed up paints, but I hadn't managed to actually paint anything since she'd left.

I was going to have to order another set of blank canvases before too much longer. It was ludicrous in so many ways, but it was the only way to keep up appearances. The pack was hanging together mostly out of sheer inertia these days. I, for one, wasn't eager to do anything to upset the status quo. As long as I kept retiring into my studio on a regular basis, there was still a chance that nobody would think to ask if I was still painting.

Once they asked, I wouldn't be able to lie. I'd have been willing to lie—it seemed that there wasn't much I wasn't willing to do anymore—but they'd smell the deception immediately. When you lived with people who could hear your heartbeat change and smell your body start to perspire, misdirection became the best way to avoid having to face up to truths that you didn't particularly want to share with everyone.

I heard Jasmin coming while she was still several seconds away. It gave me plenty of time to make sure I looked convincing when she arrived.

"Alec, we've got a problem. The first of the dispossessed just arrived."

I nodded, looked at my brush and palette, and then just mentally shrugged as I dropped them both into a wastebasket. It was probably time to get another set of supplies ordered anyway.

Pack life wasn't a very simple thing, and it wasn't even always very desirable. True submissives tended to stay with a pack because of the protection that packs offered, but dominants were another matter. There were occasionally dominants like Ash who were happy to lead a solitary life, but for the most part, wolves were social beings.

Most dominants wanted to belong to a pack, but more importantly, they wanted to rule a pack. When their abilities fell short of their aspirations, they often found themselves run out of the pack that they'd failed to take over. Some of them ended up joining up with the Coun'hij, the shape shifter ruling body, as one of their bully boys, but most of them were too rebellious for even the Coun'hij to put up with them.

They weren't any real danger to a healthy pack, but they posed a potentially fatal problem for a weakened pack.

Our pack was the definition of unhealthy right now, and it was small enough that it would draw challengers sooner rather than later. I'd actually been expecting the first challenger to arrive a week earlier.

I gestured for Jasmin to lead the way and then followed her out of my studio.

"Has Ash returned from Vegas yet?"

Jasmin shook her head, and the motion spoke volumes about our situation.

"No, he's still gone, and Dominic is still not doing well. I saw her and James earlier today, and she looked like she'd been run over by a truck."

It was another concern. Jasmin was putting on a good front, but I knew she wasn't in a whole lot better shape than Dom was. In a human it would have been the kind of thing that I'd have just chalked up to a virus, but shape shifters were supposed to be immune to pretty much every pathogen there was.

There were exceptions to every rule, but Rachel seemed to have whatever it was too, and that was even harder to explain away. I'd had Donovan cart Rachel into town so Dr. Samuels could run a bunch of different blood work on her, but he'd found nothing that explained how tired she was all of the time.

I couldn't send Jas or Dominic in for the same kind of tests, not without blowing some poor lab tech's mind with the fact that neither of them was quite human, but the fact that Rachel's results had come back clean was a pretty good bit of evidence that whatever it was couldn't be explained by purely physical means.

I hadn't said anything to the rest of the pack, not even to Donovan, but I was pretty sure the Coun'hij were somehow responsible. It still wasn't a very likely explanation. None of the Coun'hij were rumored to have anything at all like the ability to inflict the kind of general malaise that we were seeing, but I hadn't missed out on the fact that it was bringing down the three people who were the most loyal to me. I kept thinking that if the Coun'hij really did have a secret weapon, then pulling Dom, Rachel and Jasmin out of the power structure was pretty much guaranteed to cause our pack problems.

Despite the fact that Jasmin was moving a bit more slowly than normal, we were still making good time. We only had a few seconds before we'd be within earshot of the front door.

"What's this guy like?"

"About James' size, and he gives off enough power that I'm pretty sure he's a hybrid. I've never heard of him, though, so I don't think he's got any kind of extra ability over and above the normal."

I nodded. It was a reasonable assumption on more levels than one. Most of the hybrids who developed any kind of useful power tended to end up ruling a pack, but you never knew when someone who had been a plain-Jane hybrid would manifest a power that was sufficient to shake things up. It didn't happen often, but it did happen. More telling was the fact that this guy was the first challenger we'd seen.

Any of the really powerful dispossessed would wait to make their move until they had a better idea of what they'd be up against. The weaker hybrids would move first either because they were hoping for a lucky break or because they were pushed into doing it by someone higher up on the food chain.

"Who's with him?"

"Isaac and Donovan. I called James on my way, so he'll be bringing Dom. Jess is still gone."

I grunted. Jess wouldn't have made much difference even if she'd been here. She'd been our weakest fighter even before she'd lost her memories. Now that she was missing all of the experience she'd racked up fighting Brandon's pack for all of those years, she was even more useless in a fight.

"It's going to have to be you who leads off, Jas. I don't particularly like it, but if Dom is still as bad off as you're saying, then sending her in against a hybrid is just too risky."

It was the truth, but it wasn't the whole truth. I hated the state we'd come to. Jasmin knew exactly the kinds of games I was forced to play. If I sent Dominic in first, James would be even more pissed at me than normal, and he'd have a decent reason to be mad. Dom was seriously off her game right now. I could lead with her anyway and tell Jasmin to sit the fight out. It would be a way to guarantee that James entered the fight as soon as things started going bad for Dom, but that wasn't the way that I wanted to run the pack.

Instead I was going to send Jasmin in, knowing that she wasn't at the top of her game, and hope that James appreciated the gesture enough to jump in before things got too dire for her. It wasn't the kind of thing I wanted to do, but it was my best chance of earning some brownie points with James, and I needed to get the pack working together again.

Jasmin looked at me for several seconds and then finally nodded. "I'll do my best, but I'm not going to be able to bring this guy down by myself. You'll have to get James in the mix pretty fast or I'm going to be out of commission for a while."

We crossed into the range of the white noise generator that Isaac or Donovan had turned on when the challenger had arrived. It wasn't safe to talk anymore so I was left with nothing to distract me from my thoughts.

My asking Jasmin to lead was also telling as far as the status of my on-again, off-again ability went. I'd been told since I was little that I had the potential of developing an incredibly powerful 'extra' ability, but it had steadfastly refused to materialize until the night I'd faced off against a rival pack leader in a fight to the death that everyone knew I couldn't win. I'd been well on my way to losing the battle, and then all of a sudden, it had been like a rift opened up inside of me and sucked in power from everyone around me.

I'd brought two whole packs to their knees before the rift closed, but luckily I'd been the one to recover from the experience the fastest, which had allowed me to kill the rival pack leader. Since then, there had been a number of times when it would have been really useful to uncork my ability and bring people to their knees. Unfortunately, each time I'd reached for my power I'd come away with nothing.

When we'd gone up against a rogue cat from south of the border, there'd been the hint of something there as I'd tried to drain him of power and energy, but it hadn't been nearly as effective as the night I'd killed Brandon. I managed to slow him down a little, but I'd slowed the rest of my pack down nearly as badly, so the net effect had only been slightly positive.

The surest way for us to shut down the stream of dispossessed challengers we no doubt had coming our way would be for me to use my power to instantly level the first couple who came up against us. Unfortunately, it was looking more and more like my power was going to refuse to come when called.

Barring me being able to pull the equivalent of a tactical nuke out of my pocket, our next best bet was to demonstrate that we had a string of capable pack members that any challenger would have to go through before they'd get a shot at me. Six months ago, I would have said that everyone in the pack would have stepped forward at need to help send the right message to the rest of the shape shifter world at large. Now I wasn't so sure.

Jasmin would do her best, and her lineage granted her an extra degree of deadliness that most normal wolves couldn't hope to match, but given her current state, the best I could hope for was that she'd tire him out a little and bleed him enough to slow him down. Dom was out of the question unless I was prepared to run a much higher likelihood than normal that she wouldn't survive even long enough for Jasmin or one of the others to tap in, and Isaac was probably still pissed off at me for refusing to let him go camping with Jessica and Andrew.

That meant that things depended entirely on James. If he jumped in to relieve Jasmin and then managed to conclude the fight, we'd send a strong message that any other challengers would have to go through Jasmin and James just to get to Isaac. If James couldn't bring the fight to a resolution, then there was a chance I'd be pulled in to save James and we'd be telling everyone that all they needed to do to take our pack over was beat Jasmin, James and me.

Jasmin and I came around the last corner before the front reception area, and I got my first look at the shape shifter who was going to do his best to kill us over the next few minutes. He was a tall redhead, maybe even a little bigger than James, and he looked old enough that I suspected he was more dangerous than Jasmin had initially thought. Nobody made it into middle age as one of the dispossessed without being a very good fighter.

James and Dom were both there, which I'd expected, but I hadn't anticipated James' mother would accompany them. Addison was usually the last person to take an interest in a fight, but whenever she did show up for something, it invariably spelled trouble. I noted her presence and then confirmed that Donovan and Isaac were also there before acknowledging the challenger.

"What brings you to our territory uninvited, unwelcome?"

The challenger smiled, but it didn't reach his eyes. "My name is Derrick, and I come here to challenge your right to rule your pack."

I nodded as though it wasn't something everyone present had known since the second Derrick had set foot in our territory.

"That is your right, but we won't do that here. There is a space out back that is more appropriate for a challenge."

Derrick nodded, obviously trying to look unshaken, but still unable to fully mask the flash of relief that went through him at my implicit confirmation that the Sanctuary pack would be honoring his challenge right. It was rare, but some packs had been known to attack a challenger en masse, killing them rather than granting the challenge.

It was a dangerous, short-term game to play, but it had been known to happen. At some point though, word of their actions inevitably got out, and when that happened, the dispossessed always banded together and destroyed the offending pack.

There was very little the dispossessed could agree on, but nearly all of them held challenge law as sacrosanct. Their ongoing ability to challenge for a place in a pack represented their only real hope of leaving the solitary existence to which they'd been consigned.

I noted Derrick's relative inexperience with actual challenges and then motioned for Donovan to lead the way. There were traditions around nearly every aspect of a challenge, and this was no different. The weakest member of the pack led the way, then the challenger, then the rest of the pack, starting with the other weaker members and ending with the alpha. It minimized the risk to both the challenger and the pack. The challenger could attack Donovan, but if he did so, he'd quickly be swarmed under by the rest of the pack. It also meant that there was a buffer of space between him and the pack's hybrids, so he had at least a chance of being able to flee in the event of deception on the part of the pack, as long as he didn't stop to attack Donovan on his way out.

If I'd had my choice, I would have put James' mother in Donovan's place. Both of them were crippled from what the Coun'hij had done to them decades ago, but Donovan ran the pack's financial affairs. More importantly, to my mind at least, Donovan could be counted on to support me, while Addison took every possible chance to make my life difficult.

A few minutes later, we arrived. The sandy square that we'd all taken to calling Donovan's Zen Garden, was sheltered from observation by trees, both above and to the sides, and offered a chance to use the terrain to our advantage. It was a small chance, but our experience fighting on the shifting medium was the closest thing we had to a home court advantage.

The challenge rules required all fights to take place outside so that other dispossessed could watch from afar if they wanted to. The Zen

Garden met the requirement of being outside, but not the bit about others being able to watch. It was another risk, but that was one of the rules that had taken a beating over the last few years. With modern technology it was getting harder and harder to keep our existence a secret, so I felt relatively comfortable running this particular risk. Still, only time would tell whether or not the dispossessed at large would agree that secrecy trumped their need to monitor challenges.

I used the brief pause afforded by Derrick walking over to the other side of the arena to look over the pack. Dominic, standing on the other side of James, looked tired, but determined. She stepped forward, planning on being the first to engage Derrick, but I waved her back as Jasmin stepped forward. James gave me a considering look, but I'd already moved on to Isaac.

Isaac folded his arms and stared at me in a way that I knew meant he wasn't going to back down. For more years than I cared to think about, Isaac had been my strong right hand, but he'd started to lose some of his trademark calm since Jess had lost her memories. I hadn't been able to decide whether the stress of trying to court Jess was getting to him, or if Jess had somehow been the source of his serenity.

Whichever it was, the loss was becoming a greater and greater problem. He'd thrown nearly a James-style fit when Jess and Andrew had told him that they wanted to go camping without him, and that hadn't been like Isaac at all. The old Isaac would have understood that Andrew was his biggest ally in the fight to win Jess' heart and would have welcomed the sign that Jess was at least interested in reconnecting with her father. The new Isaac fixated on the fact that Jess was actively cutting him out of her life and tried to bully her into including him.

I tilted my head questioningly, and Isaac frowned. It seemed like he was surprised at his own response, but he shook his head slowly and then refused to meet my eyes. It wasn't surprising to me, but it was no less frustrating for being what I'd expected out of him. It would be Jasmin, James and me after all.

Derrick reached the other side of the sand, turned around, and called up his beast with a surge of power that was greater than I'd expected out of our first challenger. One second, a fairly large man stood across from us, and then in the next instant, we were faced with a tower of muscle, fangs, and claws.

His hybrid form was at least six foot three and had to weigh in at somewhere around three hundred and twenty pounds, but Jasmin didn't even hesitate. Her wolf form exploded out and then she was in motion towards him. Jasmin played the hothead, but when it came to a fight, she was as calculating as just about anyone I knew. She moved towards him to trigger motion on his part and then carefully gauged her speed so that they met on our half of the field.

It was a shrewd action that made sure James didn't have as far to run when it came time for him to take her place, but it meant she had to duck under Derrick's first attack. Jasmin didn't normally fight a defensive game, and it put her off balance slightly. Only the fact that Derrick didn't seem entirely comfortable fighting on the sand saved Jas from a nasty slash across her side, but then she was past him and spinning around to tear into his leg.

Jasmin released him and rolled with the force of the backhand that he landed on her, shaken but obviously not down yet. She couldn't kill him fast from behind, but she didn't need to kill him, not with James waiting in the wings. Instead, Jasmin fought aggressively but focused more on bleeding him and tiring him out.

The fight was taking a toll on Jas; she had to be bruised from one end to the other, and Derrick had landed a couple of deep slashes on her left flank. She was taking a beating, but he was moving more slowly now from the chunk she'd taken out of his right leg, and he'd lost more blood than she had so far.

James leaned forward, anxious to join the fight. He knew as well as I did that the best possible outcome would be for Jasmin to win the fight, but he couldn't help himself. James liked a good fight more than just about anything else.

Jasmin was working the perimeter, burning up incredible reserves of energy as she kept Derrick in motion. She wasn't as fast as she normally was, but she still had an edge over any non-royal wolf, and it was obvious Derrick was having a hard time adjusting to just how fast she was. A sudden burst of speed caught Derrick off guard and he pushed his leg too far as he tried to compensate.

Derrick's injured leg collapsed underneath him, and Jasmin changed directions instantly. My breath caught as she launched herself into the air and then landed on Derrick with a hammer blow of force that spun him around in a half circle as her fangs latched onto his shoulder. Derrick let the momentum imparted by Jasmin's attack continue to spin him around, and he converted it into a fall that very nearly crushed her beneath him.

Jasmin had already started jumping away by the time Derrick hit the ground, but she landed awkwardly and a yelp of pain made it out of her before she rolled back to her feet. There was a hitch to Jasmin's motions now. I was pretty sure she'd broken a rib, but Derrick's right arm hung limply at his side. She'd managed to savage the muscles of his shoulder enough that he couldn't lift it, which meant that even if Jasmin couldn't finish the fight James should easily prevail. My shoulders relaxed slightly as I realized that Isaac's unwillingness to fight would remain a secret.

It was tempting to see if Jasmin could finish Derrick off, but she was noticeably slower now. If she won it would buy us some more time before the next challenger, but there was just too much risk that Derrick would kill her. I opened my mouth and quietly said James' name.

James smiled and called his beast with an explosion of power. Before James could move, two things happened that I hadn't been expecting.

Jasmin felt James transform and took another calculated risk. She launched herself at Derrick in an all-out bid to kill him. It made my stomach drop slightly, but it was a smart risk to take. She knew that James was on his way, so she had one last chance to finish the fight, and even if she failed, there was a reasonable chance that Derrick wouldn't be able to kill her in turn before James got to him.

Jasmin's action was perfect. Addison's move made me want to kill her, and it wasn't just my beast powering the fury that washed over me.

Addison reached out and grabbed James' hand. She wasn't even close to strong enough to stop him in his human form, let alone when he was a hybrid, but he deferred to her with the force of nearly two decades of habit and stopped in his tracks.

If I'd had any questions about whether or not she realized what she was doing, they were answered as she gave me a self-satisfied smile. I had two courses open to me. I could force the issue with James and Addison, or I could save Jasmin.

Addison's power play had taken the barest fraction of a second. Jasmin was still in flight, but Derrick was already reacting. His good hand was coming up to intercept her. It was going to be close, but Jasmin had known that all along. She was counting on the pack to back her play and I couldn't leave her out there unsupported, not even if it was going to put all of us in a worse position in the long run.

I tore open the cage that I used to keep my beast confined to one corner of my being and launched myself towards Jasmin and Derrick as my transformation completed. My hybrid form was several inches taller than Derrick's and I had an incredible weight advantage on my side, but even as I streaked towards the two combatants, I was reaching inside myself trying to activate the power that had dropped Brandon and his pack instantly. Even this late in the fight, if I was able to manifest my power, it would cut off the stream of challengers that we were otherwise going to have to face, but nothing responded to my desperate efforts to trigger my ability.

Jasmin hit Derrick and her mouth fastened closed on the side of his neck, but the semi-retractable claws on his left hand had already found purchase on her stomach. As his hand sank into her flesh, Jasmin let go of Derrick and dropped towards the sand, but I collided with him at the same time that she impacted on the ground.

I tried to take his bad leg into account, but I had to make sure he didn't have a chance to finish Jasmin off, so I ended up overestimating the amount of force needed to bowl him over. Derrick hit the ground with enough force to send sand spraying out all the way to the far end of the square, and then our momentum sent us rolling.

Derrick got the talons on both of his feet into my legs, but I was focused on controlling his left hand because it was the threat most able to end the fight quickly. As we stopped rolling, I found myself on the bottom with blood flowing freely from both of my legs. I was taking a lot of damage, but I ignored the pain and brought my left leg up against his chest, pushing as I kept ahold of his left hand.

I felt his talons tear free as he flipped over my head and then I rolled on top of him, savaging his legs and chest as I got into position for a kill. A second later, I had my left hand around his throat, but something stopped me from ending the fight. I knew that later I'd come up with a host of reasons why I didn't kill him, but in that instant I just couldn't bring myself to do it.

Instead of ripping his throat out, I sank my claws into his chest, puncturing one of his lungs, and then broke his left arm. It was a brutal thing to do to another person, but I couldn't leave him in a condition to resume his attack, at least not until Jasmin and I both had a chance to heal from the injuries that he'd inflicted on us.

I pulled his face around so that the yellow eyes of his beast met my blue eyes. "I'm leaving you alive so you can testify that we're honoring the rules of challenge. Make sure the rest of the dispossessed know that. You've had your shot at us. I won't spare your life next time, so don't come back."

I waited until Derrick nodded in understanding and then I backhanded him with enough force to knock even a hybrid unconscious.

There was silence as the rest of the pack watched me pull myself back to my feet. Isaac and James both knew I would be within my rights to challenge them this instant. Given the fight I'd just been through, they could probably beat me, but that would just leave whoever won the alpha of an even smaller pack and would do absolutely nothing to stem the tide of dispossessed that they both knew were on their way.

I pointed to Derrick. "James, Isaac, put him in one of the cages and then load him into the cargo truck. Donovan will hire a driver to get him several hundred miles away from here before he wakes up."

They both nodded and then started towards Derrick, but I held my hand up. "This isn't over, not even close."

I didn't wait for their responses, instead limping over to Donovan and Dominic, who were both desperately trying to slow Jasmin's bleeding. I let my human form bubble up as I pushed my beast back into the corner where I normally kept it locked up. Dominic kept pressure on Jasmin's stomach as I bent down and picked her up.

The journey back to the house took twice as long as normal, but Donovan hurried on ahead of us and had a blood transfusion prepped by the time we made it into the operating room. Rachel was there as well; she pulled on a pair of gloves and started handing Donovan clamps and suture thread as Dominic started taping up the worst of my injuries.

I closed my eyes and tried to ignore the pain, but I couldn't block out the sounds of Donovan trying to save Jasmin's life. Half an hour later, Donovan leaned back with a sigh that made me look over at him.

"She'll be okay. Her body's own regenerative powers are finally starting to kick in."

I nodded and my fists unclenched. "I'm glad she made it. I never meant to leave her in so long."

Donovan nodded, looked at Dominic as though debating whether to wait for her to leave the room before continuing, and then finally resumed speaking.

"What are you going to do? The pack won't last long if neither James or Isaac are willing to help with the challengers."

I could feel a headache starting. "Honestly? I'm not sure. I could always beat the two of them into submission, assuming we have enough time before the next batch of challengers arrive, but that isn't the kind of dynamic that I want in the pack. We'd be better off scattering and finding new packs that each need a person or two than continuing like that."

Rachel patted Jasmin's arm and then smiled. "At least Jasmin is okay. Hopefully she'll be able to get fully back on her feet before the next challenger arrives."

I nodded, but I didn't have much hope of that. The best I could do would be to call Ash back and hope that he was able to bring down the next challenger more or less by himself.

"Honestly, sis, I wish I could just send Jasmin away for the next little while. She could use a break from the craziness of pack life. Nearly anywhere would be safer than here."

Rachel looked at me oddly. For a second it seemed like she was almost looking through me.

"Alec, just because someone is far away doesn't mean they are safe. There are plenty of threats out there that won't respect someone's desire to stay apart from the violence and danger that is part of pack life. Even a normal human is in danger nearly all of the time."

I would have to have been a fool not to know exactly what she was getting at, and half of me felt a sharp stab of pain at the reminder of what I'd lost. The other half of me was angry with her for the risk she was running. I'd forbidden everyone in the pack from mentioning Adri's name and I'd sealed the order with an imperative backed up by my beast. If Rachel had come right out and said, 'Adri isn't safe,' then I wouldn't have been able to stop myself. As it was, it took a supreme act of will to stop from throwing her into a wall.

"You are skating on the very edge, Rachel."

She shook herself, almost like she was coming out of a dream, and for a moment it seemed like she wasn't sure what I was talking about.

"I'm sorry, Alec. I didn't mean to do it."

I held her gaze for several seconds before nodding. The anger had served to cushion me from the worst of the pain, but I still wanted to put my head in my hands and cry. The tears hadn't come, not even right after *she'd* left, but I'd wanted them to come and give me some kind of release.

I couldn't escape the room, not without showing how much Rachel's comment had bothered me, and I couldn't afford that kind of weakness, not right now. I couldn't escape, but I couldn't tear my mind away from *her*, from Adri, either.

The way she'd looked the day that she'd come to tell me that she was leaving Sanctuary had burned itself in my mind. The decision obviously hadn't been easy for her, but her resolve had been equally visible and it had made her even more beautiful than normal. I'd had to stand there and watch as she first condemned me and then turned and walked out of my life forever.

It had been like having an angel come down and open the door to the Garden of Eden and then push you back out into the wilderness before you'd had a chance to sample the fruit whose aroma had been pulling you deeper and deeper into the garden. I'd seen paradise, and the washed-out world to which I'd been exiled was hellish in comparison to what I'd felt when I'd been with her.

Rachel's words spun around inside my mind, and I found myself suddenly conscious of all of the ways, supernatural or mundane, in which Adri could be endangered despite finally being a safe distance away from us, from me. I'd spent so much of the few weeks we'd had together trying to convince her to flee, to find somewhere safer than Sanctuary, but I'd never considered just how much danger she would be in no matter where she went.

She was in New York. It would be hard to find another place in North America with a higher concentration of vampires than Manhattan.

Even assuming she managed to avoid being killed by a bloodsucker, there was no guarantee she wouldn't run afoul of a werewolf, and that didn't even consider the fact that the Coun'hij wasn't above using her as a pawn to get back at me for having stood Agony off.

Isaac walked into the room, simultaneously interrupting my thoughts and providing me with a way to solve two problems at once.

"We got Derrick in the cage, so even if he loses control, Donovan's driver will be safe. The truck is loaded, all we need is a location and a time and we'll make the handoff."

I nodded, and then held up a hand. "James can make the drop once Donovan has had a chance to make the arrangements. I want you on a plane within the next hour. Pack for an extended trip."

Isaac's control was still frayed, and I could almost see the thoughts flowing around inside his head. He would like nothing more than to attack me, to force me to bow to his will, but he knew that wouldn't get him what he wanted. If our pack fell apart, there was no guarantee right now that Jess would choose to go with him. He could very easily find himself in a new pack all by himself.

"Where are you sending me, and how long is 'extended'?"

"You're going to Manhattan. I've just had it rather forcefully pointed out to me that there are all kinds of dangers in the big city, and you're going to go make sure that nothing happens to the member of our pack who lives there."

Isaac's anger was rising. I was backing him into a corner where he risked death if he obeyed me as well as if he refused.

"It's forbidden by the Coun'hij for any of the moonborn to go east of the Mississippi! She doesn't even want anything to do with us. You can't order me to make a trip like that, not for Adr..."

I'd pulled myself to my feet while he was pacing back and forth, and now I found myself standing in front of him with my claws around his throat and no recollection of having crossed the distance between us.

"Be very, very careful. The imperative still stands, and if you say her name I *will* kill you."

Isaac cleared his throat and then nodded jerkily.

"This is nothing more than an overly extreme punishment. The old Alec never would have done this."

I released my hold on him and let my hand shrink back down to the one I'd been born with.

"You risked the entire pack by your refusal to fight today. Every dispossessed hybrid in North America will rightly assume that all they have to do is kill one or two regular wolves in order to get their chance at me. They'll line up for the chance to take over the pack, and you could have at least stemmed the tide slightly by stepping in and protecting Jasmin. How many challengers will we end up fighting who would have steered clear at the prospect of facing two accomplished hybrids before even having a shot at me?"

"What good will stemming the tide mean if we're still ultimately going to be worn down?"

None so blind as those that refuse to see. I shrugged and swept my arm around, taking in the manor and everything else in the area.

"I don't know, Isaac. I don't have any bulletproof solutions right now, but anything we can do to buy us more time will give us a chance to find a way out of this hole."

Donovan stepped forward and cleared his throat.

"If I may, Master Alec. It might be prudent to kill Derrick. While it's not something easy to contemplate, if he never reports back to the rest of the dispossessed, that would help alleviate the problems that have arisen today."

I'd known Donovan would make the recommendation, but it still angered me that he'd done so with Rachel in the room. I'd done everything I could to shelter her from the worst aspects of what I was. I'd failed miserably in most of the ways that mattered, but I wouldn't let her see her older brother become a cold-blooded murderer.

"No, he lives. If I kill him now, that buys us a couple of weeks; then we're back here again in the exact same situation. There's no guarantee that Isaac and James won't pull the same stunt then that they pulled today. I won't sell my soul to cover for Isaac or James' bad decision. I may be an animal, but there are some things that I still won't do, especially when they aren't guaranteed to save us in the end."

I held Isaac's gaze for several seconds, watching his anger war with his reason, and then pointed at the door.

"Pack your bags, Isaac. You're going to be gone for a while, and if you let anything happen to *her*, I'll kill you. You're starting to reap some of the consequences of your actions."

Isaac had been gone for quite a while before Dominic tentatively cleared her throat.

"Alec, you need to send me away at some point. You need to punish James—I understand that—and the best option is for me to go to New York. Otherwise you'll have to send James away, and that would hurt the pack more than having me gone."

I rubbed my temples and wished once again that I could just disappear for a couple of days.

"I don't want to send you away, Dom. I know how much you'll miss James, and the rest of the pack. It doesn't seem fair to punish you at the same time that I'm punishing James, but you're right that it would be good if we could find a way to keep James around for the next challenger who comes through."

Dom smiled, but it was a sad expression. "I know, Alec. I love James, maybe more than he loves me, and I will miss Rachel and the others, but I understand what is at stake. If this is what it takes to make James see reason, then I'll do it. I never expected that I'd find the kind of happiness I've found here in Sanctuary. *I* won't run out on you after having received such a gift."

Chapter 2

Adriana Paige
Brathingford High School
Manhattan, New York

The clock had become my constant enemy. It wasn't just that I desperately wanted school to be over with each day. I did. It was the fact that I wanted the evenings to be over with too. The only escape that had even a hint of promise was a year and a half away, and even then I wasn't sure that college was going to be any better.

Mom was the happiest she'd ever been. Work was going great; we had more money than she knew what to do with, and if she wasn't shooting the kinds of stuff that she wanted to, she was still starting to become well known inside the fashion industry. She kept telling me that this was just temporary, that she was going to work some time into her schedule to do some landscape shoots, but I wasn't so sure.

From the outside looking in, it was starting to appear as though she was addicted to the acclaim. I didn't know what to do about that other than hope that she'd pull out of it so we could at least leave the city. She'd stood by me when I'd spent half a year basically falling apart anytime I even thought of Dad and Cindi's accident. I figured that meant I should do what I could to support her while she worked through her own coping mechanism. It just would have been a little easier if I'd been going to another school, preferably not on the East Coast.

Brathingford was one of those grand experiments that someone with more money than sense had decided to undertake as a way of 'giving back' to the community. It had been billed as a school for anyone who showed promise, which was how it had gotten so much support initially from the city. The billionaire who had funded everything had run into absolutely zero issues getting the permits he needed to tear down a quarter of a city block and then rebuild it with the state of the art in teaching.

Projectors, smart boards, screaming fast Wi-Fi. If you could think of it, we probably had it, up to and including two full-sized swimming pools and a gymnastics gym that was only a slight step down from the Olympic Training Center in Colorado.

Unfortunately, the construction had run severely over budget, which hadn't seemed like a problem until a massive shock to the real estate market had wiped out two thirds of the billionaire's fortune.

Suddenly the school needed to pay for itself and the students 'with promise' had started coming exclusively from the city's wealthiest. I didn't have anything against rich people—I'd known some really, really rich people that I'd liked a lot—but the students here all seemed like they lived in a permanent bubble.

A wave of dizziness swept through me, but I'd been expecting it, so I just grabbed ahold of the table I was sitting at and weathered the spell. I still struggled a little sometimes with thinking about Cindi and my dad, but by and large the attacks had disappeared, and when they did show up they weren't really very bad.

Mom attributed it to us getting out of Sanctuary, and therefore took credit for them in a roundabout way, but they'd actually more or less disappeared while I'd been dating Alec. My heart rate shot up a bit, but I knew my limits; I took a couple of calming breaths and felt my body start to relax a little.

These days I was coping better with the loss of half of my family, but I was struggling with a different loss. As long as I was careful to limit how much I thought of *him* during the course of a given day, I tended to be okay. It was still touch and go occasionally, but it seemed like the psychiatrist had been right for a change. Time and distance was gradually taking off the edge of having lost Alec.

I picked up the thread my thoughts had been following earlier and shook my head slightly as I looked around the bright, open study space. The girls almost all sported artificial tans and six-hundred-dollar backpacks, and they had never had to worry about anything more serious than whether or not they'd get asked to Prom.

Even before, back when I'd lived in Minneapolis, I still wouldn't have had anything in common with the kids in this school. After my experiences in Sanctuary, I almost felt like we were from different species entirely. There was a world outside these walls where people fought and died without the local news stations having any idea anything was happening, and I'd been in it up to my eyeballs for a few short months.

It put all of the games that the boys and girls at Brathingford played into stark perspective. Questions of whose parents were the richest paled against the fact that I knew there were things that went bump in the night, things that were all the more terrifying because they looked just like anyone else.

I looked back up at my enemy, the self-satisfied digital clock on the wall, and sighed. It was time to go to my math lecture. Brathingford heavily utilized recorded lectures to give students the chance to 'go at their own pace,' but I still had to go to actual classes from time to time. The concept was actually pretty neat because it meant that I'd been able to finish up my algebra class way faster than I'd expected. I just logged onto the intranet, watched a lecture, and then did the assigned homework problems. Once I'd demonstrated mastery of a particular concept, the system opened up the next section for me to watch.

Nearly all of my classmates were smart, but while some of them took advantage of the flexibility to learn faster than they could have, most of them just spent more time screwing around and less time in lectures.

I was back to having absolutely no social life since we'd moved, so I just liked that it meant I could avoid interaction with most of my peers and teachers more than I could have at another school. I still had to go to mandatory lectures, though, for whichever unit I was on. At least the lectures just covered much larger blocks of material and were more along the lines of a question and answer session where the students got to ask the teachers about the concepts they were either struggling with or interested in.

I also had weekly twenty-minute sessions with a counselor who checked to make sure that my progress through the various subjects was on track for me to graduate at the end of my senior year. I figured I might as well get as much out of the fortune that Mom was spending on tuition as I could, so I was well ahead of plan in every single subject.

I packed up my school-issued electronic tablet, and the coat that just barely sufficed for a New York winter, and headed off to the auditorium that had been assigned to my math section for the next hour and a half. I arrived early enough to get a seat at the back of the class—more because I wanted a corner to myself where I could ignore everyone else than for any other reason.

Ten seconds before the lecture started, a flash of movement caught my eye and I looked up to see Isaac sit down at the front of the class. His presence in New York was so unexpected that my mind struggled to accept that it was all real rather than some kind of hallucination. My thoughts automatically went to Alec and a flash of vertigo rocked me in my seat.

I got my systems back under control, but it was a close thing. I'd already used up too much of my quota of Alec thoughts for the day. I tore my eyes away from Isaac and focused on my tablet. I already knew I wouldn't learn anything important from the lecture. My professor was young, energetic and personable, but he was more flash than fire. He was capable of answering questions and explaining the concepts in the units we'd be reviewing today, but he was no Mrs. Campbell.

I opened up a history quiz that I'd been saving specifically for this lecture, and started through the questions, but my gaze kept flowing back up to Isaac. He looked much like I remembered. He was still as massive as a college lineman and unlike the rest of the students, all of whom sported only their tablets, he also had a pair of hardback books on his desk.

I watched out of the corner of my eye as Isaac blatantly ignored the lecture, instead spending the time reading from one of the books he'd brought. I'd suspected for a while that the teachers had been instructed to give certain students more leeway than the rest of us as a way of encouraging more donations. Isaac seemed to prove my theory beyond a shadow of a doubt, and it had the fingerprints of a certain obscenely rich pack alpha all over it.

I spent the rest of the lecture debating the best course of action, but in the end I simply followed Isaac out of the auditorium and into one of the quiet, smaller study nooks that were scattered around the sixth floor. A few of the other girls from the class had stopped at one of the tables closest to the spot Isaac had staked out. They'd probably made the same deduction I had and were all kinds of excited about just how much money Isaac represented.

"Hello, Adri."

I cocked my head at him and waited for several seconds before sighing. It was all that I could do to keep my voice to a whisper.

"That's the best that you can do? 'Hello, Adri.' You show up out of nowhere and you don't feel the need to explain?"

Isaac shrugged, obviously unshaken. "I haven't been able to decide how much you'd really want to know."

"How about we start with what it is you're doing here?"

"Alec sent me to watch over you. I guess you could say you've got a bodyguard again."

Having someone else say his name was nearly more than I could take. It was surprising that there was more of an impact when Isaac said it, but it was undeniable. My breath caught, and for several seconds, it was all that I could do to fight off the vertigo.

My inner battle didn't go unnoticed by Isaac. It was almost impossible to keep secrets around a shape shifter, so Isaac got a front-row seat as I struggled to hold everything together. Isaac had always been considerate, though, so he didn't comment on just how broken I still was. He just waited for me to pull myself together and resume.

"What if I don't want a bodyguard? What if I'm doing just fine on my own?"

It was a calculated lie. Hopefully the way that I had phrased things would throw him off the 'scent' at least a little bit. The truth was that sometimes I couldn't sleep thinking about all of the things out there that could kill me.

"I'm sorry, Adri. I'm afraid I don't have a choice. Al...he didn't make obedience optional this time around. I'll try very hard to stay out of your way; but if I don't keep a close eye on you, things will get very unpleasant for me back home."

I couldn't tell if I'd succeeded or if he was just being polite and allowing me my illusions, but there were other questions that I wanted—no needed—answered.

"How are the girls? Is Jess dealing okay with everything that happened?"

The hands that he'd casually set on the table were suddenly gripping the heavy wooden edges with a force that made the entire table creak alarmingly. It was so rare to see Isaac in the grip of strong emotion that I just sat there frozen, unsure of how to proceed.

"Jess...Jessica is slowly rebuilding her life. She and her father seem to finally be reconnecting. She's adjusting to pack life, but it hasn't been easy. There are...pressures there that are hard on even those of us who remember standing off Brandon's pack together."

If I was a boy, I probably would have just left well enough alone, but I couldn't help myself.

"Things aren't okay between you and her yet then?"

Isaac shrugged, but the motion wasn't the nonchalant thing it had been a few minutes ago.

"No, not really. Every so often there is a glimmer there, but it never seems to last very long. We fought some vampires a little while ago and I thought I'd finally broken through to her, but she retreated back into herself."

The way he'd just casually mentioned vampires practically blew my mind. I'd wondered if that legend was also based on fact, but the pack had been so tight-lipped about everything while I'd been with them that I knew only barely more than nothing about the rest of the creepy crawlies out there. I wanted to find out more about the vampires, but it wasn't the right time for that line of questioning.

"I'm really sorry to hear that, Isaac. She probably just needs some time."

His smile was bittersweet, but he changed the subject with such smoothness that I almost believed that I'd imagined his near loss of control.

"Rachel is lonely, no more so than before you came to Sanctuary, but it was hard for her to transition back to being the only human in the pack. We got a new girl, Kristin, so Rachel isn't the only human any more, but Kristin doesn't interact with the rest of us very much. Rachel is pretty listless a lot of the time. Dom and Jasmin too. Jasmin hides it better than the other two, but they are all having a hard time dealing with the demands being placed on everyone."

That didn't sound very good. Part of me didn't want to ask, didn't want to know any more than I already knew. It was going to be hard enough knowing that Rachel was pining away from loneliness. Diving headfirst into a full knowledge of all of the pack's issues was just going to make it harder to hold to my resolution. Still, I couldn't stop myself from asking.

"What do you mean demands?"

Isaac took a deep breath. "I'm not sure you want to know that, Adri."

"You're probably right, but please tell me anyway."

"He's ordered the pack not to ever say your name, on pain of death, and he backed it up with an imperative from his beast. Even worse, we have a stream of challengers headed our way. Jasmin nearly died fighting the first one, because Alec was hoping that her beating a hybrid would make the other challengers scared to come up against the rest of us. He could have intervened before he did, but he waited until the last possible second to step in and save her."

Isaac paused for several seconds and then pushed the last bit out in what was obviously an effort.

"It's only a matter of time before Dom and Jess get pulled into challenge matches themselves and everyone in the pack is worried, either for themselves or for someone they love.

Everyone but *him*. He doesn't seem to feel anything but rage anymore."

It looked like Isaac was going to say something else, but I raised my hand and cut him off.

"Thank you for telling me, Isaac. You're right, though; I can't take any more right now. I'm really sorry things in the pack have gotten so bad, but all I can do right now is make it relatively easy for you to keep an eye on me. At least that way Alec won't punish you when you finally get called back home."

I stood to walk away but put one of my hands on his shoulder before I left.

"It really is good to see you again. It's hard, even harder than I'd have expected it to be, but seeing you brings back a lot of good memories, too."

I made my way over to another table, one that was still within sight of Isaac's, but which would afford me some distance so that I wouldn't have to watch too closely as five or six of the most eligible girls in the school proceeded to throw themselves at him.

I knew my thoughts weren't very charitable, but I was already struggling with larger concerns. Isaac hadn't given me very much detail behind what was going on, but it was still enough to paint a picture that was the worst of all worlds, at least as far as I was concerned.

I'd left Alec because I'd been convinced that there was no other way to wake him up to how unjust he was being to the rest of the pack. He'd let Agony and the rest of the bullies from the Coun'hij kill Alison and the others, and he'd never even blinked. I'd been convinced he loved me enough that my leaving would make him realize he was in danger of losing other things, more important things.

Hearing that my actions had produced the opposite effect made me want to curl up in a ball somewhere quiet and just sob for days. I hadn't wanted to leave Alec; I'd loved him then and I still loved him now, but I hadn't been willing to sit by and watch him lose his soul to 'necessity.' I'd deprived myself of something I needed almost as badly as food and water, and he'd gotten worse instead of better.

Yet again I wondered if I'd made the right decision, but ultimately there wasn't anything I could do about it now. Him having ordered the rest of the pack not to talk about me was plenty sign enough. I'd known I wouldn't be able to go back, but having that simple, terrible fact confirmed hurt with a searing heat that made it hard to breathe.

Chapter 3

Adriana Paige
Upper East Side
Manhattan, New York

I exchanged cell numbers with Isaac on the ride home. My school was just a 'short' ride down the number 6 train and then a jog over on the L line. The relative proximity of the school to Central Park East had a lot to do with its success when it came to filling its classrooms with the children of millionaires and billionaires.

Isaac hadn't been able to find a vacancy in my building, but he'd apparently purchased a unit in the building down from mine. I knew how much we were paying for our two-bedroom unit on the twenty-third floor, so when Isaac casually pointed at the penthouse suite at the top of the building in response to my question as to where he was living, I nearly choked.

I knew Alec was rich, but it still boggled the mind that he'd casually drop millions, if not tens of millions, of dollars on a whim like that.

Isaac had faithfully accompanied me inside and up to my floor and then watched as I'd unlocked my door and disappeared into my apartment. I closed the door as I reflected on just how odd it felt to have a bodyguard again. There had been a couple of weeks back in Sanctuary where I'd had someone from the pack with me at all times, and although it had taken some getting used to, I was now remembering the incredible sense of security involved in having a very capable, very deadly shape shifter at your side. That feeling of safety helped offset the whiplash of emotions I'd been through since seeing Isaac earlier in the day.

Mom was waiting for me, and she had an honest-to-goodness apron on for the first time that I could remember in weeks.

"Hi, sweetie. How was school?"

"Same old, same old. A bunch of yuppie rich kids with more money than sense."

That earned me a frown. Mom was shelling out some seriously crazy cash right now between our apartment and my school. She was bringing at least that much in with her photography work, but every so often her conservative Midwestern upbringing would rear its head and remind her just how much she was spending on a monthly basis.

She seemed to think that I was mostly joking when it came to my criticisms of Manhattan's number one school, but my comments still occasionally made her think twice about the spend.

"I really wish you'd put forth a little bit more effort when it comes to fitting in at school, Adri. A school like Brathingford can open up a lot of doors for you, but you'll have even more options if you'll actually make friends with some of your classmates."

"I know; they're all in line to rule the world someday, but I don't really care about ruling the world, Mom."

She looked up from the lasagna she was preparing and gave me a considering look. "What do you want then, Adri?"

That was the rub. I actually knew exactly what I wanted. It was the same thing that kept me up late, night after sleepless night. I could admit I wanted it inside the privacy of my own mind, but it wouldn't do any good to tell Mom that I longed to be back in Sanctuary with Alec—but not the Alec who sacrificed his friends and family, the Alec who stood in front of anything that would harm the pack and protected all of us.

Even if my mom had agreed to let me go back to Sanctuary, the Alec I'd envisioned during the short time we'd been together hadn't really existed. There was no point in broaching a subject that would just leave us both unhappy, not when it was so impossible.

"I don't know. For now, I'd just like to get away from the city."

"Adri, you hated Sanctuary. For nearly the entire first month we were there every other word out of your mouth was a complaint about Utah. You just don't deal with change very well, sweetie. Give New York a chance; it will grow on you just like Sanctuary did by the end."

I shrugged and turned to go to my bedroom but my mom cleared her throat.

"Adri, honey, we're going to have a guest for dinner tonight."

I should have known something was up when I saw that Mom was cooking. She didn't have dinner with me very often these days because she spent a lot of time networking with other people in the industry. Those people seemed to come in two categories: 'important' which meant they ate at some four-star restaurant, or 'reasonable' which meant that Mom could bring them back to our place and order takeout to eat while they brainstormed ideas.

Mom bringing someone back to the apartment and actually preparing a meal for them automatically told me this wasn't a work thing, or at least not *just* a work thing. I waited silently, refusing to help Mom along with her explanation.

"Russ is one of the financial backers for the Lasserti show. He saw me setting up before the shoot and sent me two dozen roses before the night was over. We've seen each other a couple of times since then, but I thought it would be good for the two of you to meet each other."

Her words kind of hung in the air and it felt to me like they'd created an impenetrable barrier between us. I turned to walk away. "I'm not feeling very hungry. I'll just study in my room and leave the two of you alone to eat."

"Adriana Paige, you get back here right now. You're not going to snub Russ. He's a nice guy, and this is important to me."

I hadn't wanted to get into a fight with Mom, not when we had so little time together, not when she was all I had left, but her words gave the anger floating around inside me a focus that had been missing since we'd arrived in Manhattan.

"Really, Mom? After everything that you said about first Brandon and then Alec, you're really going to bring this guy in here and tell me that he's a 'nice guy'? I know the kinds of shoots you've been doing, especially lately. Any 'financial backer' for one of those is going to be worth millions. You can't have it both ways. Either rich guys are jerks who can't be trusted, like you told me when we were in Sanctuary, or they are nice guys."

My mom opened her mouth to respond but I kept right on talking. "How nice can this guy be if he hangs around fashion shows? He's probably just trolling for some hot model to sleep with."

I'd slowly been moving towards Mom as I'd spoken which meant that I was within arm's reach, but her slap came as a complete surprise.

"How dare you. You don't know Russ, and I don't appreciate what you're saying about my judgment."

My hand came up to cover the stinging on the left side of my face, but the blow was nothing compared to what Agony's men had done to me.

"It's not just your judgment that I'm questioning, Mom. Dad hasn't even been dead for a year yet. I've spent the entire time since he and Cindi died trying to piece myself back together, but apparently you've just been waiting for someone richer to come along."

She slapped me again, but I didn't care. In some ways the physical pain helped. It took away some of what I was feeling inside, lessened it somehow. I walked out of our apartment and didn't look back, even when my mom called after me.

I texted Isaac while I was still in the elevator.

Changed plans...leaving my place...really needed to get out of the house...u don't need to follow me.

Isaac's response came only a few seconds later.

You have somewhere you need to be or do you want to just come here?

It was perfect and a terrible idea all at once. I sat outside his building for a couple of minutes trying to decide before finally responding.

Okay...brt

The doorman opened the door for me with a nod and a, "Hello, miss," and then I was to the huge granite desk that dominated the center of the entryway. The slender, very proper-looking woman behind the desk looked up as I approached and then smiled.

"Are you Adri?"

"I am. Did Isaac already call down?"

"Yes, he did. My name is Nancy. I'm the night clerk for the building. Mr. Nazir has asked that I key his private elevator to you. If you'll come this way, I'll scan your thumbs, and then he can confirm the new access protocol once you arrive there at the top floor."

I followed Nancy across the polished rock floor and then waited as she turned a key to call the elevator down. Inside there was a biometric scanner that exactly matched the one outside and another lock. Nancy used a different key to open the panel next to the scanner and then entered a long code on the keypad.

"Please place your thumbs on the scanner, one at a time."

Once the machine had registered my prints, she put another code into the keypad and then locked the panel again.

"The elevator will now go to Mr. Nazir's residence. Once he has approved your entry then next time all you'll need to do is use your thumb to call the elevator and then scan it again to go up to the penthouse."

I thanked her, and then once the doors had closed and the elevator started up, I spent some time looking around. I didn't have any idea what a swanky elevator was supposed to look like, but I suspected that this one fit the bill. The marble floor combined with the stainless steel walls and the hardwood trim to give the feeling of new money.

A few seconds later, the doors opened and my mouth dropped open at just how spacious Isaac's new place was. The ceilings were at least ten feet high, and there were oversized windows looking out at Central Park which made it feel like I was practically outside as soon as I stepped out of the elevator and pulled my shoes off.

Isaac came into view from off to my left, wearing nothing but a towel, and waved. "Sorry, I was in the shower when I heard your text come through. Once I knew I wasn't going to have to follow your scent trail through the urban jungle, I figured I might as well jump back in and finish up."

"That's okay, just point me to an out-of-the-way corner and I'll stew privately."

Part of me was taking in Isaac's massive, ripped chest and thinking that the new Jess must be more disciplined than the old Jess if she was able to say no to Isaac after seeing him shirtless, but mostly I was still way too numb to appreciate any guy, let alone Isaac who'd become almost like a brother back in Sanctuary. My heart still longed for Alec too much, even though I knew that was over.

"I can do better than that. This place has four bedrooms and I've already staked one of them out for you. It's this way."

I followed Isaac through the living room which had some of the thickest, softest white carpet I'd ever seen, past a media room that looked like it could seat twenty, and then he opened an oversized door into a bedroom that was more than three times as big as my current room. I stepped inside and spun around in amazement.

One wall was all tinted glass, once again providing an amazing view of the park. The king-sized bed had an airy canopy and a soft cream bedspread. The wall opposite the bed had a large flat screen TV mounted to it and there was a massive, cozy-looking beanbag chair on the floor at what looked like the perfect viewing distance from the screen. A large desk with a computer sat in the corner where the windows met the interior wall, but I found myself turning and looking the opposite direction so I could take in the attached bathroom and huge walk-in closet.

The shower was likewise spacious, all done in frosted glass and some kind of breathtaking white stone with silver fittings. The closet was nearly as big as my room and had three large boxes already sitting in it.

Isaac had trailed along behind me with one hand on the towel to make sure it stayed put. He pointed at the boxes as I turned back to look at him.

"Rachel sent those. They arrived today. I don't know for sure what's in them, but knowing her, I expect your wardrobe from Sanctuary makes up at least some of the contents."

I shook my head in amazement. "Are you sure about this, Isaac? I mean this room is incredible."

He shrugged. "It's all Alec and Rachel's money, and Alec seemed more concerned with getting me here and set up somewhere close to where you live than what the ultimate price tag might look like. None of the other three rooms are really any less crazy, and honestly, if you're comfortable here, then there's less chance I'll have to follow you around the city just because you're looking to kill some time."

I suddenly remembered the downside to a bodyguard. Every time I was thinking about going somewhere I'd have to balance how much I wanted to go there against the fact that it would be an imposition to Isaac.

He seemed to read my mind and waved my concerns away. "This is my first, and maybe only, trip to New York. I'm happy to go wherever you want to go; this just gives you more options when you really don't feel like going out but need to get away."

Given recent developments with my mom, there was a big chance I'd need a refuge. I managed a nod of thanks, which earned me a smile from Isaac, and then he pointed at the boxes again.

"I'll go get dressed while you see what goodies Rachel sent you. If you need anything, I'll be in the study."

"How do I find the study?"

"Adri, the house isn't that big. Just walk around and you'll find it eventually. It will give you a chance to explore."

Isaac smiled again and then walked away, leaving me alone with Rachel's boxes. I put my coat and backpack on one of the shelves to my left, and then I opened up the first box. Isaac had been right; all of the incredible clothes that Rachel had bought me on our Vegas trip were packed away, some of them still with tags on them. I'd known she was buying too much stuff, but I hadn't realized just how much she'd snuck past me until the first time I'd seen it all together in one place like this.

I really couldn't take it all home; Mom would ask way too many questions, and it wouldn't all fit in my closet there anyway. I took a deep breath and started hanging things up in the closet. The stuff I'd never worn before was easy, but the second box held the stuff that I'd worn while I'd been living with Alec and Rachel.

FORSAKEN

I knew Rachel would have had it laundered before packing it up and sending it to me, but in some indefinable way it still *smelled* like Sanctuary. Even worse, each article of clothing reminded me of Alec in some way or another. I'd worn the brown hiking boots on our trip up to the top of the mountain that sheltered the estate. The paint-speckled tank top had borne witness to the one and only time Alec had taken me to his studio and tried to teach me how to paint.

It was both harder and easier to deal with than I'd expected when I first opened the box and saw all of 'my' clothes sitting there. Easier because I didn't pass out or even really have to fend off a serious panic attack. Harder because it was like I was having to leave Alec all over again.

I was crying before I managed to finish cleaning out the second box, but it was the good kind of crying. It left me feeling tired and wrung out, but somehow lighter. I cleaned the remnants of my mascara off my cheeks and turned to the last box. There was a handwritten note inside the box, on the top of all the clothes.

Adri,

This is all of the stuff that I was planning on giving you for Christmas. I expected you to be able to wear it on the skiing trip. I figure you probably need the cold-weather gear there in New York even more than the rest of the stuff I'm sending. I'm sorry. I would have just sent it right to you, but I didn't know how you'd feel about that. You seemed pretty determined to cut all ties with us when you left.

If you see this then I guess that means you and Isaac are getting along better than I'm afraid you will. I'm sorry about all of this. Alec wouldn't even talk about his decision before he sent Isaac to you. I'm sorry the pack is intruding on your life again, but I'm glad you'll have someone there to watch over you.

The handwriting was unmistakably Rachel's, and for a few seconds I almost broke down into more tears, but I managed to hold myself together, if just barely. I'd forgotten about the trip that Alec had planned on taking us all on over Christmas. It took everything I had to keep myself from imagining what the trip would have been like, but I sternly kept my mind in the present as I put away a dozen incredibly soft sweaters and other assorted articles of clothing.

I wasn't sure what to do with the boxes, so I wandered through the house looking for Isaac's study. The rest of the place was just as incredible as what I'd seen so far. The floors all seemed to be a combination of lush carpet or heated stone, and the furniture had the simple elegance that you only got when you were ready to really open up your wallet.

Again and again my gaze kept coming back to the huge windows that seemed to occupy every single exterior wall. I'd started to feel almost...claustrophobic since we'd moved to New York. That wasn't quite the right word, but more and more I'd begun feeling like there wasn't any way to get away from all of the people around me. There were too many of us packed in much too small of a space, but I didn't get that feeling here. Looking out over Central Park with the light dusting of snow that covered all of the trees, I felt for the first time like I could deal with living in the city as long as I had access to a place like this.

The study proved to be a massive room that had gigantic bookshelves on two walls and a desk with the biggest leather chair I'd ever seen. Isaac had a large antenna rigged on one edge of the desk and was typing commands into a terminal.

"What do you want me to do with the boxes now that they are empty?"

"Just pull them out into the hall and the maid service will take care of them sometime tomorrow."

"You have a maid service, too?"

Isaac nodded absently. "Yes, a very exclusive, bonded service comes in four times a week to keep everything tidy."

Yet again with the whole bit about blowing my mind.

"So what are you doing right now?"

Isaac pushed himself back from his desk with the air of someone who was having to make a conscious effort to bring themselves back to reality.

"Sorry, I was in pretty deep there. In short, I'm trying to create a more secure route to use for communications back to Sanctuary."

"What, like encryption?"

"Yes, but that's only one layer of what I'm doing. The encryption piece is pretty easy. The hard part is making sure the communications can't be tracked back here. In Sanctuary I've already got a pretty bulletproof system in place along with hacks into a few key bits of telecom equipment that allow me to monitor when someone starts getting close enough that I need to rework the paths. That isn't an option here, at least not in the time I'm willing to spend on it."

My head was already starting to hurt. Isaac was going to get way over my head, but after the way that my mom had rocked my world earlier that day, I really didn't want to just hide out by myself in my new room.

"Can you use less tech speak?"

Isaac smiled like I'd just issued a challenge and then pointed to the antenna. "Essentially, I'm going to hack some of the nearby wireless routers. I'll bounce our traffic from one wireless device to the next so that there is a long trail that the Coun'hij or the police would have to unravel in order to trace everything back to here."

That I could follow. "So how will you know if they start coming after you?"

"That's actually the interesting part. Essentially, I go in and overwrite each router's firmware. The package that comes from the manufacturer is more bloated than most of them realize. I put a dummy interface in place that matches up with what the owner is expecting to see and then bury the true protocols further down. It lets me make sure that there isn't any kind of logging going on as well as forcing the router to connect to other routers."

"So you've made it so that there isn't anything in place for them to track back?"

"More or less. They could eventually figure out what I'm doing if they opened the device up and accessed the ROMs, but the only way they will really get me is if I load my firmware up onto a router that they've already turned into a giant trap. I'm going to suborn the closest couple of hundred devices over the next three or four days, and then I just won't go after any new devices that come online."

I could kind of follow the fringes of what he was saying, and it seemed like a smart way to do things, but I could already see a problem even with my limited understanding.

"So what happens when all of the devices you hack end up breaking or disappearing? Your network will vanish at that point."

Isaac nodded, seemingly impressed. "Yep, you're right. That's why this isn't a great long-term solution. It's one of the reasons that I didn't use it for our Sanctuary security protocols, that and the fact that we don't have anywhere near enough wireless routers close enough together there to make it work. This won't last forever, but it will at least work for a couple of years, and by then, if you don't decide to go somewhere else for college, I'll have had enough time to put something more permanent in place."

Isaac casually threw around terms like 'years' and 'college'. It made it sound like this arrangement was going to be longer-lasting than I would have expected. I opened my mouth to prove him a little bit on that point, but my phone vibrated with a text.

Russ is gone, I made excuses for you. I'm sorry that I sprang things on you like that. Where are you and when are you coming home?

I had to hand it to Mom; she trusted me more than she had back in Utah. I suspected it was because she'd seen me make a really hard choice and she was still confident that it was the right choice.

I looked up and saw that Isaac was looking at me.

"It was my mom, trying to extend the olive branch."

He nodded understandingly. "You want to talk about it?"

"Not really. I mean yes, but no all at the same time. She wanted to spring some new guy on me that she's dating. It's hard on so many levels. I want Mom to be happy, but it feels like she's betraying my dad. It's been a little while since I've felt so conflicted about something."

I wanted to go on, but I stopped myself. Isaac had always seemed so sure of himself. There was zero chance that he was going to be able to relate to me when it came to this particular problem.

Once again, it was almost like he was reading my mind. It had frustrated me beyond measure sometimes back in Sanctuary the way the pack had been able to do that, but at times like this it was nice the way it helped smooth over some of the bumps on the road.

"It's hard when you can't decide how to feel about something, or when your feelings are all tangled up and headed in opposite directions. It makes me feel…well, there's a word in Italian that captures it, but nothing in English really feels adequate to the job."

This was a different side of Isaac than I'd ever seen before.

"How are you conflicted? Jess?"

"Yeah, that one is at the top of the list. Before Oblivion wiped her memories away, I really loved her. I would have done almost anything to protect her, but I failed her when I let him hurt her."

"There wasn't anything you could have done. Alec acted so fast that you were trapped pretty much as soon as it happened."

Isaac shrugged. "Maybe. It's hard to say for sure. There were things that I could have done, they just might have ended badly for either Alec or for me. I think the hardest part is that I can still see so much of the Jess that I used to know in this new Jessica. I want what is best for her. I want her to be happy, but I want so badly for her to be happy with me. Sometimes it pushes me into bad decisions."

I'd moved closer while he was talking and was sitting on the edge of the desk now. I reached out a hand and placed it on Isaac's shoulder. "Things will work out there eventually. One way or another, they'll work out."

He took a deep breath and nodded. "I know. Intellectually I know that this will all eventually fade away into something that isn't so important, but it's hard sometimes still. The whole Alec thing doesn't help at all."

He'd caught me completely by surprise, and hearing Alec's name threw me for an incredible loop. It might have been because of the emotional rollercoaster I'd been through while unpacking, or it might have just been that I'd used up my full allotment of willpower for the day already. In the end, the why didn't matter as much as the impact.

My head spun and I nearly fell off the desk. Isaac steadied me, catching me before I could drop to the ground.

"I'm sorry, Adri. I'll do a better job from here on out. I won't mention him anymore."

I already knew from the panic attacks with Dad and Cindi that I had a brief period of immunity right after a spell struck me, so I shook my head and carefully sat back on the desk.

"No, tell me what you meant. I'm okay for a few minutes."

Isaac cleared his throat and then shrugged. "It's hard to describe exactly. I think the best way to put it is that there is a constant pressure on me to decide."

"Decide what?"

"How far I'll go for Alec, how loyal I am to him, how much he can depend on me."

It was another sign that my departure hadn't had the effect that I'd been hoping it would.

"He...Alec puts pressure on you?"

Isaac shook his head. "No, actually he's been pretty careful not to push me too far for the most part lately. He hasn't made an issue out of it, at least not yet, but I still feel a need inside to figure out whose side I'm really on."

"Does it really have to be like that? Do you have to be on someone's side?"

The smile he gave me was bittersweet. "Yes, I'm afraid so. I don't necessarily see eye to eye with Alec on as many things as I used to, but he's right. Our world is too savage for an individual to survive unaided. There has to be a boss, and I either need to start backing him again like I used to, or I should get out of the way."

"Are you sure that's the answer? Maybe you keeping yourself more in the role of an observer will help convince Alec that he's going too far."

Isaac took a slow deep breath and then shook his head a final time. "Alec is convinced of what he's convinced of. He's not going to change a single bit of his beliefs. All that is left is for the rest of us to decide whether we stand with him or against him. There isn't a middle path."

Chapter 4

Alec Graves
The 'Old Anderson Home'
Sanctuary, Utah

I'd debated the purchase for weeks before going through with it. The price had amounted to little more than petty cash, but I'd still almost not proceeded with the deal several times. It didn't seem like a very healthy thing to be doing, but I also couldn't help but provide one last bit of assistance to Adri and her mom.

My purchasing their home at a slight premium over what they'd paid for it several months ago had allowed them to retire the loan to the bank and move on with life. Unfortunately, it left me with a unique piece of real estate that I didn't know what to do with.

That wasn't quite fair; I knew exactly what I wanted to do with it. I just knew that it would be a very bad idea.

I stood outside their door...my door now, for at least an hour before I finally fished the key out of my pocket and used it to let myself in.

The bare wood floors and tired white walls seemed too small to have ever contained *her*, but there was no denying the scent that teased at my senses as soon as I entered the house. It was like coming home and torture all at once. My beast surged nearly to the surface as I fell to the ground, but I just barely managed to keep myself from transforming.

It wasn't the rage that I was used to feeling. Instead of being angry, my beast was more frantic, like he was desperate to get out so he could look for her. There was a tiredness to his efforts though. It shouldn't have been so hard to retain control, but I was exhausted, too. Not physically, at least not so much. It was more a mental and emotional weariness that was making it hard to retain my normal shape.

I remained curled up on the floor for several minutes, but Donovan's call provided the distraction I needed. I forced myself back upright and answered my cell phone.

"What is it, Donovan?"

I knew I was being rude. Donovan had just pulled me out of a near breakdown, and even if he hadn't saved me he still would have deserved better than that. It was becoming a recurring theme. I was picking the more self-destructive option far too often lately. I knew I needed to pull it together, but I couldn't seem to quite bring myself to do so.

"Master Alec, I'm sorry to disturb you, but I thought that you'd want to know that Ash has stabilized."

Donovan might as well have slapped me. He was right to call. Part of the reason I'd fled the house after the challenge match was how close I'd come to getting Ash killed, but as soon as I'd arrived at Adri's house I'd forgotten about him as if he'd never existed.

"Thank you, Donovan. I'm glad to know that he'll be okay."

There was a lot more that could have been said. This fight had been particularly brutal. Jasmin hadn't been up to a repeat yet. She was walking around under her own power, but it would still be at least a couple of days before she'd be able to jump back in the ring against a hybrid. Actually, the more I thought about it, the more it seemed like she was healing more slowly than I would have expected.

With Jasmin out and Isaac in New York, the rotation had been Ash, James and then me. I could have thrown Dominic or Jess into the mix, but I figured that neither James nor Isaac would appreciate having their girlfriends put in danger like that. Not when neither of the girls was likely to be able to do more damage than Ash.

Nothing in challenge law specifically forbade weapons, but that was more because a wolf couldn't possibly use any kind of weapon while shifted rather than because anyone thought that weapons were an acceptable route to go down.

Ash defied convention with his fighting style, just like he did with so many other things. He'd pulled his handgun out and gotten three shots off almost before our latest challenger even realized the fight had started. All three shots had landed. They were good, center-of-mass hits, but even a normal hybrid had a level of redundancy to his internal systems that made it hard to bring them down. Before Ash could get a fourth shot off, the hybrid had crossed the distance between them and opened up the entire left side of his chest.

The only thing that saved Ash was the fact that James didn't hesitate even slightly. James hit the challenger only a split second after Ash went down and made it around behind him for a kill shot less than a minute into the fight. James had still taken a respectable amount of damage, but it meant that I hadn't had to get involved, and that should buy us the tiniest bit of breathing room. The next challenger would assume that he'd have to face Jasmin, at least, and maybe James or Isaac as well, before he'd have his shot at me.

It sounded good on paper, but I already knew that I was grasping at straws. The deluge of challengers had only just started and there were hybrids out there who could take James apart in seconds. They were waiting still, letting others of the dispossessed feel us out, but it was only a matter of time. I could order Isaac back and it would help a little, but the fact of the matter was that we were too small of a pack to survive for very long now that we didn't have the deterrent of Brandon's pack. Nobody wanted to take over a pack that was a heartbeat away from being destroyed by another pack, but now that wasn't a worry anymore.

There were smaller packs that weren't being cased out by the dispossessed, but each of them had an alpha who was really, really scary, and that was the crux of our problem. Without a power that I could call at will, we were just so much lovely bait. More likely than not, the only reason we hadn't seen more challengers so far was the fact that we'd held off Agony and his lot as well as we had. Everyone was still worried that we were going to produce some kind of secret weapon and nobody particularly wanted to be its next victim. That kind of deterrent only worked for so long before people decided you *weren't* using it because you *couldn't* use it.

Donovan had waited while I followed my thoughts to their logical conclusion, but the silence had stretched out long enough that it was obvious to me that he had something else he wanted to say.

"What is it, Donovan? I've known you long enough now to be able to tell when you have something to tell me that you don't think I'm going to like hearing."

"It's more of an observation, or maybe a series of observations and a question."

"Out with it, please. You're usually right when you get to the point that you think I need to hear one or more of your observations."

"You haven't painted in weeks. Not since right after Agony and his men left."

"I'm in my studio nearly every day, Donovan."

Donovan cleared his throat, but he didn't let his reluctance stop him from calling my bluff. "If I may, sir, sitting in your studio is not the same thing as painting. It is important for you to continue to nurture your talents. Even in our current circumstances it is unwise to let the violent aspects of our nature consume too much of your time and attention. Without balance you risk becoming no better than one of the Coun'hij murderers."

It was an unusually strong nudge from Donovan, but more importantly, it wasn't fair. I hadn't done any of the kinds of things that Abaddon or Marco would have done in my situation. Either of them would probably have killed at least one of the girls already as a way of trying to bring James and Isaac to heel. I knew that Donovan was trying to help, or failing that just as scared as the rest of the pack, but I could still feel my beast surge to the fore of my being as my fist clenched.

"You said you had more than one observation."

"Indeed. I'm sure it is no surprise when I tell you that we can't continue on the course we're currently on, not for long, not without suffering consequences that none in the pack really want to deal with."

It was all I could do to keep my voice even. Donovan had been like a father to me, and he deserved a certain level of respect, but I was having a harder and harder time lately according him his due.

"I'm aware of that, Donovan."

"Indeed, Master Alec. The question is what you're going to do about it."

"I don't have any answers right now, Donovan. I can't see a way out of what is coming towards us."

"I know I'm exceeding my station, Master Alec, but with all due respect, you're the Kir'shan of the pack. You can't just passively wait for someone to hand you a solution. You need to come up with an answer and fast. That's not a responsibility you can shirk for much longer."

"Be careful, Donovan. Mallory has already pushed me too far. Don't you pile on, too."

I hung up on Donovan before I could say something that really couldn't be taken back and then looked up to find that I'd put my fist through the wall. I didn't remember doing so, but there was no arguing with the results of my rage.

Donovan wasn't being fair, but that didn't mean there wasn't a kernel of truth to what he'd just said. I'd been avoiding the call that I knew I had to make next, but avoiding it wasn't going to make things any easier.

I took a couple of calming breaths and dialed the number that I'd started seeing in my dreams.

"Bishop residence, this is Shawn."

"Hi, Shawn. It's Alec."

The pause between my greeting and his response wasn't promising, but I waited him out.

"Hey, Alec. It's been a while. I thought maybe I'd get a call from you after everything that went down with Agony, but you seem to be playing your cards even more close to your chest than normal."

"Yeah, I probably should have given you a call. Agony's visit was even worse than I'd expected it to be. Right after he left…something else happened that threw me for a loop. I guess I haven't been myself lately."

Calling another pack, even when I wasn't talking to the alpha, was always a bit of a verbal sparring match. Shawn was a good sort, but the formal communication between packs these days was so intermittent that everyone was reluctant to give up too much information. The Coun'hij tended to find ways to make all kinds of tidbits come back to bite people later on.

"So what really happened when Agony visited? I've heard the rumors, just like everyone else. Agony's men came back looking like they'd been through a meat grinder, but you lost some people. That's not how I expected things to go down. I expected that you'd either unleash whatever you used to take Brandon down or Agony would pretty much wipe out your entire pack."

That was the rub. If I was going to be able to recruit Shawn's help then I was going to have to come clean and risk the information getting out sooner rather than later.

"The rumors are right; I manifested a power when I faced off against Brandon. Not before the challenge, literally in the middle of the fight. It was some kind of vortex. I pulled energy out of both packs and essentially leveled everyone there."

Shawn let out a low whistle. "That's a big deal, Alec. Agony and Oblivion both have to touch someone to use their powers on them. This puts you in a class above them. You'd be up there nearly with Puppeteer."

"Maybe not quite as high up there as you think. All of that power leveled me, too. The only thing that saved me was the fact that I was the first one to my feet afterwards."

"Is that why you didn't use it to take Agony and the rest down?"

I couldn't go back from here, but I needed Shawn's help. The pack couldn't continue on like it was.

"No, I didn't use it because, so far, it isn't something that comes when I call it. Donovan thinks I just need more time for it to finish developing."

I could almost hear the cogs spinning inside Shawn's mind.

"You don't have much time left, Alec. Only losing three people when Agony came calling is probably holding some of the dispossessed back from challenging, but you guys didn't make a very good showing on the first guy who came through."

"I know. Agony's visit did a real number on us. I've got people who are one step away from cutting and running right now and it's all I can do to hold things together."

"That's not a good situation for you guys to be in, not with everything else going on. The dispossessed are going to be lining up to take a shot at you. How many challenges have you had so far? Two? Three?"

"Two so far, but you're right; they are just going to come faster and faster. Best-case scenario right now is that they'll wear us down. Worst-case scenario is that somebody really nasty comes through and rips through us sooner rather than later."

Shawn sighed. "That about sums it up, but it doesn't explain why you're calling me."

"We need help. You guys have the largest pack in North America right now. If you could loan me a couple of hybrids and a few wolves to help even things out as far as the power structure inside of our pack, it should go a long way towards deterring some of the challengers. I just need more time to get my power to finish manifesting."

Another pause, this one long enough that I started to get uncomfortable. Shawn literally had the fate of my friends in his hands.

"If my dad agreed to your request it would be tantamount to declaring that our two packs were allied against all comers."

"I know."

"Then you know that the only reason the Coun'hij has allowed us to get so big is that Dad has remained steadfastly apolitical ever since the dustup between them and your dad. If Dad throws his weight behind you, we'll have Agony here inside of a week, and he'll bring every spare enforcer they've got. At best we'll have a repeat of what you just went through, but on a larger scale. At worst we'll have a repeat of what they did to your dad."

I'd known what Shawn's answer would be. That was part of why I'd waited so long to make the call, but I had to ask. If we didn't get some kind of help, we weren't going to make it very much longer.

"I just need time, Shawn. If my power finishes manifesting we have a very real chance of breaking the Coun'hij once and for all."

The call quality was good enough for me to hear Shawn pacing. He'd started about the time I'd brought up my power, but as he stopped moving around, I knew he'd made his decision.

"I'm sorry, Alec, but me sending down some of our people will just get a lot of people I care about killed and it won't buy you the kind of time you need. It would be like throwing a bucket full of ice into hell."

I felt my beast surge up nearly to the surface, felt my vocal cords lengthening slightly, but I stopped the transformation before it could go any further.

"You can't know that, Shawn. A few days might make the difference."

"I'm sorry, but I do know it, Alec. I know that sounds crazy to you, but it's the truth. Even if you're right and your power isn't as developed as it's going to get, even if it comes whenever you call for it, you're still not going to be a match for the Coun'hij, not with Puppeteer in the mix. You'd need something else, someone else that could offset the army he'll bring to the table."

I took another deep breath, trying to keep myself under control, but it was getting harder and harder.

"That's not the only reason. What aren't you telling me, Shawn?"

Shawn paused for several seconds and then sighed. "Truth be told, Alec, nobody is going to be willing to go help you, even if my dad was willing to take the risks. Your family has always enjoyed a lot of support among the rank and file, but after Agony's last visit people are wondering if you sacrificed a third of your pack just so you could keep your own skin intact. People are already doing a compare and contrast between what you did and what your dad did. You're not coming off very good."

My phone creaked as my grip tightened to dangerous levels, and I had to consciously force myself to relax at least the hand that was holding my phone.

"So you're not going to do a damn thing for me?"

"There might be one thing, but I don't even know if it will work. That girl I heard talk of a while back, is she still in the picture?"

It was more than I could take. I retained just enough presence of mind to cover the mic on my phone before I put my hand through another section of the wall. I forced my hand back to normal, shrinking it down and losing the claws, and then put my phone back up to my ear.

"No, she left just after Agony came by."

"I'm sorry to hear that, man. That's rough."

"It's okay, I'll get over it."

I could almost hear the exhaustion creeping into Shawn's voice. It made no sense, but I could tell that he was suddenly all but dead on his feet.

"Like I said, I'm sorry. That might give me something to work with. I'll see what I can do."

I tried one last time. Even as I opened my mouth I knew it was the wrong thing to do. Shawn wasn't going to change his mind now, but I couldn't stop myself.

"Shawn, I need tangible help, not some nebulous promise. I'll go to your father directly if I have to."

"That won't get you what you want, Alec, and it will just back Dad into a corner. He doesn't do very well with changing his position once he's made up his mind. Look, I've got to go. Hopefully I'll get a chance to talk to you again."

He hung up on me before I could get anything out, and the sound of dead air ripped away the last of my control. My transformation shredded my clothes and then I cut through a large chunk of the wall with my claws before Adri's scent hit me. I'd somehow become accustomed to it even during just the few minutes I'd been there, but my hybrid form had sharper senses than my human body.

I collapsed onto the floor, surrounded by the smell of Adri and the destruction I'd just wreaked on the one link I still had to her.

Chapter 5

Adriana Paige
Brathingford High School
Manhattan, New York

Things with Mom were still strained, but it hardly mattered because I still only saw her a couple of times a week. If that had been the only problem in my life, things actually would have been pretty good.

Isaac had made even more of a ripple at Brathingford than I'd expected him to. He was undeniably good-looking and the definite scent of Alec's money had to help, but at least part of his appeal was the way that he'd kept himself so aloof from the girls who were slowly lining up to throw themselves at him.

It would have been humorous if not for the fact that I knew some of the girls really were interested in him. Isaac was unfailingly polite, but he never initiated a conversation with anyone but me, and he generally made an excuse about needing to study a few minutes after any girl approached him.

Isaac spent way more time with his nose in one of his books than he did talking to me, but the grapevine seemed convinced that the two of us were dating. Rather than making the rest of the girls just throw their hands up, that information actually seemed to anger some of them. *I* knew that Isaac was shooting them down because of Jess, but there didn't seem to be any way to get Lexus and her friends to believe that it wasn't me that was stopping them from completing their latest conquest.

Honestly, I was starting to get tired of it all. These girls had everything: money, looks, popularity, you name it. I knew I wasn't in their league, but that didn't mean I particularly liked being reminded of how much they outclassed me. Mom was making more money in a month than Dad had made in a year, but we still couldn't compete financially with Lexus and her friends. I knew that trying to compete was stupid, but I'd recognized one of the sweaters that Rachel had sent in her care package. It was the kind of thing I'd never have worn six months ago, designer and decadent in a way that almost defied reason. I'd done a quick check online and confirmed my suspicion. Rachel had bought me a two-thousand-dollar article of clothing.

When we'd had our school pictures a few days ago I hadn't been able to resist wearing *the* sweater. I told myself I was wearing it because I wanted to look really, really nice for my picture, but a small part of me had known that Lexus would probably recognize my little piece of near haute couture, and I'd taken just the tiniest bit of satisfaction over the fact that it would bother her.

Today I was wearing my own boring, old clothes, which had never impressed anyone, but they'd never occasioned amused glances like I was getting right now. It took me a couple of hours before I noticed the hot pink flyer making its way from one girl to another. I wouldn't have thought anything of it, but the giggling and nasty looks seemed to follow the flyer.

I finally got up and moved away from my usual study spot. Isaac faithfully followed along behind me as I headed towards the stairs. We were nearly there when I suddenly realized that there wasn't any reason for me to guess at what was being said. I had my own personal super spy.

"Isaac, what were those girls saying?"

"I'm not sure you really want to know. Maybe you should just ignore them and let it all blow over."

If he'd actually wanted to keep me from knowing he should have told me they weren't saying anything.

"Please, just tell me."

Isaac sighed and then pointed down the hall. "Maybe I should just show you."

There was a large bulletin board hanging between the elevators. Normally I just ignored it, but Isaac walked straight to it, pulled down a hot pink flyer, and handed it to me. It was a picture of me, but not just any picture. Somehow someone had gotten ahold of the picture I'd had taken just a couple of days ago, the one with the ridiculously expensive sweater that Rachel had bought me. Below the picture was the caption, 'Will Slut for Sweaters.'

I literally saw red for a few seconds. I closed my eyes, counted to ten, and then turned to Isaac. "Who was it? I know you'll have overheard enough to know which of those spoiled brats did this."

It was obvious that Isaac didn't want to come clean.

"Adri, this kind of thing never goes down like you think it will. If you let her pull you into a mudslinging contest you're just going to regret it in the end."

He was right. It really, really pissed me off, but he was right. There was absolutely nothing that I could do that would punish her like she needed to be punished. I could start nasty counter-rumors or convince Isaac to hack into her tablet, but that would just invite more problems and another round of retaliations.

"Just tell me who it was."

"It was Lexus."

I took a couple of deep, calming breaths, pulled the flyer out of Isaac's hand, and hit the elevator call button.

"Can I ask where we're going?"

"We're going to tell the administration about these flyers and then we're going to go from floor to floor and pull the rest of them down."

The office secretary promised to quietly get the staff and faculty to confiscate any flyers they saw, which I knew was probably still a losing battle, but at least it would force Lexus and her friends to be more circumspect.

I thanked the secretary and then headed to the top floor of the school and started working my way down. Isaac tromped along behind me, obviously hoping that I wasn't going to try and push him into helping with some kind of scheme to get even with Lexus and her friends.

The second floor was the worst; the bulletin board there was completely covered with the hateful hot pink abominations. By the time we got down to the first floor, I had a stack a quarter of an inch thick, and I was even angrier than I'd been when we left the office.

As I pulled down the last flyer and threw the stack into the trash, I saw a green poster off on one side of the front door. There was something about it that caught my eye, but I couldn't place it until I was standing right in front of the poster. It was for a band called Fatal Angst and featured a list of show dates and locations, but that wasn't what was tickling the back of my mind.

There was a picture of the lead singer down one side and he looked alarmingly familiar. I tugged on Isaac's arm, causing him to look up from the book he'd opened up almost as soon as we'd stopped moving.

"Isaac, does the guy on this poster look familiar to you?"

"Hmm? Yeah, I guess he does. He looks kind of like Albert from back home."

I was suddenly sure that it really was Albert. I'd almost forgotten that he was in a band. He'd said they were starting to get some heat down in Vegas, but I never would have guessed that they were going to blow up like this.

"We're going to this show, Isaac. I mean I'm going. You can come if you want, but I'm definitely going."

"Okay. I'll go online and check for tickets tonight. Alec may as well pay for that, too."

It wasn't until we were back in the elevator and headed upstairs that Isaac looked up from his book and gave me a questioning glance.

"Does this mean you're over Lexus and her friends?"

"No. Right now I'd happily push all three of them off the top of a building, but there's nothing I can do about them, not really. I'm going to keep telling myself that this school is just a tiny little pond and that once I graduate I'm never going to see any of these people again. And then I'm going to go to a concert."

I went to the rock show figuring I'd blow off some steam at the very least, but secretly hoping I'd get a chance to see Albert. I had no idea whether or not I'd even like the music that his band played, but I was ready to brave the crowds in the hope that I'd get to spend a little bit of time with him and get another taste of home.

The venue wasn't huge, but it was bigger than I'd been expecting. There were at least a thousand people there and Fatal Angst put on quite a show. They ranged from lyrical, haunting stuff that leaned heavily on Albert, to aggressive, high-energy, electronic sounds that got the whole crowd jumping up and down. The band was good, but the thing that kept blowing my mind was how different Albert looked.

The geeky math tutor who had been working the tutor lab with me a few months before had been replaced by a confident rock star, complete with a tattoo and a couple of piercings. Albert had always had a slender build, but sometime since I'd seen him last it had morphed into the kind of too-skinny frame that some performing artists seemed to get while on the road because they weren't taking good enough care of themselves.

I let Isaac convince me to stay in the back of the crowd where he could keep an eye on me for the first hour or so in return for him promising to get me right up to the stage by the end of the show.

He hadn't liked it, but he lived up to his part of the bargain and I was center stage, almost close enough to reach out and touch Albert, as he started into the last song, another of the aggressive numbers that had people crowd surfing and generally rocking out.

Isaac was obviously uncomfortable, but I let the music take me over and joined in the fun with everyone else. I looked up at one point about halfway through and saw Albert looking at me. I smiled and thought that I got a bit of a smile in return, and then almost before I knew it, the band was taking their bows and filing off the back of the stage.

I followed Isaac over to one of the walls as the lights came up and the rest of the crowd started breaking up.

"Sorry, Isaac. I know you've probably got a ton of other things you'd rather be doing, but can we wait for a little while and see if Albert comes back out?"

"Yeah, no problem. I wouldn't mind seeing him myself. I noticed he wasn't in school anymore a few weeks ago, but I didn't realize that this was where he'd gone."

We sat for several seconds in companionable silence, both playing on our phones. About twenty minutes after the show had ended I heard someone walking in our direction and looked up to find Albert standing in front of us with a big smile on his face.

I threw my arms around him so fast that I nearly knocked him over.

"You have no idea how good it is to see you. New York sucks."

Albert gave Isaac a nod as he wrapped an arm around me. "I thought about you when we booked the tour dates out here, but I figured there was zero chance we'd actually run into each other, and I had no way to get ahold of you after you left."

I blushed. I'd never been real big into the social media scene, but I'd cut even my limited interactions down to nothing after I left Sanctuary. It hadn't seemed fair to Alec to leave but then keep up contact with everyone else in Sanctuary other than him.

"Yeah, things kind of happened fast. I left without really having a chance to say goodbye to anyone."

Albert gave me a considering look, one that said he'd heard all of the rumors that had probably circulated after I'd left and that he was pretty sure I wasn't telling him the full truth. I did my best to move the conversation along so that he wouldn't get a chance to grill me.

"Your show was really, really good. When did you guys become famous?"

His chuckle was just as self-deprecating as always. "I'm pretty sure we're still not famous, but things started moving along pretty well a little while ago. We put some of our stuff up where people could buy it, and the next thing we knew, we started getting monthly royalty checks. It's not enough for all of us to retire in comfort on yet, but it was enough to support us on a six-month tour. My parents freaked out when I told them I wanted to drop out of school and really try to make a go of things with the band, but I managed to get them to meet me halfway."

"Meaning you're touring but still doing homework so you can graduate?"

His smile was just as cute as I remembered it being.

"Pretty much. That and I've got a two-year window before I need to be making obscene amounts of money or I'm supposed to go to college. The fact that I was already eighteen and making enough money to support myself was probably the only reason I managed to get even two years out of them."

I was still reeling from the idea of *Albert*, of all people, telling his parents that he wanted to drop out of school and become a rock star.

"So, can Isaac and I buy a big-time rock star something to eat?"

Albert shrugged. "I don't know about a big-time rock star, but you can buy Albert the high-school dropout something to eat. I haven't eaten since last night."

Isaac suggested an all-you-can-eat buffet, which I thought was a really good idea considering how skinny Albert was looking these days. We jumped on the subway and half an hour later we were sitting inside a modest-looking restaurant. The conversation on the way there had been pretty light, but a few seconds after we all made it back to our table with our food, Isaac looked down at his phone and sighed.

"Sorry, guys, I need to take this. I'll just be right outside."

Albert watched Isaac leave and then took a long pull of his Mountain Dew.

"So...you and Alec?"

"Wow, you don't waste any time, do you?"

His smile had hints of the shy math geek I'd known before, but he managed a breezy wave.

"I'm a big-time rock star and we can get away with that kind of thing. At least that's what the rest of the band keeps telling me."

Something about Albert's presence dulled the sting that Alec's name usually inflicted on me.

"Alec is in Sanctuary, and I'm here. That kind of says everything that needs to be said."

Albert shook his head. "Come on. I'm a geek at heart, but even I know better than that. Girls only simplify relationships as a way of confusing the issue. You guys aren't in the same city, but that doesn't necessarily mean you aren't talking to each other."

"In our case it does. I haven't talked to anyone from Sanctuary since I left. Other than Isaac, I mean, and him showing up here was a complete surprise."

"So you guys not talking, was that your idea or his?"

I was starting to get less and less comfortable with the direction he was guiding the conversation, but I managed to keep my voice pretty normal when I finally sighed and responded.

"It was my idea."

"Your idea, but you're not sure it was the right thing to have done?"

Maybe I hadn't done as good of a job keeping my unhappiness out of my tone after all. I picked up a piece of garlic bread and bit off a corner as a way of buying myself time.

"I'm conflicted about a lot of things where Alec is concerned, but I made the only decision I could at the time."

Apparently I'd finally given Albert the answer he wanted to hear. He dipped a shrimp in some marinara sauce and popped it in his mouth.

"Can we not talk about Alec? I mean there have to be like at least twenty other people in Sanctuary. I haven't heard anything about any of them for a couple of months now."

Albert swallowed his shrimp and then stuck his tongue out at me.

"You're behind the times. It's eighteen now. Twenty was before you and I left town. I guess technically, right this instant, it's seventeen because Isaac is standing outside pretending to talk on his phone while he keeps a careful eye on the two of us."

My ears heated up. Albert hadn't gotten any less observant since leaving home to play with a rock band.

"Aren't you rock stars supposed to be shallow and self-centered? You're not supposed to catch on to stuff like that."

Albert shrugged and grabbed another shrimp. "I grew up in Sanctuary. You develop an odd kind of sixth sense when it comes to weird after living there for a couple of years."

"Things are complicated for me right now. Isaac is out here kind of watching out for me. If you ask him he'll probably tell you he's checking in on some of Alec's business interests, but you're right, he's here because of me. Don't spread that around though."

"I won't say anything about Isaac's current whereabouts. Actually, I'm glad to see him and know that he's keeping an eye on you. We had three people disappear a little while after you left."

My face froze, but Albert was reaching for a shrimp, so I was pretty sure he hadn't seen my reaction.

"Oh, no! Who was it this time?"

"Sam, Jack and Alison. You know, I hadn't really connected those three to the other disappearances, but now that you mention it, every single person who used to hang out with Brandon is gone now. Sanctuary is starting to rival Sunnydale when it comes to missing people."

It took me a second to get the reference. Cindi had been a big-time *Buffy* fan so I'd seen every episode at some point or another, but I didn't even know what had happened to her DVDs.

"You know, you're really going to ruin your rock star mystique if you keep making those kinds of references."

Albert tapped his chin for a few seconds and then nodded. "Should I switch to *Vampire Diaries* instead?"

"I'm not sure. I'm not in the loop very well so I don't know if it's considered geeky or cool. It's very contemporary, though, so maybe you'd better steer clear just in case it is geeky."

"Okay, I'd better retire my 'What Would Damon Do' bling."

He was funnier now, less shy and more confident, too. My shoulders started to relax.

"Very funny. Seriously though, I'd like to hear about everyone we left back there."

"I'm not sure what to tell you. Not a lot changes in just a few weeks. Brandon and the rest are gone, so there was a massive hole at the top of the social food chain. Britney Samuels made a valiant effort at capturing the top spot, but then just kind of seemed to lose interest."

That made me a little sad. Britney had always wanted to be popular. If that had lost its appeal for her then she probably was going through a bit of an identity crisis.

"Ben disappeared too, but not like the others. A couple of people claim to have talked to him. Supposedly he's out here on the East Coast somewhere working on cars or something like that. The tutor lab was still ticking along when I left, but Mrs. Campbell was a little at a loss for what she was going to do to fill out her staff with you and I both having left so close to each other. Who else did you want to know about?"

I opened my mouth to respond but it clicked shut almost of its own accord. I wanted to know about Alec, but not really, not enough to deal with the pain it would involve. Besides, it was unlikely that Albert could offer any more insight into Alec's mind than Isaac already had.

"I guess nobody. I hadn't realized how small my circle of friends was until just now."

Albert shrugged. "Don't let it get you too down. You only lived in Sanctuary for a few months and I've always said that it's quality that counts more than quantity. I'm your friend, so you can't have been in too bad of shape."

I reached over and punched him gently in the arm.

"Careful, Mr. Rock Star. If this all keeps going to your head then I'll have to dissolve our friendship."

"You know that isn't going to happen, Adri. The tattoo and the piercings are pretty much all just a smokescreen to make the fans think that I've got the chops to sing. Inside I'm still the same quiet math geek I've always been."

I hadn't expected the conversation to take that turn.

"If you're still the same math geek you've always been then why did you choose all of this?"

"What guy doesn't want to be a rock star? Granted, I'll probably never change the world or anything as a performer, but there's an excitement there that you don't get anywhere else."

"Excitement…and girls, obviously."

"Not really. I mean there could be if I wanted there to be. A couple of the other guys are nearly out of control right now, but for me there's only ever been one girl I was really interested in."

My face heated up. The adulation from his fans apparently was doing more for his assertiveness than I'd realized.

"It's admirable that you haven't just jumped into bed with a bunch of groupies. I think we can continue to be friends despite your newfound fame and fortune."

Albert had worked his way through his shrimp and now was starting in on his pizza.

"Newfound fame I can maybe give you. Fortune is still a long ways off. Some of the guys are starting to push for us to take a deal from one of the record companies that are sniffing around. You know, cash in right now and start living on more than two or three dollars a day."

"But not you?"

"No, the way that I see things we're already building a good following on our own. As crazy as it sounds, people really like our stuff. I think we should release another couple of albums and see how we do as independents before we make a final decision as far as signing with a label. They can offer wider distribution, but they'll take three-fourths of the proceeds."

"So for now you tour the East Coast and live on ramen in the hopes of future millions."

Another bite of pizza and then a pause while he chewed.

"This food is good. I mean it's probably just mediocre, but wow, it tastes good right now. Yeah, that pretty much sums it up, but you've missed the biggest bonus of all."

"What's that?"

"Well, since I don't have to answer to a label, I can schedule our tour stops wherever I want. I'm thinking that we're suddenly going to be swinging back through New York a lot over the next few months. Do you mind if I look you up?"

I knew he wanted more than just friendship, but I found myself answering before I'd even paused to consider all of the implications.

"That would be really nice."

Chapter 6

Alec Graves
Graves Estate
Sanctuary, Utah

Shawn's nebulous aid hadn't materialized and I was getting nervous. We hadn't had another challenger since the one who had ripped Ash up and I was pretty sure we were past due for our next fight.

I was in Donovan's study running through our monthly extended business update when I got a call from Ash.

"Alec, we've got another car inbound. It's not one that I recognize."

"Okay, Donovan and I are on our way. Can you call Dom and James?"

"Sure thing. You want to play things like we did last time?"

That was the question, a very important, high-stakes question, and despite having agonized over it for the last week or so, I still hadn't made up my mind. Ash healed only a little faster than a human would have. We all healed more slowly from wounds inflicted by other shape shifters, but Ash really was one of the weakest wolves I'd ever met. In a straight up fight he was completely overmatched, which was no doubt the reason that he'd become so proficient with guns.

When he had the drop on someone, he had a chance at besting them, but it was virtually guaranteed that our last challenger had already let Ash's particular cat out of the bag, and he still wasn't moving as smoothly as he normally did. I waved for Donovan to go get Jess, partially as a way of buying myself some time and partially because things hadn't been the same between us since he'd pushed on the Shawn issue.

"Are you ready to lead off another match?"

"Honestly? Probably not, but I don't know that we've got any other options really. If we don't create a defense in depth we're all pretty much screwed. That means that Jasmin, Jess, Dom or I need to lead off, and throwing Dom or Jess out there is like throwing kittens off a bridge."

I was far enough away from Donovan that he shouldn't be able to overhear my conversation. I closed my eyes for a second and asked one of the questions that had been preying on my mind for the last few weeks.

"Ash, why are you still here? There is really nothing stopping you from taking Kristin and heading for the hills."

I could hear him pop the magazine out of his handgun and then slam it back home with a sense of finality.

"We have a deal, Alec. I know you don't have your crap together right now. Hell, the entire world knows that you're not at the top of your game. You may be only going through the motions, but you're at least doing that much. The rest of the pack has seen some crazy action over the last couple of years, but in a lot of ways they are still kind of naive when it comes to how the world works. You saved Kristin when you'd have been a lot smarter to have just sent us on our way. As long as you don't throw me under a bus, I'm going to stand with you and just hope your power clicks into place sooner rather than later."

"That's the biggest long shot I've heard of someone betting on in a long time."

Ash's chuckle wasn't very comforting. "Yeah. We're all probably going to end up dead, but I'm still going to bet on you. The reason the Coun'hij is in power is because too many people were more interested in trying to get their own slice of the pie. If more of us had united solidly behind your ancestors, then there's a chance we'd be living in a very different world. You're still plenty screwed up right now, but even screwed up, you're still better than most of the alphas out there. Besides, you're the only hybrid right now who has a chance of standing up to those butchers. You're not there yet, but there's a chance, which is more than anyone else has going for them right now."

I nodded, even though he couldn't see the motion.

"Thanks for your honesty. The rotation is going to be you, then James, then Jasmin, then me."

"I'll be ready."

By the time Ash's mystery car pulled up in the driveway, all of the shape shifters other than Addison and Andrew were gathered and waiting. Addison hadn't liked being excluded from the challenge matches, but James had backed me up on the ruling, so for once she was doing what I'd told her to do.

The woman who got out of the car looked like she was in her very early twenties. She had long blond hair, was a little taller than average, and moved with the calm assurance of someone who knew her limits and was comfortable working inside of them. She looked us over, shrugged her trim shoulders, and then walked up to me and put her hand out.

"My name is Natasha Annikov. I'm not here to challenge you, I've got a proposal for you instead."

If she'd chosen that moment to pick up a two-by-four and hit me, the blow probably would have landed. I was that surprised. The rest of the packs had started cutting Donovan out of the grapevine shortly after my father had been killed, so he and I had very little good information when it came to the other packs. Shawn occasionally let something slip, and Donovan sometimes managed to collect an important tidbit through more conventional channels, but by and large I was operating blind. Most of my resources had been aimed at keeping me in the know when it came to Brandon, and I was woefully unprepared for the larger arena in which I found myself.

I looked over at Ash and he nodded almost imperceptibly, so I knew she was really who she said she was, but that didn't mean I necessarily knew what to do with her.

"On behalf of the Sanctuary pack I welcome you to our territory. If you're really not here to commit violence, then we'll happily extend our hospitality to you."

"Surely you can smell the truth of my words, Alec. You're reputed to be a respectably powerful hybrid."

I knew my smile didn't make it all of the way to my eyes.

"You smell like you're telling the truth, but your assurances weren't very comprehensive, and even if they had been, it wouldn't necessarily surprise me if the heiress of the Tucson pack was able to lie without giving off any of the normal signals."

"You're being overly kind. We've had to shrink our territory down a lot over the last few years. It would be fairer to say that we are the Sierra Vista pack these days."

That had been one piece of information that I had known, but frankly she took me by surprise with her admission. Most dominants were touchy about the size of the territory they controlled.

"May I show you to a room?"

Natasha nodded as she walked around to the back of the car and popped the trunk. "That would be much appreciated. Where would you like me to park my car?"

Dominic stepped forward. "I'd be happy to park it for you and then bring the keys to your room."

James scowled a little. He knew that Dominic was a submissive both by nature and ability, but he still didn't like it when she waited on people. Natasha bestowed a smile on Dom as she handed her the keys and pulled out a single bag.

"Thank you, I'd really appreciate that."

I turned to Donovan and raised an eyebrow. "Where would you suggest we put Miss Annikov?"

Donovan smoothly took Natasha's bag and motioned for her to precede him. "I think that the Lilac Room is the best option we have available right now."

My beast tried to make its presence known, but I stomped on the flare of power before it could manifest into something strong enough to show how much he'd rattled me. The Lilac Room had remained empty since before Rachel had shipped Adri's clothes back to Manhattan. He was purposefully reminding me of Adri's time at the mansion.

"The Lilac Room it is. Ash, you're with us. Everyone else is free to go back to whatever they were working on previously."

It took only a couple of minutes for the four of us to make it to the Lilac Room. Once we arrived, Natasha looked the room over and then nodded at the soft purple accents and antique furniture.

"This will serve just fine. I hear that you prefer to be direct when possible, so I'd like to get to the point of my visit. Is this the group you'd like to hear me out?"

A petty part of me wanted to send Donovan away, but it really would have been pure spite to do so. Donovan was the conduit through which almost all of our intelligence flowed. It would be stupid to cut him out of this particular discussion.

"Yes. Do you want to have the discussion here or would you like to go somewhere else?"

Natasha looked around, as though confirming that there were enough chairs to seat us all, and then motioned for us all to sit.

"Here's fine. Do you have a privacy box somewhere that we can turn on?"

She waited while Donovan turned on the white noise generator located next to the door, and then joined the rest of us in the tiny breakfast nook off to one side of the room.

"I'm going to be blunt. I'd like to call you Alec and you can call me Tasha if that's okay."

Despite all of the minefields inherent in dealing with the representative of another pack, I found a smile trying to work its way out onto my lips. I was starting to suspect that Tasha would have had a hard time being anything other than blunt.

"That's fine. Ash is to your left and Donovan is to your right. Donovan held things together after my father died. Ash is a recent addition to the pack."

She nodded respectfully at Donovan. "Your reputation is only a tad short of legendary. My mother has mentioned many times just how impressed she was with the way you managed the crisis after Agony's first visit."

Tasha likewise nodded to Ash and then shifted slightly in her chair, almost like she was wishing that she didn't have to go through with whatever it was she'd come to say.

"To be perfectly frank, I have a very good idea of how much of a bind you're in. You're a small pack, but even worse, you're not all pulling in the same direction. You've had two challenges so far, and during the first one, the dominants were at odds with each other enough that the pack alpha had to get involved in only the second round. There aren't very many ways that fight could have gone down that would have been worse for your pack from the standpoint of long-term survivability."

My beast tried to rise up to the surface in answer to her allegation of weakness, but once again I brought it to heel. Everything she'd said so far was nothing more than the severely unfortunate truth.

"The second fight went a little better, but only because Ash here skated right up to the very edge of what he could get away with and shot the challenger full of holes before James jumped in with both feet. To put it simply, you don't have a big enough deterrent, and it's only a matter of time before you get worn down from the constant fights and someone either beats or kills you. The latter outcome is far more likely."

She said that last part looking directly at me. Again, I wanted to get mad, but that would accomplish absolutely nothing.

"How long do you think we have?"

"A month, maybe two at the outside. It's hard to say for sure because I don't know if your second hybrid is coming back and I don't know which challengers you'll see when. Even giving you the benefit of the doubt, nobody your size has lasted much longer than that without some kind of doomsday weapon at their beck and call."

Tasha took a deep breath and continued. "My pack isn't much better off unfortunately, just for different reasons. The Coun'hij is keeping it quiet, but we've started to see a decided uptick in the number of forays up from south of the border. It's not just about the number of cats we're seeing come up; it's also a factor of just how strong some of them are."

It wasn't the kind of admission that any wolf wanted to make voluntarily. Once there was a perception of weakness it was almost inevitable that attacks would follow. She was putting the future of her friends and family in our hands.

"I've heard rumors that you killed a southerner a little while back. Most of the packs seem to be dismissing the piece of the story that indicates that this cat was extremely dangerous, but I'm not. If anything, I suspect the rumors are understating just how powerful he was."

I leaned back in my chair, trying to buy myself a little distance mentally in which to think. She was trolling her bait very carefully and she most definitely had my attention.

"Why aren't you discounting that piece of the gossip?"

"Because he came across our section of the border and he wasn't quiet about it. He tore through us like we were a bunch of children, and the only reason he didn't stay and wipe my entire pack out is that I bluffed him into thinking the Coun'hij had a group of enforcers on their way already."

Tasha smiled at the stunned look on my face. "Exactly. You had six effectives, seven with Ash, assuming that I'm right in thinking he was in the mix for that one. Nearly half of your pack are hybrids, but we hit him with fourteen people and my mother got in a couple of blows that would have knocked any normal cat down for the count. He shrugged them off and just kept coming."

Ash spoke up. "You're not talking normal fisticuffs. You're implying that your mom hit him with her ability and he shrugged off the equivalent of a double Taser shot?"

"Actually, the last time we measured her ability she was closer to four times what a normal Taser hits for, and yes, that's exactly what I'm saying. My mother leads from the front and she hit him twice. Either discharge should have put even a very powerful hybrid down, but the cat we were up against shrugged both attacks off and went on to kill four of our pack. He almost killed my mother too."

If what we'd just been told was true, then the Tucson pack was in almost as bad of shape as we were. The border packs tended not to get challenged as often as the rest of us simply because most of the dispossessed weren't keen to take control of a pack that would be faced with having to repulse regular forays from the cats out of Mexico.

Even if they managed to avoid a string of challenges like what we were facing, they were still underpowered to be trying to stem the tide of southern shape shifters looking to escape northward. Especially if Tasha was right about the attacks becoming more numerous.

Tasha gave the three of us a minute to digest the information and then continued. "I think that this Anton that you took out was the same cat who gave us so much difficulty. If I'm right, that means whatever ability you manifested to kill Brandon is still working, at least intermittently. As I said earlier, I've come, quite literally, with a proposal. If I were to become Mrs. Alec Graves then we could unite our two packs and solve most of the problems facing both of us in one stroke."

Chapter 7

Alec Graves
Graves Estate
Sanctuary, Utah

Ash and Donovan were each giving their best blank looks, but it was all I could do to keep my composure. As soon as the words had left her mouth, my beast surged forward in a bid to force a transformation. I held on to my shape, but it was a close thing and the edge of the table didn't survive.

Tasha looked down at the tabletop that I'd just crushed and pursed her lips. "Maybe I was a bit too straightforward. I'm not trying to back you into any kind of corner. Go ahead and take some time to talk it over. I'll be fine by myself for a little while."

I nodded stiffly and motioned for Donovan and Ash to follow me as I exited her room. A few minutes later we were safely ensconced in the privacy of Donovan's study.

"Okay, what do the two of you think?"

Ash thought for a couple of seconds and then shrugged. "It has potential. The Coun'hij has traditionally left the border packs pretty much alone because they are so vital to the security of the U.S. There's always a chance they'll still come after the Tucson pack regardless, but we'd have a much better chance of completing that kind of merger than we would with, say, the Chicago pack. A lot will depend on what kind of guarantees Tasha's mother is willing to offer. Everything I've heard is that she's one tough cookie."

Donovan cleared his throat and then proceeded at my nod. "The rumors are right. Jaclyn Annikov is incredibly dangerous. Many years before you were born, there was quite a bit of pressure inside the pack for your father to court her because she is nearly unbeatable in a fight. I've seen her in action, and Agony would never have dared provoke her the way he did your father."

This was news to me. Donovan was generally careful of how much he told me when it came to the thinking that had led up to my father's fight with Agony. Sometimes it seemed like he was worried I'd be influenced into following the exact same path. Not that he was particularly happy with the path I was currently on.

"So what happened?"

"Your father fell in love with your mother, and Jaclyn fell in love with Tasha's father. They both took humans as their mates, following their hearts rather than seeking out the most powerful hybrid they could find as so many of their peers had done."

I was pacing now, but I couldn't decide whether or not to be angry that Donovan had kept that information back from me for so many years. My feelings toward Donovan were nearly as conflicted right now as they would have been towards a biological father who'd started trying to push me down the road he thought was best for me.

"Was that the only reason the alliance didn't go through?"

Donovan shook his head and sighed in unhappiness. "Some of your father's advisors were worried that the move would be viewed as being too aggressive by the Coun'hij. It was an all-or-nothing type of gambit that was almost certain to cause an open confrontation between us and the Coun'hij, and they weren't positive that we could stand off Puppeteer."

"Do you still have contacts with the Tucson pack?"

"A few. We came so close to merging that most of the pack had a friend or two in Tucson at some point or another."

"What can the two of you tell me about Tasha? How powerful is she?"

Ash shrugged. "I have some suspicions, but that's all they are. Jaclyn keeps a very tight lid on her people, so there is very little information out there when it comes to her pack members, but there's even less information than normal on Tasha."

I pinned Donovan to his chair with my gaze for several seconds before he answered. "Ash's suspicions are correct. Jaclyn has been ruthlessly suppressing the information, but Tasha hasn't ever manifested a hybrid form. Some of her pack believe it is her father's legacy, but you would tend to disprove that theory. I know that Jaclyn is very worried about the future though. She so completely outclasses the dominants in her pack that she's been able to protect Tasha from most of the infighting, but once Jaclyn is gone, it is almost certain that Tasha will lose her position and be relegated to a role out on the fringe of the pack."

I nodded, understanding a bit more about her plan now. "So by combining our packs Jaclyn strengthens her position against the ongoing incursions from the south, and by buying me time to manifest my power, she'll also be ensuring her daughter's future after she's gone. It's not a bad plan, assuming that the Coun'hij will let her get away with it, and the dispossessed are a nonissue because she can drop any of them pretty much instantly."

I had to hand it to Tasha and her mother both. It was bold, almost to the point of recklessness, but it was the best option available to them. Sending Tasha to deliver it was risky. It would only be a matter of time before our whole pack knew that she was only a wolf, but without her presence here their plan wouldn't have had any chance of succeeding.

"What are the downsides?"

Donavan was first this time. "Your mother won't be willing to leave Sanctuary. Forcing her to do so would set her progress back decades."

I nodded and turned to Ash, who didn't look entirely happy to be sitting in the hot seat.

"When you get right down to it, Jaclyn doesn't really need anyone but you. You're the one who guarantees her daughter's position. The rest of us are just foot soldiers to help beat back the cats. Anytime you try and integrate two packs you're going to have some really, really nasty fights as the dominants try to sort out the new pecking order. Doing it on short notice, like we'd have to do for this to work, just makes all of that twenty times worse. If you go through with this, there's a very good chance that a couple of us will die."

The thought had already crossed my mind, but it was good to have Ash's perspective on it. He had spent a good chunk of his life being kicked around by Onyx, so he sometimes had a different take on the power struggles inherent in pack life than I did. I turned to go, but Donovan spoke up before I could leave.

"Master Alec, we haven't mentioned the most important consideration. This alliance will only go through if you marry Miss Annikov. Jaclyn Annikov is too shrewd to risk her daughter's future on an alliance that doesn't bind you as tightly to her as possible. Should you marry Miss Annikov, her mother will be watching you like a hawk. Any sign that you plan to do other than remain faithful to your vows after her death would lead her to take severe steps."

"I'd figured as much already. Let's keep all of this between the three of us for now. Also, anything we can do to keep Tasha clear of Addison would probably be worthwhile to pursue. We all know that she's the biggest leak we have, and I'd rather not start the negotiations out by letting Tasha's cat out of the bag."

I left Donovan's study and headed to Rachel's room. Dominic looked up as I entered the room and motioned for silence as she walked me back out into the hall.

"How is she doing, Dom? Any sign of improvement?"

Dominic shook her head, obviously distressed by Rachel's condition. She'd assumed the bulk of the weight of caring for Rachel as my poor little sister got worse and worse.

"No, Alec. She spends most of the day unconscious now. There's no fever, no symptoms at all other than a complete listlessness worse than anything I've ever seen."

"What did Doctor Samuels say when he came by?"

"He still doesn't know what's wrong with her. I helped him draw blood samples, but it was obvious that he didn't even know what tests to run on them next. Alec, I don't think it's a natural phenomenon."

I sighed. It was one more thing that I wasn't staying on top of, and out of all my priorities Rachel should be at the very top, but I didn't know what else to do for her. I'd hired a team of twenty doctors from across the country and hooked them up to a continuous video conference in an effort to find someone that could figure out what was wrong with her. Doctor Samuels came by once every other day or so to run whatever tests his peers came up with, but more and more I was convinced that Dom was right. Whatever was wrong with Rachel wasn't something the doctors were equipped to deal with.

"Can I have a few minutes alone with her?"

"Of course. Just call me on your way out and I'll come back and keep an eye on her."

"Thanks, Dom. I really appreciate it."

Dom offered up a tired smile and then slowly walked away. Whatever was after Rachel was still after Dom as well, and while she was dealing with it better than Rachel, she was still getting worse, too.

One more thing to worry about. I turned and went into Rach's room. Rachel had pushed the sleeves of her pajamas up, revealing arms that were much too skinny. Rachel had always been slender, but she'd really lost weight recently.

I watched for several minutes as Rachel restlessly tossed and turned, but she didn't wake up and I didn't want to deprive her of whatever little benefit she might be getting from her troubled sleep.

"I'm sorry, Rachel. You deserve better than this, but I don't know what else to do for you right now. Hang in there; the doctors will find something soon."

I stood to go, but Rachel's eyes snapped open and she grabbed my hand with surprising strength despite her emaciated form.

"Dominic."

"Calm down, Rach, you'll hurt yourself. I'll call Dom and she'll be back in just a minute."

Rachel shook her head desperately and suddenly her grip on my hand felt fevered.

"No, Alec. Dominic needs to take the center. If she doesn't, then everything stands at risk."

My mind spun wildly for several seconds before I realized that Rachel had to be hallucinating. I sat back down and patted her hand.

"It's okay, Rach. I'll help Dom take the center and everything will be okay."

She grabbed my shoulders and pulled herself up nearly to a sitting position. "I know you don't believe me, Alec. I can see it. You need to though, it's important."

There was something about her tone and expression that stopped my response before I could open my mouth. It was like something other than my little sister was looking up at me from behind her eyes.

We locked gazes for several seconds and then Rachel fell back into her bed and closed her eyes. I checked her pulse as I dialed Dom, but Rachel seemed to just be resting easily now. Dom arrived a couple of minutes later, but didn't have any better idea of what to make of Rachel's cryptic demands than I did.

I thanked Dom again for taking care of Rachel and then left, wandering more or less aimlessly through the house until Kristin intercepted me outside of the theater room.

"Alec, we need to talk."

I stopped and looked at her, which seemed to unnerve her more than I would have expected.

"I can walk with you. Where were you headed?"

My shrug didn't seem to help her state of mind any. "I'm not sure. I didn't really have a destination in mind."

Kristin looked at me for nearly half a minute. "I've never seen you not know exactly where you were headed. Usually you're rushing somewhere and heaven help anyone who gets in your way."

"I guess I'm having an off day. What did you want to talk about?"

She shook herself slightly, as though trying to distance herself from a world where I didn't know where I was headed.

"When Ash and I were on the run from Anton I had a dream about us being attacked. The next day he attacked us and it went down almost exactly like my dream. The only differences seemed to be tied back directly to me having told Ash about my dream. I can't control it and it's only happened once since then, but I'm pretty sure my dreams are a form of precognition. Ash can back me up if you don't believe me."

"What did you dream? You're not the type to overshare, Kristin, so you wouldn't be telling me all of this if you hadn't just had a dream that you figured you needed my help to deal with."

"There's going to be another challenge soon, a huge black hybrid. In my dream I saw the challenger standing over Ash. James was streaking towards the fight, but before he could get there the hybrid ripped Ash's heart out of his chest."

Her voice broke a little as she related the details of Ash's death.

"You told Ash what you saw?"

"Yes, but he just asked me if I'd seen any of the actual fight and then shrugged. I think he thinks that his knowing about the dream will be enough to save him, that he'll do something different this time."

They were still feeling their way forward in their relationship, but I knew they really cared about each other. Kristin would do whatever she thought she had to do when it came to saving Ash. I stared at her for several seconds but she met my gaze without blinking.

"He could be right. Knowing that the challenger will kill him might give Ash the edge he needs to come out on top this time."

Kristin balled both of her hands into fists and took a step towards me. "The dream didn't have any of that kind of information in it. Ash would have already gone into that fight knowing that it was for keeps. How is he going to avoid it without more information than he has right now? You need to keep him out of the fight with the black hybrid."

"Who do I send in first instead? Jess is still pretty much worthless in a fight, Dom practically has to rest when she gets to the top of a set of stairs, and Jasmin isn't in much better shape than Dom right now."

"I don't know, Alec. You're the boss; you need to figure it out. Send James in, or get Isaac back here and throw his butt into the ring. If you don't come up with an alternative then Ash is going to die and I'm going to hold you responsible!"

A threat like that wasn't a good idea at the best of times, but in my current state I didn't have even a prayer of stopping the transformation that ripped through me as my beast took exception to what she'd just said.

Ash had done his work well. Kristin was scared out of her mind—I could smell her fear and most people would have been paralyzed by the intensity of her feeling. Despite that, she threw herself backward, drawing the handgun holstered under her left arm while she was still in the air. Her training was already superb, but she didn't have a prayer; I outmatched her physically by too great a degree for her to compensate for my inborn abilities.

My right hand closed over the top of her pistol before she could finish bringing it around. Her backward lunge had bought her a fraction of a second, but it still wasn't enough to compensate for my greater speed. I'd covered the distance between us in a single step and my left hand was already shooting forward towards her when I heard the safety click on Ash's gun.

"You both need to stand down. Kristin, you need to apologize to Alec. Alec, if you hurt her, I swear I'll kill you. You're fast, but I've got you dead to rights and this isn't my normal nine mil. These rounds will go all the way through you and laugh as they blow big exit wounds out the other side."

I effortlessly ripped the handgun out of Kristin's grasp and then turned towards Ash with a flare of power that left no question as to who was dominant, but I didn't try to close the distance between us.

"Were you planning on using those rounds this morning before Kristin told you about her dream?"

Ash shook his head slowly, but his gun never wavered. "No, I had my normal caliber loaded up, but it's becoming apparent that they don't work very well on hybrids. Too much tissue to go through before you can get to something important."

"So this might make the difference?"

"Maybe. There's only one way to know for sure."

Kristin hissed something angry at the two of us but Ash quieted her with a wave. "All of the considerations we talked about earlier today haven't changed. If we can't establish a bit of depth to our lineup then we're screwed. Even Tasha's proposal will need a little bit of time before it will have a noticeable deterrent effect."

I let my shape shrink back down to my human form, ejected the magazine, racked the slide, and then handed the weapon back to Kristin as I pocketed the magazine and spare round. She snatched the weapon out of my hand and then leaned forward, talking quietly enough that her voice wouldn't carry to Ash.

"If you put him in the ring against the black hybrid and he dies then I'll come after your mom and Rachel."

My beast just about broke loose again, but I suppressed the transformation with a grim determination. Ash was still on edge and I couldn't afford to do anything that looked threatening. Instead I leaned forward and whispered into Kristin's ear.

"What is to stop me from killing you as soon as Ash falls? Be careful what kind of threats you issue. You're not ready to play with those kinds of stakes yet."

"You're not a murderer, Alec. Not by nature or choice either one, not while you have people who love you."

I looked down at her and let my eyes bleed over to the ice blue of my beast. "How can you be so sure of that?"

"I'm sure of it because you're not that different than I am, and I won't do those kinds of things as long as Ash is around to anchor me."

I pushed past her and walked away, but anger still lapped at the edges of my control even after the two of them were safely several corners behind me. The last thing the pack needed right now was a willful human throwing her hat into the power structure. It was all I could do right now to keep the rest of the pack from killing each other. If Ash didn't get Kristin back in check enough that she stopped threatening noncombatants, there was going to be hell to pay.

I debated lifting weights, but with as little defense in depth as we had right now it was too risky. I just couldn't take the chance that another challenger would show up while I was still exhausted from a workout. Eventually my aimless feet brought me out to the gardens behind the house.

Once I stepped out into the cool winter air, I knew where I'd end up eventually, but I just couldn't stop myself. The memories were painful, but they hurt precisely because of how incredible they'd been back when they'd happened. I couldn't help the fact that Adri's leaving had poisoned them to a certain extent, but I knew that I needed to start trying to move on.

Tasha's appearance in Sanctuary today had driven that fact home, even if it ultimately accomplished nothing else. Grief over Adri's departure was causing me to make suboptimal decisions in almost every aspect of my life, but even recognizing that fact hadn't halted the slow-motion meltdown that was my life.

The grotto was just like I'd remembered it. The slightly cooler December temperatures were enough to send some of the vegetation on the rough rock walls into a state of dormancy, but Andrew and Donovan had carefully staggered the plant life such that there was something in bloom at nearly any time of year.

The potted rose bushes were something else that I'd been avoiding ever since Adri had left. Lagrimas del Angel represented the culmination of two generations of work. The full, white petals edged in purple were so close to perfect that a casual observer could have been forgiven for thinking that we'd actually managed to achieve perfection, but the true beauty of the plant wasn't its visual presence.

I took a deep breath and let the scent of the few remaining buds float into my lungs. Lagrimas somehow made everything around them smell better, so today I was sampling the solid, unmoving smell of the walls and the tiny trickle of water that made its way down the rock face. It was a heavenly bouquet, but I knew it was a pale imitation of what it could be.

Adri had turned the grotto into something unearthly. The first time we'd been together here had been in a shared dream. We'd been so lost in our own heads that we hadn't realized there was anything unusual about the experience.

Since then it seemed as though most of our milestones had been here. It had been here that she'd started to understand what I was for the first time, but she'd bravely seen past the beast to the man behind it. The night of Ashure Day Dance, Donovan and I had put floating lights into the reflecting pool and carpeted the entire grotto with Lagrimas petals.

I let my mind drift back to that night, to the way it had felt to hold her in my arms, and I found a quiet sliver of peace underneath all of the pain that the memory triggered. Somewhere along the way I'd lost Adri's trust and respect.

There wasn't anything I could do about that now but try to live up to the person that she thought I could be. It was a formidable challenge given the inherent savagery of pack life.

I lowered myself down to the floor of the grotto, and put my back against the rock wall. As the minutes passed, something tickled the back of my mind. It was almost like I was on the verge of some kind of mental breakthrough. I could feel the thought, whatever it was, working its way up from my subconscious.

A split second before it seemed like I'd have my realization, my phone rang. It was James.

"Alec, we've got another car inbound. I think we'd be pushing our luck to expect that this one isn't a challenger. Do you want Tasha there?"

I took a deep breath and reminded myself that it wasn't James' fault that my thoughts had just gone skittering away.

"Don't make it a command, but please have Donovan stop by and extend an invitation for her to be there if she'd like. You can handle rounding up the rest of the pack?"

"Yeah, we're all getting plenty of practice at this kind of thing."

A few minutes later, I was back in Donovan's Zen Garden waiting for the rest of the pack to arrive as a cool breeze caused the trees to slowly sway back and forth. Tasha pulled me off to the side a few seconds before Donovan and James arrived with the challenger.

"Alec, I caught a look at your latest arrival. James agreed to have Donovan lead him around the long way so I could brief you about whatever I knew. This guy's name is Raphael and he's really bad news. Honestly, I figured you had at least a few more weeks before this caliber of challenger started showing up."

"It had to happen sooner or later. What makes this guy so dangerous?"

"In a word, he's Agony-lite. He can't do permanent injuries as quickly as Agony can. It seems like he has to concentrate harder to make it happen, but the effect is essentially the same."

I nodded, my mind feverishly fitting the pieces together. "He's here now because he figures he can intimidate the rest of the pack into standing up to any future challengers. He doesn't just figure he's a better fighter; he figures he's got the kind of deterrent we're currently lacking."

Tasha was pacing now, obviously following the same chain of logic I was. "You're probably right. He's not the scariest dispossessed out there, but he's got a chance of making it work. He could have been part of the Coun'hij if he'd wanted to, but he turned them down because he knew he'd always be playing second fiddle to Agony."

"Where do you and your mom stand with regards to an alliance with the Sanctuary pack if he were in charge of things?"

"Why, are you thinking of stepping down?"

I shrugged. "Possibly. It depends on a lot of factors. If there is an option that preserves the pack and just requires that I become one of the dispossessed that might be the lesser of all evils."

"The Coun'hij would see you dead inside of a year. It wouldn't matter how good of a job you did hiding; they'd find you and kill you once you didn't have the protection of a pack."

"That still might be the lesser evil."

Tasha didn't look happy about my train of thought, but I knew that wouldn't impact her answer. She'd been groomed to rule her pack since she'd been able to walk. She knew all about hard decisions.

"I wouldn't marry someone like Raphael. He'll keep people in line through torture more even than by intimidation. I wouldn't bring that into my pack and subject my friends and family to dealing with him. We'd either find another way or we'd fail, but I wouldn't consider him an option."

"Fair enough. Sounds like it will be a fight then."

Raphael had already shifted to his hybrid form by the time Donovan and the others brought him back to Tasha and me. His words came out with the deep, almost alien sound of a throat that hadn't been designed with speech in mind.

"Are you so scared of me that you wouldn't even greet me with your pack, Graves?"

"Quite to the contrary. I had other, more pressing business to attend to than meeting one unimportant dispossessed challenger who will probably be dead before the sun sets."

We both knew it was all nothing more than blatant posturing, but I could still see that my comment had angered him. He relied on his reputation and someone claiming they didn't know who he was seemed to drive him nearly into a killing rage.

"Come face me and we'll see who lies dead at whose feet."

"I don't fight the trash. You can challenge as per your right, but we'll have to verify that you're worth my time before you'll get a shot at me."

"I think you'll find that your pack is even less willing to fight me than most. I promise you all now that anyone who stands against me today will pay for their actions once I've taken over this sorry excuse of a pack."

I confidently turned my back to him, knowing that Donovan, and probably Tasha would remain facing him and that they'd give warning with plenty of time if he moved towards us. James, Jasmin, Dominic, Jess and Ash all gathered around me. I pulled out my phone and loaded up the special app I'd had commissioned more than a year before.

I drew a circle and then started moving the names of each member of the pack around into the positions where I wanted them. Everyone nodded, and then it was time to lay out the order of who would go when.

I started putting the list together just like Ash and I had discussed, and then paused as I looked at the diagram I'd put together. Ash was in the center of the arc I'd drawn, and for some reason Rachel's words came back to me.

Dominic wasn't ready to go up against a hybrid—she wasn't even in a position to go up against a regular wolf—but I couldn't get what Rachel had said out of my mind. My finger moved, almost of its own accord, and I found myself putting Dominic at the top of the list, followed by James, Jasmin, and then me.

James hissed in displeasure when he saw the list, but Dominic put a hand on his arm and nodded slowly to me. A few seconds later we were all spreading out around the square of sand and then Dominic sprang towards Raphael.

My heart jumped up to my throat as I saw just how slow she was. She never even had a chance. Raphael sidestepped her attack and sank a claw into her side, pinning her to the ground.

James started towards the two of them, but Raphael held up a hand. "Stop, or I'll kill her."

It was the one threat guaranteed to immobilize James, but it worked equally well on the rest of us. Raphael repositioned, keeping

Dominic pinned to the ground, as he brought his right hand up to her face and slowly sliced her left cheek down to the bone. The slow, measured motion left no doubt in my mind but that he was using his power on her. The wound was going to scar, and there wasn't anything any of us could do about it.

Raphael stood up, Dominic dangling from his arm. "She stood against me, and now she's felt the very first taste of the retribution I'll be visiting upon her once I kill Alec. The rest of you would be best off standing down and letting me kill him now."

Dominic hung limply from Raphael's left hand. She was heart-wrenchingly still and I started to worry that he'd hit something critical when he'd sunk his claws into her chest. Raphael dropped Dominic into the sand as he slowly turned in a half circle, taking in the rest of the pack.

James stepped forward, obviously intent on vengeance for what had just been done to Dom, but then things happened almost too fast even for me to follow. Dom rolled back to her feet and sprang onto Raphael's back, all four sets of claws scrabbling for purchase.

Raphael spun around, trying desperately to knock Dominic off his back, but she had too good of a grip and hybrid arms weren't hinged in such a way as to let them get at anything behind them. It boggled the mind that Dom had been able to hang motionless in Raphael's claws, pretending to be unconscious despite the pain, but she'd managed it and sprung the ultimate ambush.

Dominic mewled in pain as Raphael threw himself backward, slamming her into the ground, but she didn't let go. She clung to his back as he rolled away and then regained his feet. I could tell that Dom was taking a beating, but she gamely held on to Raphael's back until she saw her chance and then she took it.

One moment she was clawing frantically to try and keep her perch and then suddenly her jaws fastened around the back of Raphael's neck. There were still another several minutes of desperate motion, but in that instant Dominic had secured her victory.

As soon as Raphael hit the ground, the rest of the pack swarmed around her, congratulating her. Relief that Dom had survived washed through me, and then sorrow that she'd been scarred, but most of all I found myself thinking of the respite she'd just secured us. Raphael, a powerful, dangerous hybrid, had just been killed by one of the weakest members of our pack. With Tasha here to report on the events, word should spread quickly enough to deter at least some of the dispossessed currently lined up to take a shot at us. I looked over at Tasha and saw the same thought in her eyes.

Maybe we were better matched than I'd realized.

Chapter 8

Adriana Paige
Upper East Side
Manhattan, New York

Life had gotten a little better after dinner with Albert. The girls at school were just as bad, but I found I was able to keep things in perspective more so than before.

Isaac and I had settled into a comfortable routine, which mostly involved me hanging out at his place whenever my mom wasn't around. Albert occasionally texted me after they'd finished a big show, or when a new song seemed to be coming together better than he'd expected it to.

All in all, it seemed like he was doing well, and somehow knowing that he was out there helped me to deal with all of the stupid craziness of being in high school and having to deal with other high-school girls.

Isaac tended to get a little antsy if I left my building without him, so I'd taken to hanging out in my lobby each morning until he showed up to escort me to school. I was downstairs, trading texts with Albert while I waited, when I got the second best surprise since I'd arrived in Manhattan.

It wasn't Isaac who picked me up, it was Dominic.

"Sorry, Adri. I know this is a bit of a last-minute kind of change, but Alec wanted Isaac back, so he flew me out to take his place late last night."

Dom yawned and then gave me a cheery smile, but I found my eyes pulled mercilessly over to the side of her face.

"What happened?"

"Another challenge match. Alec has tried to keep me out of them so far because I've been so tired all of the time, but something made him put me in on this one."

She'd given me a lot to process already. I was reluctant to dive into the inner workings of the pack, but that was trumped by my concern for Dom.

"What do you mean 'tired all of the time'?"

"I can't really explain it. Rachel and I seem to have it the worst, but I think it's impacting Jasmin, too. I'm just always tired. I'm weaker and slower than normal, too. It's been going on for weeks. Don't worry though. I can still defend you from a lot of the nasty stuff out there; we'll just have to run away from more of it than normal."

I shook my head and pointed to her building. "I don't care about having a bodyguard; I care about the fact that you're sick. You should get back to the penthouse and spend the day in bed resting."

"I'm fine, Adri. I've spent a number of days in bed resting over the last little while, and it hasn't made any difference. I'll be fine. Also, I really worry about you in this city. I've already crossed over an old vampire trail, and I've only been in the city for four or five hours."

There it was again. Vampires. It made sense that there would be a heavy concentration of supernatural parasites in New York, but the thought of walking past them and not even being able to tell what they were gave me the willies.

"Okay, you can come with me, but I'm serious about you not overdoing it. If you start feeling like you've done too much, I'm putting you in a cab and sending you back here."

Dom's smile still transformed her face into something angelic. The angry, red scar didn't change that, but it was still concerning.

"So tell me about this challenge match."

"I'm not sure there's much to tell. Ash was still injured and Jasmin wasn't quite back to normal so Alec sent me in first. I did awfully. It had been so long and I felt so weak that the challenger didn't have any problems dodging my spring. Once he pinned me though, I realized that my best hope was to play dead, so I waited until he let go of me and turned around to face James. Once his back was to me, I attacked."

Dom looked around and then leaned in closer to me. "I managed to kill him myself. It isn't the kind of thing I'll probably ever be able to repeat, but it should help buy the pack some breathing room. If a hybrid as powerful as Raphael falls to our submissives then there will be some who decide we're too dangerous to challenge."

I forced myself not to show the horror I felt at the thought of gentle, kind Dominic killing someone. I knew she could still smell the shock on me, but as long as I didn't frame the feeling with words she probably wouldn't know for sure what it was that had disturbed me so.

"What about your cheek? Shouldn't it have healed by now?"

Dom's sad smile had an air of tranquility to it that surprised me. "No, it will never fully heal. Raphael had a power that was very similar to what Agony wields. I have a matching set of marks here on my ribs, but James still thinks I'm pretty, so they don't matter."

I was angry now. How could Alec send Dom, one of the weakest members of the pack, in to fight something as monstrous as this Raphael must have been?

"That's terrible, Dom. I can't believe you can be so calm about everything that happened. What was Alec thinking?"

There was fire behind Dom's gentle eyes now and I suddenly found myself wondering if I'd ever seen her really mad before.

"Alec did what he had to do. These challenge matches are life and death for the pack. Alec saved my life years ago and I won't turn my back on him now. Not when he needs me, not when the pack needs me. I love you almost like a sister, Adri, but you don't know what he is up against right now. It's not that you're stupid, but you're ignorant of just how much evil abounds in the world."

I opened my mouth to respond, but nothing would come out. We stood in silence for a couple of minutes and then Dom gestured out at the streets. "We should be on our way or you're going to be late for school."

I almost didn't know what to do. We started off to school, but that wasn't what was bothering me. Dom had never been mad at me. I'd never even seen her get mad, not like that, and I didn't know how to fix things now that I'd ruined our morning.

Arriving at school didn't do the trick, but I found my respect for Dominic growing as I watched her during the day. Dom needed to register still, so we stopped off at the office first thing after we arrived. Alec and Isaac seemed to have done whatever spadework was required already. Dom handed over a check and gave the office lady her name.

As I watched the secretary do a double take at Dom's scar, I hoped that I'd been less obvious than that. It didn't stop there though. Every guy or girl we passed during the day had the same kind of response, but it didn't seem to rattle Dom in the slightest. She had better hearing than I did, so I knew she could hear the whispered insults that started around noon, but even being called Franken Freak didn't ripple the pool of calm that seemed to reside at her center.

A couple of hours after we finished up lunch I found myself reaching out and putting a hand on Dom's arm.

"Dom, I'm really sorry. You're right; there's so much I don't know. I didn't mean to take anything away from your accomplishment; I'm just worried about you."

Dom's smile was more hesitant than normal, but she looked into my eyes, seeming to weigh my sincerity for several seconds before nodding.

"You are forgiven, Adri. I know it's hard to watch someone you care about put themselves in harm's way, but that's the reason I have to do what I'm doing. James, Alec, all of the others are in just as much danger as I am in, more possibly."

There wasn't really a response to that. If someone you loved was in danger how could you do anything other than your absolute best to help them?

Dom patted my hand and then pointed to her scar. "I know this distresses you, but it really doesn't matter. All of the girls mocking me are more foolish than they know. Up until I met James, my looks brought me nothing but problems. If I'd built my sense of self around them I would have been very unhappy. It's the same with the exhaustion that is robbing me of my usual strength. There will always be those around me who are more dangerous than I am. What matters isn't what I can do or how pretty I am. What matters is whether or not I'm doing my absolute best to live up to my beliefs."

Something she was saying reached inside me and smoothed away some of the hurt I'd been carrying around with me for what already seemed like forever.

"Dom, do you hate me for leaving Sanctuary, for leaving Alec?"

Her smile was incredibly gentle. She paused, as if letting me fully take in the sentiment behind it, and then shook her head.

"I'm not going to lie to you, Adri. Life has gotten very difficult since you left. Not all of that is because of your departure, but some of it is. Even so, I don't hate you. You did what you felt like you had to do, and I respect you for it."

It seemed a weight had come off my chest. It was somehow easier to breathe now, and a matching smile made it up to my lips.

"Thanks, Dom. That means more to me than you know. What can I do to help make up for my earlier words though? Is there anywhere in New York that you've ever wanted to visit? We can spend the evening sightseeing if you want."

There was a flash of something that I was pretty sure was hope, and then Dom's face settled back to its normal pleasant expression.

"No, Adri, you don't need to do anything else to make things right between us. We should return home after school and do homework."

"That's not what you really want to do though, is it? Please tell me. I'd really like to do something other than just study tonight."

I could see Dom's hidden desire working on her, slowly chipping away at her reluctance to inconvenience me.

"If you won't let me make a gesture to make up for earlier, at least let me go with my friend somewhere that she wants to go."

Dom's smile was back. "Okay, I'll tell you my secret. My favorite author is doing a book signing tonight. Ever since Rachel told me about it I haven't been able to stop wishing there were a way that I could go meet her in person. She hardly ever makes it into the United States, but it is really out of the way."

"That's perfect. We're going to a book signing tonight, and that's all there is to it!"

Dom hadn't been kidding when she said the signing was out of the way. I texted Mom to let her know I'd be out late, and then we jumped on the number 5 train and headed out to Brooklyn. We swapped trains twice and then jumped on a bus in order to get to our destination, which proved to be a massive underground parking garage.

I thought it was an odd place to hold a book signing, but Dom apparently had done a little bit of research on her flight, and it wasn't uncommon for this particular garage to host multiple events during a given week, sometimes simultaneously.

We arrived to find a line that snaked up a couple of levels and an outrageous din that I was sure had nothing at all to do with the book signing. Dominic pulled three books out of her backpack as we stepped into line and started our slow journey towards wherever it was that the author was actually signing copies.

When she saw my interest in the books she was holding, Dom handed me one to look at. I opened it up, but it was written entirely in Spanish. "Vanessa Valencia. I've never heard of her before. What kind of books does she write?"

Dominic shrugged, seemingly at a loss for how to describe the books. After several seconds she took the book back from me and sighed.

"I think you would probably call it literary fiction. The part that calls to me is her characters. They are all so real, such ordinary people, but during the course of the novel there is always at least one who finds himself."

"What do you mean 'finds himself'?"

Another shrug, I was starting to see that we were talking about something that was important to Dom. Her natural shyness generally meant she had a harder time talking about something when it was central to who she was.

"It's a little bit like what we talked about earlier. The characters in her books decide what is really, truly important to them, and then they make the sacrifices that are required for them to live up to their beliefs. I think more than anything else that it was Mrs. Valencia's writing that gave me the courage to flee north and eventually find Alec's pack."

I nodded, not because I really understood, but because she'd told me enough to get me started. I made a mental note to get a translated copy of all three books, and then asked Dom about James and his latest modifications to his car.

Dom didn't love cars and tuning them anywhere near as much as James did, but she loved James, so she was quite capable of talking about his passions for long blocks of time. With the conversation safely turned to something less intimate, we both relaxed a little for the next half hour.

Dominic was halfway through describing how a turbo worked, when she suddenly tensed up and grabbed my arm.

"Adri, I smell vampires."

I leaned in close so we could exchange words without other people overhearing. "How many, and are they close?"

Dom paused for several seconds, and then shook her head. "Not close. The scent is very faint, so it's hard to say for sure, but I think there are two or three individuals in what I smell."

I looked around, trying not to be too obtrusive in my scan of our area of the parking garage, but I didn't see anyone that made me think 'Oh crap. There's a vampire.'

"Faint like they aren't nearby, or faint like the scent is very old? There isn't much chance for the elements to wash away the scent down here, so an old scent trail could stay around for a long time."

She seemed to consider my words for several seconds before nodding grudgingly. "You could be right, but we should go anyways. It's too risky for you to be here."

Dom tugged on my arm, but I pulled back. She could easily pick me up and carry me back outside, but that would attract exactly the kind of attention she spent so much time and energy avoiding. She would need at least a modicum of cooperation from me if she was going to get me back up to the surface without making a scene.

"Dom, I know you're worried, but there's got to be at least a thousand people here. Unless you think we're really in immediate danger then we're going to stay and get you your autograph."

It was obvious I'd hit upon the perfect argument to make her pause, but even so I wasn't positive it would work on her. A few seconds later she sighed and nodded.

"Very well, we'll continue forward, but if the scent gets stronger then we're getting out of here, and I don't want you fighting me."

"You've got yourself a deal."

The next few minutes were pleasant. We talked about Sanctuary, but Dominic was a natural when it came to skirting around topics that would cause me unhappiness. The noise from whatever the other activity was that was going on at the same time was rising and falling now, but I still hadn't figured out what it was. There was a crowd. I could distinctly pick out cheers and even an occasional whistle. That was the piece that was cresting every now and then, but there was a metallic bit to it as well. It sounded like someone had buzz saws going at the same time.

We went down another set of stairs and I was finally able to see the cause of all of the commotion. There was a rough circle walled off a dozen feet or so away from where our line snaked past. It took me a couple of seconds to realize that the kids standing around the circle were pressing up against Plexiglas shields, and that the circle contained half a dozen remote-controlled robots busy trying to destroy each other.

Seven or eight other robots had already been dispatched, some of them in multiple pieces, lying at various places inside the arena. I couldn't see very well from where I was standing, but even so I could tell that the designs were incredibly varied, everything from hammer-wielding contraptions to ones with spinning discs and even giant claws.

I was both simultaneously impressed by the ingenuity of the combatants, who were frantically controlling them with massive remote controls, and amazed at the sheer work they'd put into something that was being destroyed in spectacular fashion. I started to turn around to talk to Dominic some more, but stopped and felt my mouth drop open as I realized I knew one of the boys standing around the circle.

I started toward the circle, but Dom grabbed my arm before I could make it more than half a step. "Adri, where are you going?"

"I'm not going far, Dom. You stay here. I'll make sure I don't get out of view, but I need to go check something."

Dom let go of my arm with a worried look. I smiled reassuringly at her and then started back toward the circle. It only took a few steps to become certain I'd been right.

"Ben!"

He turned around and looked at me with confusion on his face for a split second before breaking out in a smile. He met me halfway between the arena and Dominic and actually gave me a hug with the hand that wasn't holding a massive remote control.

"I never in the world would have expected to see someone else from Sanctuary at this thing. Since when are you into battle bots?"

I shook my head and smiled again. I was smiling hard enough that I knew my face was going to hurt before long.

"I'm not into robots, I'm here with Dom. There's some kind of book signing going on for one of her favorite authors."

Ben nodded. "That explains it then; you never struck me as much of a gearhead. What are you doing in New York?"

"My mom moved us out here a little while after all of the craziness…"

It was the wrong thing to say, and I knew it almost as soon as it came out of my mouth. Agony's trip had been extremely unpleasant for me, but it had been as bad or worse for Ben. Despite all of Alec's effort to keep me at arm's length because he was worried I'd become addicted to his touch, I'd almost stopped believing it could really happen.

My doubts had been washed away when Ben had touched Jasmin and felt the full force of the Ja'tell bond. He'd been utterly addicted to her, but Agony's visit had prevented Jasmin from seeing Ben again for days after the bond had been formed. Ben had thought Jasmin was just stringing him along, so he'd left town, choosing a clean break rather than letting the addiction get even worse.

We sat in silence for a couple of seconds before I pointed at his remote control. "So you didn't just come to watch; you came to compete, too?"

Ben brightened up instantly. "Yeah, this was my first go at things and I made it past the second round, so I'm actually pretty happy with how I did."

"There are multiple rounds to this?"

His laugh was different than I remembered it being back in Sanctuary. It was lighter, more relaxed than before. I found my smile getting wider.

"Yeah, there are four rounds. This is the last one. It's getting boring now. Nobody has any surprises left so it's moving a lot slower now than it did for the first few rounds. I was starting to think about heading out. Let me get my robot and I'll walk with you."

'Getting his robot' proved to be a lot more involved of a process than I'd expected it to be. It was literally in multiple pieces.

"What happened?"

"One of the buzz saw robots managed to dart under me when I rolled over top of some loose parts. The next thing I knew, it had cut both of my axles."

I shook my head in astonishment as I helped him pick it up. It had to weigh at least forty pounds, which meant that getting it home was going to be a real pain now that he couldn't roll it along ahead of him.

"Do you mind if we walk up the line a ways? I don't want Dom to think I completely ditched her."

"Sure, no problem. You're going to have to help me carry it back up to the street though; there's no way that I can manage it by myself. I'm starting to think that next time I'll bring spare axles."

It felt like Ben's robot got heavier the further we hauled it. We didn't make it all of the way to Dominic. Actually, we didn't even come close, but we covered enough distance that she wasn't going to lose sight of me, which would help calm her back down. I'd been stealing glances at her while I'd been talking to Ben, and she'd been getting more and more concerned as the line had taken her further and further away from me.

"So what are you doing out here? What school are you going to?"

Ben shook his head. "No school. Honestly I don't know why I bothered with school back in Sanctuary as long as I did. I got a job with a sweet auto body shop. They've got a pretty exclusive client base and we do all kinds of crazy stuff. Today I installed a pair of turbos and then started drawing up plans for a secret compartment in an SUV."

"What do they need secret compartments for?"

"I don't know, they don't tell me that kind of stuff. The customer is always right and all that. Rich people can be pretty eccentric, though, so who knows what it's for. Remember all of the crazy stuff Alec used to do? I keep in touch with a couple of people back in Sanctuary, and the word there now is that he's got some new girl throwing herself at him. She's staying at his house and picks him up from school. Just more craziness."

I opened my mouth to respond and suddenly felt like the floor had moved on me. Ben caught me before I could hit the ground, but even so, it was plenty embarrassing.

"Are you okay, Adri?"

"Yeah. It's stupid, but sometimes I get kind of woozy when I think about him. Things...well, they didn't end well when I left Sanctuary."

It was only a partial lie. I did sometimes get unsteady on my feet when I thought about Alec, but this had more to do with learning that he'd replaced me. Already.

Ben sometimes played the stupid gearhead when it suited him, but he wasn't an idiot. It took him only a fraction of a second to run back through our conversation from right before my near collapse and figure out exactly who I was talking about.

"Sorry, I didn't mean to take you back down memory lane. Are you doing okay otherwise? I mean, as long as you don't think about him."

I almost snorted at the incomprehensible thought of going more than an hour or two without thinking of Alec, but Ben didn't deserve that. Instead I just nodded.

"Yeah, overall I'm doing okay. My school is full of a bunch of stuck-up snobs, but I saw Albert a little while ago, and Dom flew out today, so that's helped. I was kind of surprised, actually, that it helped as much as it did. I only lived in Sanctuary for a few months, but I guess it set its hooks in me pretty deep."

It was Ben's turn to look like he was thinking of other times and places. "Yeah, I guess it does. I lived there my whole life until I ran away, so I don't really know any different, but I find myself thinking about home a lot more than I thought I would."

He'd been the one to bring it up, so I decided to go ahead and turn the tables on him. "How are you doing, Ben? I mean really."

"I'm okay. Work really is cool. They didn't even bat an eye when they found out I wasn't quite eighteen yet. All they seem to care about is whether or not I can do the job. I've actually been clean since before I got here. Whatever

Jasmin did to me was a real mind job, but it had one benefit. I don't even feel the urge to use, at least not the normal stuff."

"You miss her?"

"I don't think 'miss' is the right word. More like crave. One of the guys at work does some hypnosis though. I've started doing a few sessions with him and that's helping a little. Mostly I just fight every hour not to jump on a bus and head back to Utah."

There wasn't a lot you could say after an admission like that. We both sat there in silence for a minute or so before I remembered to look up and check on Dom. Even from so far away, I could tell she was getting nervous. There was a massive wall that the line snaked around which was going to carry her out of view if we didn't move pretty soon.

"Do you mind if we move a little further up the line?"

"You know it would probably be easier to just wait here until she gets done and comes back this way."

I nodded and then bit my lip. "I know; it really would, but it's just...well, you know how there was always at least one or two odd things going on at Sanctuary at any given moment?"

Ben's chuckle didn't have very much amusement in it. "Let me guess, this is another one of those odd things?"

"Yeah, I'm afraid so. If you want to just stay here you can, but I need to move up there a little ways."

"No, I'll come with you. I should have known. Alec always seemed to be in the middle of at least half of the crazy stuff back home. It only stands to reason that Dominic would have brought her share of crazy here with her."

We lugged Ben's robot another fifty or so feet until we got far enough around the wall that, not only could we see Dom, we could also see the table where the author was signing books. I set down the robot with a groan of relief.

"This thing is heavy, Ben. Was your strategy to just drive over top of the competition and crush them?"

He rolled his eyes at me. "No, but some of the robots tip you over as a way of bringing you out of the game, so I made it heavy enough that the crane and wedge types would struggle to execute their strategy."

Whatever Ben was about to say next was interrupted by a chirp from my phone. Ben motioned for me to go ahead and check my texts, so I fished my phone out of my pocket and smiled when I saw that it was from Albert.

You at another rave?

I shook my head and showed Ben the screen. "Albert's band did a show in Manhattan a little while ago. I told him I'd never been somewhere where everyone had lights on their fingers and he told me I'd just been to my very first rave. I think he's making fun of me."

Ben smiled and nodded. "Yes, he's absolutely making fun of you. I suspect a real rave would have made you hyperventilate. Tell him I said hi."

Nope. Doubleheader—warring robots and a book signing. Ben says hi.

Albert's response came back only a couple of seconds later.

Are the robots signing the books, too? I'd pay to see that! We're going to be back in New York sometime in the next couple of weeks. Can I swing by and see you then?

The question of 'us' again. I knew nothing had changed, that Albert was going to want more than I wanted, but there was always a chance I was misreading the signs.

I told you we could hang out last time I saw you.

I know. I just wanted to make sure nothing had changed. Off to a crazy after-party—see you later.

Ben shook his head when I handed him my phone to read the exchange. "Albert as a rock star. I kind of wish I'd seen that with my own eyes. With stuff like that going on, I can almost believe anything. Bring on the werewolves and vampires."

FORSAKEN

I looked back yet again and wished I hadn't let Adri talk me into splitting up. They were far enough away from the bedlam of the robot competition that I could hear most of what she and Ben were saying, but knowing that *I'd* know they were in trouble as soon as *she* knew she was in trouble wasn't actually very comforting.

The lady behind me let out another long-suffering sigh, so I took another couple of steps, closing the distance that had grown between me and the people in front of me. My nose wasn't providing much help when it came to monitoring Adri's status. The stale scent of vampire hadn't gone anywhere. In fact it was oddly stronger sometimes than others. My beast knew the scent meant danger and she was acting up more than normal. I could feel my power snap out of me and then recoil back and lash out again.

My beast usually didn't act up as much as the wolves inside the rest of the pack, but today she was in rare form. So far none of the people in line seemed sensitive enough to realize anything was out of the ordinary, but I knew from past experience that if Adri had been standing next to me the flares of power would have been making her very uncomfortable.

I took another step forward and then turned back and checked on Adri again. She and Ben seemed to be getting along well. I could just hear her laughing at something as Ben handed her phone back to her. The laughter sounded a little forced, but she still looked more relaxed than she had earlier in the day.

Another sigh from behind me triggered another step, and then suddenly I was able to see Mrs. Valencia. She was sitting at a table, which was exactly what I'd expected, but there was an expanse of empty space between her and the front of the line.

I would have known if I'd dropped one of my books, but I still found myself double-checking that all three of them were safely in my hands. Adri had been gracious to agree to accompany me, but she didn't understand just how momentous an occasion this was for me. I knew I probably wouldn't get a chance to exchange more than a couple of words with Mrs. Valencia, but I still knew it would be one of those moments in life that I would treasure for however long I had before death caught back up to me.

I'd told Adri that Alec had saved me, that he'd given me the kind of life that I'd never even hoped—much less expected—to have, but that was only part of the story. It had been the characters in Mrs. Valencia's novels who had given me the courage to set out towards the United States in the first place. I owed a debt of gratitude to Alec that I would never be able to repay, but there was an earlier, in some ways greater, debt that I owed Mrs. Valencia.

FORSAKEN

My father had been wrong about so many things, but he was right about the need to repay debts. I had no special power and would never develop one. A few of my kind developed the ability to track their prey regardless of how much time or space came between us and them, but we weren't ever blessed with the amazing, multi-form talents the wolf hybrids sometimes manifested.

I didn't need the ability to see into the future, though, to know what my destiny had been. I'd been firmly slated to an early, unremarkable death long before I ever made it out of my teenage years. In so many ways every day of the past couple of years had been a gift, one for which I remained profoundly grateful.

I took another few steps and then, almost as if time had skipped forward, I was the next in line to talk to Mrs. Valencia. I took a deep breath, trying unsuccessfully to calm the power arcing around me, and then crossed the barrier of empty space between us. She looked up and smiled as I approached, but there was an odd hitch to the motion as she saw my scar.

I couldn't help the brief flash of disappointment that coursed through me. I'd meant everything I'd said to Adri. I was mostly adjusted to my maimed face, but I was still human. It hurt a little bit when someone I didn't know responded like that, but it was worse when it was Mrs. Valencia reacting so poorly. I'd somehow thought that she'd be above those kinds of concerns. I sighed a little and then held out my books as I finally reached her table.

"Thank you for writing these, Mrs. Valencia. I…well, they made a big difference in the course of how my life would have gone."

She took the stack of books and opened the first one, but she wasn't moving as fast as she had with the person who'd been standing in front of me in the line. She cocked her head to the side and looked up at me as she signed the first book.

"I have people tell me that frequently at these kinds of things, but I think you really mean it. You're quite a ways from home, aren't you?"

I nodded my head in surprise at her insight. "Yes, I'm out visiting a friend. My home is in Utah."

"That's not what I meant, child. You're not from Utah, not originally at least. You originally come from somewhere much farther away than that."

Another nod, this one full of discomfort as my internal alarms started sounding.

"How could you know that?"

"I have been on the face of this earth for a very long time. I know things most people don't know. For example, I know you can slip this form and run on four feet."

That last bit had been said in something less than a whisper, another clue that she knew more about the moonborn than she should have. No normal human would have been able to hear her words, even from just a couple feet away. She was putting me in a difficult position.

"You're not supposed to know that unless you're one of us."

Her smile was sad. "There are many things which I would do much to unlearn, but the presence of moon's children isn't one of them. Your secret is safe with me."

"How did you learn of us?"

"You hide yourselves from the vampires, who in turn hide themselves from the humans. Did you never consider that there might be others who hide themselves from you?"

She'd just finished signing my second book, but she'd done so in an absent manner. We both knew the conversation was the important part of what was happening. My beast was bubbling just below the surface, shedding power as it worried about her implication that she wasn't human, but instead another, unknown threat.

"Is my friend in danger from you?"

She looked down the line, and smiled again. "No, child. Your friend isn't in any danger from me, at least not danger that I can control. Your concern for her does you credit."

The third book was signed, but she reached over to a pile of bookmarks and picked one up. "Would you like me to fix that for you?"

She'd pointed at my cheek, at the angry scar that had caught her attention earlier.

"That depends on the price involved."

"You're wise to ask. In dealings with one such as me, the price is often more than one realizes at the time payment is agreed. I will extract no price beyond a few hours of your time, and a promise that you won't tell anyone about me. In fact, I believe I can teach you a new skill that you'll find very valuable. I expect that skill will extract some additional cost over the years remaining you, but that will flow from natural consequences. I won't stir the pot up and make the terms more onerous than they would have been otherwise."

I opened my mouth to respond and then shrugged as I realized that I didn't truly know if I wanted my cheek fixed. "I'm not sure."

She smiled, almost as if I'd passed some test, and then wrote a phone number on the bookmark and tucked it into the top book.

"That is understandable. If you decide in the affirmative, call me, but know that I'll be in New York for only a short time. It may be many years before we have another chance to meet up again."

She handed me my books and then turned to motion the next person in line forward. I accepted my possessions back from her and then headed back toward Adri and Ben. My head was spinning. I'd come here hoping for a couple of words from someone I respected more than almost anyone else, and instead I'd gotten so much more than I'd even dreamed was possible. I wanted to tell someone, Adri or James maybe, about the experience so they could give me advice as to whether or not I should trust her, but secrecy had been one of the conditions of her help. I couldn't break that condition until I was firmly resolved that I wouldn't be going to her for help.

I could have traveled all the way back to the penthouse in a daze, nearly worthless as a bodyguard, except that in that instant I suddenly knew where the vampire smell was coming from.

Dom didn't look like herself as she walked back to Ben and me. I'd watched out of the corner of one eye as she'd gotten her books signed, and I'd noticed that she'd spent two or three times as long with her author as everyone else was getting.

I wouldn't have expected Dom, of all people, to suffer from celebrity shell shock, but it was obvious that she wasn't firing on all cylinders. There had been a second there as she'd gotten closer to us where she'd practically tripped over her own feet. She stopped a couple of feet away from us and carefully put her books back inside of her backpack.

"Hi, Ben. I'd heard rumors you were out here somewhere on the East Coast, but never expected that Adri and I would run into you."

Ben nodded and pointed at the robot we'd packed all this way. "Yeah, I'm working at a garage. They let me use the tools after hours, so I put together this beast and entered the competition."

Dom's smile was very nearly her normal, gentle expression, but I knew her too well to be deceived. Something was bothering her, and it went beyond just a case of hero worship.

"Well, I'm sorry to see that you didn't win. Maybe next time you'll come out on top."

Ben shrugged and gestured back the way we had come. "It's okay. Half the fun is building the robot. I've got a bunch of ideas already that I can't wait to go back and try and implement. Do you mind helping Adri and me lug this thing back up to the road? Once we're up there I can call one of the other guys from the shop to come pick me up, but he'll complain if I make him hunt for us down here."

Another plastic smile. "Sure. Adri, if you can carry my backpack I think I can get this side by myself. Mrs. Valencia actually told me there's a shortcut off this way."

I didn't buy it, not for a second, but Ben seemed to already be mostly thinking about the modifications he was going to do to his robot. He just nodded and picked up his end of the robot. I watched as Dominic picked up her half and then I started around her so I could walk closer to Ben.

Dom grabbed my arm with her free hand and steered me gently, but firmly, back behind her. It suddenly clicked for me that she was in full bodyguard mode, and she was viewing Ben as a threat somehow. I opened my mouth to tell her she was being silly, but the look she shot me was so fierce that I shut up and let her do her job.

A couple of minutes later we entered a stairwell and Dom made her move. She pushed the robot forward, running Ben into the wall, and then grabbed him by the throat.

"Why are you working with vampires, Ben?"

"What? Why did you just do that? I don't know what you're talking about!"

Shock had frozen me in place for a second, but I stepped forward now. "Dom, calm down. Ben's not working with any vampires."

Dom looked back at me for a second, and her eyes weren't the gentle brown orbs that usually graced her face. Her beast was only barely controlled and even I could tell it would take only the slightest provocation to push her into a transformation.

"The smell I kept telling you about is coming from him. He's not a vampire, not yet at least, but he's associating with them. Even worse, he just lied to me."

Ben opened his mouth, probably to tell Dom to let him go, but whatever he was about to say was cut off as she picked him up by his throat, easily holding him up against the wall despite the fact that she was using only one arm.

"You've lied to me once already, Ben. I'll know if you lie to me again. I'm going to let you down now, but if you lie to me again, I will kill you."

I was pretty sure Dom wouldn't actually kill Ben, at least not without more provocation than he'd demonstrated so far, but her voice was so deadly serious that I didn't blame Ben for believing her.

"The guys I work for at the garage are decent but really, really odd. I thought that was all it was until just now when you said I was working with vampires. It fits, not just their schedule, but sometimes I see them doing things that are crazy like lifting parts into place without needing a crane."

Dom's voice was subtly different than normal. I'd heard something similar out of Alec when he was at the point of transforming into a hybrid, but Dominic had never evidenced the kind of control that would let her arrest a transformation partway through the process.

"Truth. Very good, Ben. Do you intend to hurt Adri?"

"What? No, of course not. Why would you think that?"

"Because there is no such thing as a decent vampire. Eventually they will suck you into their web, it's just a matter of time. I can't do anything about that right now, so I'm trying to figure out how far they've sucked you in."

Ben had been in shock up until that point, but I could tell he was getting angry. "Look, I'm not involved in anything. I'm not going to hurt Adri, and you can't just throw me around like that."

Dom took a step forward and Ben backed up slightly, pressing up against the wall in an unconscious attempt to keep some distance between the two of them.

"Do you know of anything that's currently in motion that could result in Adri being hurt?"

"You mean besides the fact that you've gone ape-crap psycho since the last time I saw you? No. I'm not involved in anything illegal or dangerous or whatever."

It boggled the mind on so many levels, but suddenly pieces started snapping into place for me. "Are you sure, Ben? What about the secret compartments? Couldn't those be used to run drugs and stuff?"

He didn't want to believe me. I could see it in the set of his jaw.

"I don't know why I thought this time would be any different than the others. Every time I get involved with any of Alec's crew I end up screwed over in some way or another. I'm not quitting this job. It's the best gig I've ever seen. Just leave me the hell alone."

Ben pushed past the two of us and tromped up the stairs. I started to follow him, but Dominic stopped me.

"I'm sorry, Adri, but he's dangerous now. He wasn't before, at least not any more than anyone else that has been embroiled in vampire nets, but he's angry enough right now that there's no telling what he'll do if you follow."

We sat there in silence for a couple of minutes with Dom holding onto my arm to make sure I wouldn't follow, before I mentally gave up on the prospect of trying to find Ben and apologize.

"I just wish Ben and Jasmin could get a break. Every time I stick my fingers into that particular situation it seems like things get even worse. I know you were just trying to protect me, but I wish you could have played things a little cooler than that."

Dom looked embarrassed now. "I'm sorry. You're right; I shouldn't have come on so strong. I guess the things Mrs. Valencia said rattled me more than I'd realized."

I shook my head in astonishment. "I think that went beyond just being rattled, Dom. I don't know what she said to you, but you picked Ben up with one hand like he weighed absolutely nothing. I thought you said you were feeling weaker and more tired than normal."

We'd turned and started back the way that we came, but Dom missed a step as she processed my words. "You're right, Adri. Normally I couldn't have done any of that. It was suddenly like my beast was so much stronger than it's ever been before. Maybe that's why I was so aggressive with Ben."

"So you're cured?"

"I'm not sure what it means. I'm not sure of much as things stand right now. The questions are arriving much faster than the answers."

Chapter 9

Alec Graves
Sanctuary High School
Sanctuary, Utah

Now that we didn't have the constant threat of Brandon's pack hanging over us, the pack had started developing hobbies that expanded beyond what you could do just at the estate. The fact that we weren't all confined to the estate quite so much helped ease some of the tension in the pack, but like so much else right now, it was too little too late. With Dom in Manhattan and Rachel confined to bed, we had plenty of extra vehicles, but Tasha had still started dropping me off at school each morning and picking me up in the afternoon.

It had an element of staking out her territory to it, which I didn't particularly love, but it did have the benefit of keeping the girls at school at arm's length. It also had the benefit of giving me a few private moments each day with Tasha. I hadn't expected things to progress as well as they had so far.

Physically, Tasha was superficially similar to Adri. She had blond hair, a slender build, and was more than just merely pretty. As far as temperaments went, though, the two of them were markedly different. Where Adri had been accepting and gentle, Tasha was challenging, and when someone couldn't back up their position she wasn't above calling them an idiot.

Adri hadn't understood pack life because she'd only ever had a ring-side seat. She'd wanted me to be better than the savagery that was part and parcel of being a shape shifter. Tasha had lived in that ring her entire life and understood exactly how hard I'd had to work to create even the superficial bubble of civilization around the Sanctuary pack.

I exited the school and saw Tasha waiting inside her car for me. I suspected she actually came to pick me up just as a way of getting away from the estate. She seemed to keep busy, even from an entire state away, helping her mother manage their financial holdings, but I could already tell she was more social than I was. She didn't go hang out at Sanctuary's one and only bar or anything, but driving through town and seeing honest-to-goodness humans seemed to satisfy some unspoken need for her.

"So what great bits of knowledge did you learn today?"

I shook my head at her recurring question. "School is just like any other way of learning knowledge. You rarely learn something that moves the world all on its own. It's more a gradual process. At the end of it all, you realize that you're better equipped in some area than you were when you started the process."

"Ah, finally a decent answer out of you, Alec. That means I can go on to my next question."

As always, there was a hint of mocking laughter to our time together.

"If school is merely a method of acquiring knowledge, then why haven't you optimized your efforts the way you have in most other aspects of your life?"

It only took a second for me to realize what she was getting at.

"You're saying that I'm wasting my time by going to school."

"Maybe not in so many words, but yes. High school isn't optimized for learning; it's optimized for a broader set of things. I would suggest that you don't need much of what this school is still able to offer you. Get your GED if you must, but your time would be better spent running your pack."

I didn't like the idea, but I suddenly realized I couldn't think of a single rational reason to stay in school. I could learn faster on my own, or with hired tutors. It was meaningless as far as helping me get into a college. College might have been an option if my father had still been alive, but the alpha of a pack couldn't be gone for nine months out of the year.

There wasn't even a social reason for me to be spending so much of my time each day sitting in classrooms. I hadn't interacted with the rest of the student body very much even before we'd killed Brandon's pack. Since then, everyone had been polite but distant. I suspected they were worried that they might somehow run afoul of me and suffer a similar fate.

Adri had pierced my armor in part because she'd come from outside Sanctuary and arrived without the deference that most of the town offered my family almost instinctively. There wasn't anything saying that something like that couldn't happen, but ultimately, could I justify bringing another human into my world? It had been more than Adri had been able to handle. Odds were that any other normal human would have an equally hard time fitting into my life. What was worse, they would always be a liability. I'd never thought about Adri in those terms before Tasha arrived, but it was impossible not to see the differences between the two of them when it came to their suitability to life as the mate of an alpha.

Adri had been completely defenseless. Tasha wasn't a hybrid, so she was only a step above

Adri when it came to being able to protect herself, but that one small step would still translate to fewer problems inside the pack. More telling was the fact that Tasha had been raised to rule a pack. I'd loved Adri. I still loved Adri if I was brutally honest about it, but from a practical standpoint Tasha was right. Marrying a shape shifter had destroyed my mother. There was every reason to believe that it would do the same thing to any other human I tried to bring into my life.

The silence had stretched out long enough that it would have felt uncomfortable with almost anyone else, but Tasha was content to wait for me to think through her points. I finally shrugged and motioned that we should get started back home.

"I can't argue with your logic, but I find myself oddly reluctant to abandon school right now."

Tasha smiled as she dropped her BMW into gear. For once the mocking undertone was gone. "That's a good enough answer for now. As time goes on, you'll either come up with a real reason or you'll realize your reasons are purely emotional."

I nodded, but the truth was that I already had a pretty good idea that my reason was emotional. That didn't mean it was invalid though. That was one of the places where I was suspecting we didn't see eye to eye.

We drove in silence for several seconds before Tasha ventured another question. "Do you trust me yet, Alec?"

I shrugged. I'd already pretty much expected her to turn the tables on me at some point in our conversation.

"I'm not sure it really matters whether or not I trust you yet."

She took her eyes off the road and gave me a frustrated look.

"It absolutely matters. We're not talking about some kind of business joint venture where we've only got a couple of million at stake. We're talking about a complete merger between our packs and a marriage between you and me. Trust absolutely has to be at the bottom of all of that, or we all may as well just slit our throats right now."

"Okay, point taken, but the truth is that I still don't know how far I can trust you. Based on your actions so far, you're either honest or a very accomplished liar. Do you trust me?"

Tasha nodded without taking her eyes off the road this time. "Yes, I do actually. I have the advantage of being here where I can watch your interactions with your pack, all of whom have known you for your entire life. You're honest. You're a decent leader, too, except for the way you keep oscillating back and forth between trying to build some kind of consensus and being more authoritative."

"So you're all in then?"

She shook her head. "No, I wouldn't go that far, but I can see my way to dealing with some of the issues I think you bring to the table with you. The real question now is how I go about managing to convince you that I can be trusted. Mom figured that if we waited long enough the pressure from the challenges would convince you that you didn't have much of a choice but to jump into bed with us. Dominic bought you more time than I expected with her little miracle win though."

Tasha didn't realize it, but it was comments like that which were still putting the biggest brake on our relationship. I didn't think I'd be falling in love with her any time soon, but I could have gotten past that. Plenty of people had married out of duty in the past, but I wouldn't put my friends and family in a position that was worse than we were in now. I still got the impression that the other members of my pack were little more than counters on a board for her.

I waited in silence for another couple of minutes, and then, as we pulled past the gate into the estate, she seemed to make a decision.

"Okay, the only way this is going to progress is if one of us takes a risk and exposes themselves to something that could really come back to bite them. Since you seem to need the convincing, I'll take the risk."

I raised an eyebrow expectantly. She took a deep breath before continuing. "We've been killing any werewolves we run across in our territory for years now."

That in and of itself was a pretty hefty admission. The Coun'hij had outlawed werewolf hunts as part of the agreement that brought Puppeteer firmly onto their side. It had been all but inevitable really. He'd been much too powerful to let wander around loose, and no other pack had wanted anything to do with him, not after he'd lost control of one of his minions and gotten his original pack's alpha killed.

"So you guys hunt werewolves. Everyone kind of expects the border packs to march to their own tune. I could maybe make life a bit more difficult for you if I went to the Coun'hij and told them, but short of them agreeing to let Puppeteer overwhelm you guys in a sea of werewolves, it won't change the fundamental balance of power. They still don't have anyone who can take your mom one on one, and you're still too small of a group to really threaten their powerbase."

She was nodding, already seeing where I was headed. "Right, and I would have known you'd see things that way, so I risked very little by telling you, because you would have known that the Coun'hij is hardly likely to embrace you like a prodigal son. Even if you do turn informer for them, it's not going to outweigh the risk you represent as a rallying point for the rest of our people."

"Right, so you haven't risked much of anything yet, Tasha."

"What about if I invite you on a hunt with us? That's how your dad and my mom started down the path to an alliance, you know. Mom chased a pair of vacuums up into Utah and your dad heard about it somehow. He brought four of his most trusted hybrids far enough south to help trap both of the werewolves in a dry canyon somewhere around here. When the dust finally settled, the combatants from both packs were plenty the worse for the wear, but both alphas respected each other for being willing to do what was right, even though it could have created waves for them with the Coun'hij."

I shook my head in amazement. It hadn't been one of the stories that Donovan had shared with me. It was possible he hadn't known how the first tentative steps had been taken towards an alliance between the two packs, but it did sound remarkably like something my dad would have done.

It wasn't that much more of a risk than what she'd already done, and it actually put me and the rest of the Sanctuary pack in more danger. Agony and the rest would love nothing more than to catch us hunting a few werewolves and use it as a pretext to destroy the entire pack.

Even so, it would give me a chance to take the measure of whoever came north from her pack, and it would provide an opportunity to see how their dominants and our dominants interacted.

"Okay, I'm in, and I'll see what I can do to get at least a couple of the others to come with us."

"Perfect, have Donovan get your jet warmed up. We've got the ideal prey already identified."

Just over an hour later, Isaac, Jasmin, Jess, Tasha and I were landing in a tiny airport just outside of Clifton, which was on the extreme east edge of Arizona. Isaac wasn't happy about Jess accompanying us, but I wanted at least one of our submissives along for the ride so I could see how the Tucson pack reacted to more than just our dominants. James had stayed home to mind the store, but honestly, if another challenger showed up he was going to just have to stall for an hour or so until we could make it back there.

Jasmin had agreed to come along with a minimum of coaxing, but it was obvious that her heart wasn't in the hunt. She was coming along because she figured something was up between Tasha and me, and she wanted to get as much firsthand data as she could so that she didn't get blindsided by whatever we had in the works.

Jaclyn met us at the airport with a trio of bulky guys who almost had to be hybrids, and a guy and a girl I was pretty sure were normal wolves that she'd brought along for the same reason I'd brought Jess. She inclined her head slightly in my direction when I walked into the tiny terminal.

"I'm glad to see Tasha was able to convince you to join us. This is Arnold, Brutus and Alexei; they are three of my dominants. Peter and Jane will be acting as scouts; I'd like to keep them out of the main fight if we can manage it."

She'd presumably followed the normal convention of introducing her pack in order of dominance, but that just confirmed what I'd expected. At sixteen, Alexei was too young to have unseated either of the other two yet. Arnold was a massively-muscled man who had to be midway through his second century. Brutus was only slightly smaller and younger. They both looked like they'd be a handful in a fight.

Peter and Jane had an alert, cautious air that backed up the idea that they were towards the bottom of the pack's power structure, but they weren't overly jumpy, which meant Jaclyn probably kept her hybrids from doing anything overtly cruel to the rest of her people.

"We've never hunted vacuums before, but we thought maybe it was time to do something more constructive than just lock horns with more of the dispossessed. This is Isaac, Jasmin and Jess. I'd like to keep Jasmin and Jess on the fringes of things as well if at all possible."

Jaclyn smiled and waved us all over to a table that already had a map laid out on it.

"We occasionally run extended patrols in an effort to make sure we don't have any vampires moving into the area. We keyed into the trail of a werewolf six weeks ago and have been slowly tracking it down since then. We probably would have gotten to it before now, but Natasha's already told you about the run-in we had with that cat."

I nodded as I stepped forward and found our position on the map. Jaclyn pointed to a cluster of buildings off on the east side of the town.

"They are probably in this area, so we'll take a foot patrol through here and see if we can find them. Do you guys have any questions before we head out?"

It was a test. She knew as well as I did that the Sanctuary pack knew next to nothing about hunting werewolves, but an insecure alpha would try to pretend they knew what they were doing. She would probably keep our ignorance from getting any of her people killed, but I wasn't that stupid.

"What tips can you give us about fighting werewolves? We don't know much more than that they have some kind of absorptive aura."

Jaclyn nodded to Brutus, who stepped forward and cleared his throat.

"They're bigger, stronger and faster than nearly any hybrid, so the best bet is to attack with greater numbers and try to keep them off balance. They have a shoulder and elbow construction that limits their ability to get at anything behind them. Similar to a hybrid, but you have to be mindful of just how fast they are when you're trying to exploit it."

I stepped back from the map so Isaac and Jasmin could get a good look at it, and Tasha picked up the thread of the explanation.

"It's hard to predict how any given werewolf will behave when they run into a shape shifter. We've seen anything from berserker attacks against a superior force to cunning ambushes and guerilla tactics. The newer wolves tend to be less dangerous though. They are smaller and act more...confused in battle."

Isaac looked up from the map and then looked around at the Tucson pack. "Any distinctive smell to them? Do we need to worry about their absorption ability?"

Peter shook his head. "Nothing unusual about the scents of the younger ones, which these all seem to be. We usually find them by watching the news for unexplained power outages on the night of a full moon. Once you've got a scent trail, it's like following anyone else, but they tend not to jump in cars or the like to obscure where they've been. They don't function very well, even in human form, so you generally find them on the fringes of society."

Jane cleared her throat. "Their scent seems to transition really slowly though. The older they get, the more they seem to have a common note to their scent, but it's really, really hard to pick out."

Jaclyn smiled at Jane and then turned back to Isaac. "To your question regarding their absorptive abilities, they don't seem to be offensive weapons, but they can be a strong defensive measure. They completely absorb any kind of electrical shock without evidencing any kind of ill effects. Some of the pack histories have accounts of werewolves attacking vampires, and as nearly as the observers could tell, the vampires weren't able to manifest any of their unusual abilities. No fire, no telekinesis."

She'd just essentially told us that her arcing ability was off the table for this fight. None of the Sanctuary pack had any kind of extra power, so it sounded like this was going to be a purely physical fight.

Seeing no more questions from any of us, Jaclyn got everyone moving out to a pair of SUVs and a limo. A group this size didn't need so many vehicles, but it meant we'd be able to keep the two packs out of close quarters, which was a really good idea until after any dominance questions had been shaken out. I climbed into the limo with Tasha and Jaclyn, despite a little trepidation on the part of my beast at the idea of being outnumbered inside of such a small space.

Peter slid into the driver's seat and raised the privacy partition. Jaclyn waited until we started moving and then offered me a bottle of water.

"You look a lot like him, you know. Your dad, I mean. He was always remarkably self-possessed. I know your beast is acting up at the idea of being in the car with both Tasha and me. I expect it knows that you're clearly dominant to Tasha, but the question of dominance between you and me hasn't been settled."

I allowed myself a guarded nod, not sure where she was going.

"Tasha told me that your pack is remarkably tight-lipped about your power, but I know you don't have control of it. If you did, you'd have already wiped the floor with one of the challengers. Given that, there isn't any way you can stand against me."

"I thought we were here as allies."

"We are, and I intend for things to remain that way, but I find it's best just to get the dominance questions out in the open right away. I'll treat you with all of the respect due the alpha of another pack. As long as you can keep from digging your heels in over something stupid, I can pretty much guarantee that we won't have any problems."

It was a bold statement, but everything I'd seen so far backed her up on it. Packs functioned best when there was a clear line of command, and her ability to instantly drop any of her wolves had obviously allowed her to craft exactly the power structure she wanted inside her pack.

"Assuming you continue to be as reasonable as you've been so far, you won't have any problems from me, and I'll keep Isaac and the rest of my people in line."

I kept the mental wince that the promise caused off of my face, but I wasn't excited at the thought of having to keep Isaac on a leash. He was less and less the calm pillar he'd been in years past and he was especially unhappy today.

Jaclyn gave me a long look that seemed to indicate that she knew what that promise had cost me.

"I could always step in and ensure things go smoothly on both sides if you want."

It was the kind of offer that only a few hybrids living could have made. It was the ultimate symbol of just how powerful she was, and if I accepted it there wouldn't be any going back.

"I'll police my own pack."

"Alec, I hope you don't feel like I overstepped my bounds by offering. I know what kind of position that would put you in. It's not the kind of thing you could agree to unless you'd already decided that you want to accept our offer of alliance, but I thought I'd still offer. If you've decided to join us then there is no reason for you and your people to continue to tear into each other between now and when the agreement is formalized. If Isaac became combative I could drop him with a charge of power. It would take only seconds, it would expose me to almost no risk, and he'd be back up and able to help in little more than an hour."

Their proposal had been tempting to start out with, but it was growing more appealing by the minute. There was a part of me that was tired of it all, that wanted to just hand all of the responsibility over to someone else, but I knew that would be the coward's way out. If I agreed to a merger of our packs it had to be because I was confident it was the best thing for my friends and family. My exhaustion couldn't enter into the equation.

"I appreciate the offer, but I haven't made up my mind yet with regards to Tasha's proposal. Until then, I can't abdicate my responsibilities like that."

Tasha chuckled and shot her mother a satisfied look. "I told you he wouldn't go for it. He's too much like you said his father used to be for something like that to be acceptable."

Jaclyn nodded with a sad smile, obviously remembering better times.

"I respect your desire to keep faith with your people, Alec. If I didn't think you were capable of great things then we wouldn't be having this conversation. I've spent my entire life on two pursuits. I've fought and bled to make sure the lands to the north of us weren't washed away in a flood of corruption and violence, and I've tried to build a pack that was strong enough to protect those I love. I love Tasha, but my death will leave her ill-equipped to preserve our family's legacy."

Yet again I was astonished at her openness. Every word she'd said since we'd arrived had been the truth. She was operating from a position of such incredible superiority that she didn't need to lie or manipulate to accomplish her ends.

It made me think of some of the legends about Jaldul. He'd established the monarchy for two reasons. He'd been strong enough to enforce his will in his pack, but more than that, he'd been a man of such character that he'd won the allegiance of some of the most powerful hybrids of his day. With their backing, he'd ruled from a position of strength, but it had been a strength that had been tempered by goodness and justice.

Jaclyn continued on, ignorant of the compliment I was paying her inside the privacy of my own thoughts.

"You represent a chance for me to sidestep that outcome. I can buy you the time you need for your power to fully manifest, and then the two of you can rule and preserve the legacy I'm trying so hard to leave her."

"What if my power never manifests in the way you're describing? What if it always remains an undependable wild card?"

It wasn't an admission I'd have made to very many other people. The rest of my pack had a pretty good idea that I couldn't call my power at will, but even with them, I'd mostly made sure that the conversation was framed as one of 'when', rather than 'if'.

Jaclyn's smile was sad once again. "I have my own theories when it comes to the abilities we manifest. I remember when I first manifested mine. Tasha is the only other living person who knows this, but I manifested mine because I'd found something that was too important to allow me to roll over and die. I don't know why Tasha became a wolf and her sister remained a human. I don't know why some of us become hybrids and others don't, but I'm convinced that once a certain level of power is reached that it becomes more a matter of will than anything else. I have every confidence that you'll eventually master your power, Alec. It's just a matter of you needing more time and an even greater reason to do so than anything you've found yet."

The car pulled to a stop as Jaclyn finished talking. She gave me another wistful smile and exited the car before I could respond to her almost metaphysical discourse. I shook myself slightly and filed her words away for later examination. I had a pack to keep in check and a fight pending with some of the most dangerous creatures to walk the night. Neither of those tasks were something I could undertake while distracted with other concerns.

The second SUV pulled up only seconds after I got out of the limo. I walked over and opened the door for Jasmin, who'd been driving. She looked even worse than normal. Her skin had taken on a gray cast, and she almost looked like she was struggling not to shake. I leaned forward and pitched my voice low enough that nobody else should be able to overhear.

"Are you okay? I didn't realize it had gotten this bad. We can make an excuse and you can head back to the airport."

"I'm fine, Alec. I'm not showing weakness in front of your new best buds."

"Jas, I'm serious. This isn't a normal field trip. If you're off your game as much as it looks like you are, then you need to go back to the plane."

"I'm not screwing around either. All of the signs point to the fact that you're going to shack up with the Russian princess over there, and when that happens I'm not going to be doing myself any favors if I undermine my credibility right now. This is as much of a tryout for us as it is for them. Get back over there and act like a real alpha instead of sitting here holding my hand."

My beast took exception to her tone and power bubbled up from inside of me. It wasn't threatening a full transformation yet, but if she kept pushing I'd find it harder and harder not to kick her back to the plane. The safest bet right now was distance, so I turned and walked away, hoping the entire time that she could keep from getting herself killed in this fight.

Another map was out and resting across the hood of the limo. Peter was drawing lines on the streets closest to us. He waited until the four of us were close enough to see what he was doing before he launched into his update.

"It's definitely here. Male, middle-aged, and it smells like he's been running through some fields, because there's an undertone of fertilizer there as well. You'll probably be able to pick him out as we get closer. Nothing else seems the same as the last place I tracked them to, but it's a safe bet that the other two are around here somewhere."

Jaclyn nodded and took the pencil from Peter. "Okay, I'd recommend that we split into two groups. The Tucson pack will take the north street here and move east so that we flush the things away from town if they decide to run. Remember, they are faster than a hybrid, but you should have a slight edge as a wolf. Be careful not to engage them by yourself. Three to one odds are acceptable. Four to one is better."

She paused and scanned the group, making sure everyone nodded before continuing. Isaac seemed to be operating under the same assumptions as Jasmin. He refused to acknowledge her stare until I called up power and thrust it in his direction hard enough to ignite an answering flare from him. It put him on notice that I wasn't in the mood for him to be difficult, but more importantly, it gave him a pretext for backing down that relied on the fact that I was dominant to him. It was a thin pretext, but it allowed him to avoid admitting that Jaclyn could wipe the floor with him any time she felt like it.

Satisfied that everyone had gotten her message loud and clear, Jaclyn drew another line.

"I'll take the southern road here with Tasha and the Sanctuary pack. If you see one vacuum, howl for help and pile on it. If you see two, then howl for help and stay away from them until the other group can arrive and pitch in."

Everyone nodded again and then we split up and started walking towards our respective routes. I looked back to confirm that Arnold seemed to have taken command of the other detachment and then turned to Jaclyn.

"You've done this before, so I'm happy to follow your lead."

She nodded, but it was obvious she and Tasha were both on high alert already. Feeling a bit like an amateur who had shown up unprepared to a pro game, I shut up and started paying more attention to our surroundings.

The buildings were reasonably well-maintained, but they had an air of disuse that indicated that the town had suffered in the recent economic contraction and was having a hard time attracting new businesses. This far outside of town there weren't any streetlights, but there were enough exterior lights and motion-activated security lights to provide plenty of illumination even in this form. My eyes were better than a human's still, but nowhere near as good as what I had as a wolf.

We'd been walking for several seconds before I realized what was bothering me about the night. There wasn't any ambient noise. I could hear an air conditioner kick on somewhere behind us, and it sounded like one of the buildings off to the right had some kind of slow leak in the plumbing somewhere, but the kind of organic sounds that you'd expect on the edge of the city were shockingly absent. There weren't any insects of any kind, and I hadn't heard a single dog bark since we'd arrived.

Tasha grabbed her mom's arm and pointed off to the right. It took me a second to see what had caught her eye. There were some flickering lights inside a building that had just come into view. I probably would have dismissed them as nothing more than a light that was nearly to the end of its useful life, but she was probably right. A werewolf's absorption ability always seemed to play havoc with the electrical grid.

Tasha already had her phone out and was sending a text to the other group. Jaclyn led us between two buildings and then she and Tasha both started pulling their clothes off. My cheeks start to heat up as I realized that the Tucson pack hadn't adopted my dad's innovation. We tended to go through a remarkable number of ha'bits in a given month, but avoiding the frequent nudity that most of the packs were forced to deal with paid for the stretchy garments several times over.

I'd known that Isaac seeing Dom naked or James seeing Jess would have ratcheted up all kinds of pressure inside of the pack. I hadn't stopped to consider the fact that without a ha'bit, you were more likely than not to see your future mother-in-law completely bare at some point or another.

Isaac, Jess, Jas and I stripped our own clothes off in smooth, economical motions, and then turned to find that both Tasha and her mom had transformed into wolves in a cool rush of power. It made sense. People were still probably going to comment on half a dozen abnormally large wolves this far inside the city, but it was less likely to cause a real stir than someone seeing our hybrid forms.

We followed suit and then all padded back out onto the street on four legs. Jaclyn led us closer to the building with the flickering lights as her pack caught up to us. I could hear them out there a few dozen yards away, close enough that they could support us, but far enough away to help ensure that we didn't have some kind of pissing match between the dominants.

Our group circled the building and found a door that had been ripped off its hinges. I saw claw marks on the siding and made a mental note to have someone come out and obscure some of the evidence once we were done here.

We crept into the building and found a huge, mostly-empty industrial space. Jaclyn changed forms again, presumably judging us safe from casual observation, and I followed suit. I always felt more prepared for the unexpected as a hybrid. Isaac changed, too, and then we spread out slightly, flanking Jaclyn as the wolves took the outside edges of our formation.

I heard the other pack slip inside the building and felt flares of power as the three dominants completed their transformations. A second later all of the lights outside picked up the same kind of flicker Natasha had noticed earlier. It was darker inside than I would have liked and the loss of artificial light was making things worse. There were shadows deeper inside the building that even my hybrid eyes couldn't pierce.

Jaclyn slowly started moving forward and then I caught the edge of a smell that didn't belong here. Peter had a split second to catch the same scent and whine before we were attacked.

The wolf we'd been tracking stepped out of the darkness ahead of us and my chest got tight as I saw just how big he was. He looked like someone had taken a rough, unfinished hybrid and scaled it up to at least eight feet tall while making it proportionally wider than a normal hybrid. A split second later, two bulky wolves dropped through a skylight, falling more than forty feet before hitting the ground with enough force that they probably cracked the concrete.

Everything still felt like it was going more or less according to plan until a *fourth* werewolf came out of an office behind us.

We were surrounded, and every light for at least a block died completely in the same instant. Only the fact that they gave off the cool golden glow of a living organism to our vision saved us from fighting completely blind.

Jaclyn issued her orders without hesitation. "Alec, Isaac, with me. Arnold and Brutus on the one to the south. Alexei, Jane and Tasha will have to keep the one on the east distracted. The rest of you take the one to the west. We're outnumbered, so stay in motion and try to keep out of their reach."

As plans went it wasn't a bad idea, but we all knew it wouldn't survive the first few seconds of the fight. Our best bet would be for Jaclyn, Isaac and me to overwhelm our opponent quickly so we could turn and help with the others. If it took us too long then some of our allies were going to fall. It would only take one or two of us being cut down to shift the odds so far against us that our chances of making it out alive would be almost nonexistent.

I paced Jaclyn, staying on her left side as she rushed the gigantic werewolf that had lured us into the trap. I couldn't get over how much bigger he was even than I'd been told to expect. He waited until Jaclyn was almost to him and then sprang towards her with speed that wasn't much less than what Anton had demonstrated when we'd ambushed him to save Ash and Kristin.

Jaclyn dodged to the side, scoring a slash on the werewolf's arm as it tried to spin around to follow her. I saw my opportunity and lunged forward, trying to get in behind it, but the werewolf reacted faster than I was expecting. He spun around and backhanded me into one of the steel pillars that supported the roof.

Somewhere between when the werewolf had made his move and when Jaclyn had made hers, my senses expanded in a way that I couldn't explain. I could feel a vortex of energy sitting roughly in the center of our opponent's navel and there were three others not too far away, only calling it a vortex of energy wasn't quite right. It was more like a tiny black hole that was greedily sucking in power from everywhere around it. When Jaclyn had attacked, I'd felt a flash of power that exactly mirrored the energy being pulled out of the electrical wires running all over the building.

Jaclyn had affirmed at the start of the fight that her ability wouldn't work on the werewolves, but it must have been so second nature to her to release a jolt of power simultaneous to a strike that she'd gone ahead and tried to zap it. The power arced from the tips of her claws into the werewolf and then disappear into the tiny singularity sitting inside of her opponent. The lights had flickered slightly, not the ones in the building, but lights somewhere further away, almost as though Jaclyn's ability had partially overwhelmed the werewolf's capacity to absorb energy.

It was an interesting piece of information, but it wouldn't help me right now. My thoughts had taken only a split second to register, and then I heard the splatter of blood hitting the concrete floor and got my third huge surprise since we'd engaged what I had to assume was the oldest werewolf in the group. His claws weren't just sharp on the inside edge, they were sharp on the outside edge, too. A backhand like he'd hit me with would have been a blunt blow coming from a hybrid, but he'd opened up a series of deep slashes along my chest with his attack.

Isaac danced in and slashed at the werewolf's arms before dancing back out. He'd been experimenting, trying to learn the style of fighting that Abaddon had used to best him when Agony had visited, but even so, he still almost wasn't fast enough. He ducked under a blow as Jaclyn landed a strike on the werewolf's leg.

My injury wasn't immediately concerning, so I was already rushing back into the fight, completing the third point of the triangle that we were using to try and keep the werewolf too busy to really go after one of us.

I got a glimpse of the battle around us just before I had to throw myself to one side to avoid another swipe of the werewolf's massive arms.

Brutus and Arnold seemed to be working their opponent in much the same way we were, but they were even more on the defensive. The other two werewolves had retreated back to one wall and were close enough together that nobody was managing to get in close enough to do more than just feint at them.

I sank my claws into our opponent's side and then jumped away, but not fast enough to completely avoid taking an elbow to the side of my head. Jaclyn took advantage of the distraction I'd provided to rush in and sink both sets of claws into its arm. She rode the momentum the werewolf's spin imparted and used it to keep just outside the range of its other arm.

"Get the other arm if you can!"

It still seemed like a risky tactic, but I could see her logic. If we could immobilize both arms at the same time then we'd only have to worry about its leg talons and teeth. I'd already finished rolling back to my feet, and I darted in, but Isaac got there first. He got both hands around the wolf's right arm, but he didn't commit strongly enough and it shook him off after only a split second.

Jaclyn was forced to let go and spring away within heartbeats of Isaac losing his grip on the vacuum, but they'd created an opening for me, and I didn't second-guess the opportunity. I landed on the werewolf's back and managed to set both sets of feet talons and one hand into the rock-hard slabs of muscle before a violent spin nearly threw me free again.

I was too low to reach its neck with my fangs, so I sank my left hand further up and freed my right hand. It was like trying to scale a vertical cliff in the middle of an earthquake. Every time I tried to reposition an appendage I nearly got bucked off, and my presence made it harder for Isaac or Jaclyn to get in and land any kind of strike.

I couldn't get to anything really important from behind the werewolf, its ribs were just too strong. I was bleeding it out, but I was starting to wonder whether or not I'd get tired and lose my grip before it passed out from blood loss. I needed to get high enough to get to its neck and end this.

I pulled my right foot free and tried for a new foothold when it happened. The werewolf backed into another of the steel support pillars, driving the air out of my chest and cracking at least three of the incredibly strong ribs on my left side. I might have still managed to keep my seat if my head hadn't hit hard enough to leave me seeing stars.

It was like I'd just gone up a weight class. Nothing this thing was doing was anything I hadn't run into before, but it was just so much stronger than me that I was having a hard time staying in the hunt.

Jaclyn and Isaac chased our opponent off me before it could take advantage of how dazed I was. I pulled myself back to my feet and started towards them again when I saw it start to happen.

Alexei and the wolves had managed to divide the two vacuums they were fighting, and although they were all bleeding and showing signs of exhaustion, it looked like none of them had been seriously hurt yet. I would have chalked it up as our team being ahead on points, except for the fact that I got a good look at Jasmin as she nipped at her opponent and then backed away to avoid another slash that would have opened her up from nose to tail.

She was frustrated. This kind of hit-and-run combat went against every instinct in her body. Hybrids learned to bleed out their opponent where possible before going for the clinch that could end the fight. Wolves, the really, really good wolves at least, quickly figured out that doing anything halfhearted was a good way to miss your opportunity. Jas had been fighting Isaac, James and me for years. For her, this was just that same kind of fight against an opponent that was a little bigger and quicker than her pack mates.

I'd sparred against Jasmin for far too long not to see the signs. She'd decided she had her opponent's measure and that it was time to end the fight. I knew I was endangering Isaac and Jaclyn, that with just two of them that they weren't going to be able to keep up the pressure, but I couldn't stand by and do nothing.

FORSAKEN

I sprinted towards Jasmin and the other wolves with every ounce of speed my hybrid form could muster, but I was still a dozen yards away when Jasmin planted and made her move. It was one of the most impressive lunges I'd ever seen. Her timing was perfect and she was fully committed, but she'd acted out of reflexes that had been trained before her current state of weakness had set in.

Her trajectory was perfect but it lacked that extra edge of speed that had characterized Jasmin for as long as I could remember, and that was her undoing. Jasmin was still a few inches away from her werewolf's throat when its claws came around and knocked her out of the air.

I could see the trajectory of the werewolf's other hand. That thing was going to continue the spin it had just used to bat her aside, and then it was going to sink the claws on its left hand all the way through her and into the floor. I willed my legs to move faster, reached with all that I was towards the werewolf in a futile effort to save Jasmin, and then something flickered inside of me. It wasn't quite like the singularity in the werewolf ahead of me; it was more like a conduit, but it still futilely tried to pull at the life force of the werewolf.

It was like standing in a wind tunnel. My singularity was less powerful than its singularity, but that was okay, I'd never expected it to help me today. I took one last step and threw myself into the werewolf with all of the force I could muster.

I knew it was a vain effort. The best I could hope for was that the impact would ruin its aim, that the claws would miss Jasmin by a few inches, but that wasn't what happened. I hit with my shoulder solidly under its armpit and somehow countered the force of its spin.

Jasmin rolled out of the way as the werewolf's right hand came back around, carving furrows into the floor, and then the talons on my left foot sank six inches into its leg. In a display that was more aggressive than anything else I'd seen out of Jess since Oblivion had wiped her mind clean, she lunged, grabbing our werewolf's right forearm and pulling in an attempt to overbalance it.

It was the final, infinitesimal straw and the werewolf's left leg came up off the ground as it overbalanced and started to fall. I took advantage of the fact that it wasn't going to be executing any crazy changes in direction and pulled myself further up its back in a sharp, violent motion. In the instant I had remaining before we hit the ground, I set my claws and talons as deeply into it as I could and tucked my chin.

The impact when we hit knocked the wind out of me again, but this time I was ready for it and simply held on and waited for my ride to start rolling to its feet. In the split second between when the werewolf started the motion and when it was set enough to change direction, I let go with both hands, reached forward, and ripped its throat out.

The rest of the fight was bloody and by no means guaranteed, but we managed to come out victorious and, even more astonishingly, managed not to lose anyone. I'd been bucked off a second later, but I hadn't stuck around to wait for it to bleed out. Instead, I'd dashed over to Alexei, Jane and Tasha's werewolf with Peter only a couple of steps behind me.

With five of us focused on the next werewolf while Jasmin and Jess kept the first one distracted until it finished bleeding out, we managed to bring it down fairly quickly. Alexei pulled it out of position and then Tasha had hamstrung it. Once it lost its usual mobility, Peter and I hit it from behind and brought it down.

The last two fights ended at nearly the same time, but they'd been the ones where we'd almost lost someone. Brutus and Arnold had been slowly wearing their opponent down over the course of the whole fight, but they'd been equally tired and bloody. Brutus had been a second too slow on one of his dodges at the very end, and the werewolf he'd been fighting had opened him up from his stomach all the way up to his right shoulder. The shock had forced him back into his human form and only the fact that the strike had missed his heart and left lung had kept him alive long enough for Jane to stabilize him.

Arnold had ruthlessly taken advantage of the opening that the werewolf had allowed to develop while it was attacking Brutus, and darted in and clinched with it from behind. That sliver of the fight was over a few seconds later.

Peter had bypassed Brutus and Arnold's fight and gone to help Jaclyn and Isaac along with Jasmin and Jess. He'd gotten a little too close there at the end, but had bought Jaclyn the split second she'd needed to get in and hamstring the oldest werewolf.

Both packs had blood and medical supplies back at the planes, but I hadn't been positive that either Brutus or Peter would make it that long. Jaclyn had yelled her goodbyes as her entire pack, save Tasha, had boarded their plane and then taxied away within seconds of the door closing.

It had been a more abrupt end to our first joint operation than I'd expected, but I'd understood her reasoning. A severely wounded wolf or hybrid was perfectly capable of completely losing control of their beast. It usually resulted in death for the injured shape shifter and an incredible amount of collateral damage. Jaclyn's presence on that plane was the best way to ensure nothing got out of hand while they were in the air.

Tasha and I watched the plane take off and then headed back over to where Jess was bandaging up Jasmin. Isaac was already taped up and resting but neither of the two of us had been bleeding bad enough to require immediate aid.

She'd pulled jeans and a tank top on while still in the limo, but both were covered in blood now. I grabbed gauze and tape and tried to see to her first, but she playfully knocked my hands away and started working on my chest.

"So, just out of curiosity on the part of your potential future wife, how did you do that?"

"Do what? Survive my first werewolf fight?"

"No, how did you stop that thing from killing Jasmin?"

"You saw that?"

"Yeah, I saw it. I expect Peter did too which probably means the rest of my pack will know about it before the plane lands."

"I'm not sure. I hit it with everything I had, but I didn't expect it to even notice the impact. All I can figure is that it stumbled a little. That, or maybe it had been injured more than anyone realized."

Tasha gave me a considering look before moving around to deal with the huge gash in my left lat.

"It didn't look like a stumble from where I was standing."

Chapter 10

Adriana Paige
Upper East Side
Manhattan, New York

Dominic wasn't happy with me. She wasn't pissed, but she didn't approve of the hijinks I was dragging her into. She was on the phone with James, and based on what little bit I could overhear, he wasn't a fan either.

Her smooth alto voice had been getting more and more frazzled as the conversation went on. I finally walked over to her room and gently took the phone away from her.

"James, this is Adri. I know this sucks, but I don't know what to tell you. Alec told Dom to keep an eye on me and if we're going to avoid a super-awkward, creepy vibe that will completely ruin my social life, then this is the best bet."

"So you're going to force my girlfriend to cheat on me just so you can date some guy?"

James' voice was even more surly than normal, but I took a deep breath, perfectly aware that he'd hear it, and hit him with the zinger I'd spent the last half an hour perfecting.

"No, James. She's not cheating, she's chaperoning. If you really think Dom is going to do anything with some random guy, then you don't know her as well as you should. I know the situation isn't ideal, but the alternative is that I just stop dating anyone because Alec is making you guys babysit me. I'm not giving him that kind of control over me, so if you have any problems with what's happening then I propose you go to Alec and ask him to give Dom permission to leave me alone tonight."

That shut him up immediately. I'd been getting the vibe that there was more unrest than normal in the pack, but apparently Alec was still the uncontested top dog. I waited for a couple of seconds to see if he'd respond before looking over at Dom and raising an eyebrow. She was shaking her head so my course was clear.

"Goodbye, James. Dom will call you when we get done with the date. I'll try not to keep her out too late."

I hung up the phone and handed it back to Dom. My closing jab hadn't been very fair. Given that the guys had to be in Brooklyn for a late show, I knew that we wouldn't be gone for very long, but James was just one of those guys who begged for you to let some of the air out of his tires.

Actually, I hadn't been fair on a couple of levels. James was a jerk sometimes, but I'd been meaner than I normally would have been. The problem was that he'd touched on some of what bothered me so much about the date with Albert that was scheduled to start in less than an hour.

Albert wasn't just 'some guy.' He was a very good friend, but it wasn't like he was the love of my life or anything. I didn't feel entirely good about how I'd pushed the issue with James, not given that I was pretty sure I was going to have to tell Albert that I didn't really want to date him.

The real problem was exactly what I'd said on the phone though. I really liked having Dom around, but if I wasn't careful I'd just swear off guys altogether and I knew that wasn't healthy. I didn't really want to date right now, but I needed to keep the option open or I'd just end up more lonely and bitter than I already was.

It all made a ton of sense on paper, but I couldn't help but feel like I was..I don't know. Cheating wasn't the right word for it, but I still felt some kind of bond with Alec and something about the thought of dating other guys still made me uncomfortable.

Dom walked out of her closet and sighed unhappily.

"I have absolutely nothing to wear here. I didn't expect to miss Rachel's handiwork quite so much. For a while there, every time I walked into my closet there was some new surprise waiting for me."

I needed to respond, but I couldn't quite seem to get any words out. Dom gave me a concerned look.

"Are you going to be okay, Adri? I know James seems unhappy right now, but it's not like he's going to fly out here and confront you. By the time I make it back to Utah, he'll have had plenty of time to cool off. I appreciate you ending the conversation; I don't think I would have been able to get off the phone in time for our date otherwise."

I put my hand on the top of my head and sighed. "Yes—no—I don't know. I feel really bad about all of this and having you thank me for pissing your boyfriend off isn't helping. I mean, I should feel guilty about that, and I do. It's just that there is *so* much right now to feel guilty about. It's all throwing me for a loop. Why is this so hard?"

Dom walked over, sat on her bed, and pulled me down next to her. "It's hard because you still love Alec. There isn't any use denying it; there have been plenty of signs over the last week or so."

I shrugged uncomfortably. "I was the one who walked out on him. It doesn't feel like I should be able to say that I still love him after doing that to him."

"That doesn't change the facts of the matter. You still love him, and I can understand why you left without necessarily agreeing with all of your reasons. In many ways, you left *because* you love him."

This was the first time Dom had come so close to condemning me for leaving. I didn't want to know the details, but I knew I should be brave and face her criticisms.

"You don't think I should have left. What should I have done differently?"

Dom pursed her lips and thought for a few seconds before shaking her head. "The real question is whether or not you still feel like your original reasons for leaving are valid."

She was right. It was hard to nod. The decision to leave Alec had been the hardest thing I'd ever done. In some ways it was even more difficult to reaffirm the decision now that I knew how much grief it had caused the rest of the pack, but I couldn't see any other course of action that I could have taken in good conscience.

"I guess so. It's hard knowing my leaving hasn't helped, has made things worse in a lot of ways, but I couldn't just stand by and do nothing when I thought Alec was headed down such a dark path."

"There is your answer. What I think doesn't really matter, Adri. You stayed true to yourself.

That is what is most important. How can I claim to still be your friend if I criticize you for being the best you that you can be?"

I found myself smiling a little. I gave Dom a hug and pointed at the hall. "There is a perfectly well-stocked closet in my room. You and I are close enough to the same size that there's bound to be something in there you can wear. Not only that, if you're going to wear something out of my closet then it will give me an excuse to wear one of those ridiculously gorgeous sweaters Rachel bought me."

A few minutes later we were both dressed in jeans and sweaters courtesy of Rachel. Dom had picked out a soft gray sweater and I'd picked out a green one that was almost the same shade as the dress I'd worn to the Ashure Day festivities.

I'd told Albert that he and his band mate could pick us up at my house, because I hadn't wanted to have him come up and think I lived here. It was the perfect refuge from the city, but that didn't mean I was comfortable with other people knowing that I hung out here. It felt like a lie, like I was pretending to be rich.

As we walked from Dom's building over to mine, I started to become uncomfortable even with the idea of Albert and his friend coming upstairs to pick us up. It felt a little odd to have a boy come to my house while my mom was nowhere in sight.

"Hey, Dom, do you mind if we just wait downstairs for the guys?"

"That's fine. Something wrong?"

I shrugged. "I'm not sure. I guess I'm just feeling odd. This is my first date since Alec. Isaac and I hung out with Albert a little while ago, but this feels different."

"No worries, Adri. We can wait wherever you want, but I like the idea of inside better than outside. I never thought I would miss the heat so much, but this city has some really cold weather."

My feeling of unease started to fade away after the boys picked us up. Albert's friend was an overly skinny redhead named Daniel who was the band's drummer. I kicked myself for not having dressed down a little when I saw them. They'd obviously made an effort to look nice, but their wardrobes ran heavily toward rock star casual. Albert didn't seem to mind though, and Daniel didn't complain because he was too busy trying to come up with something to talk about with Dom to notice if the sky had fallen.

We walked to the Metropolitan Museum of Fine Art, and then all sighed in relief once we were out of the cold. It was obvious the boys wanted to start out in the section of the museum that housed all of the medieval armor and weapons, but they graciously agreed to let us girls lead the way up to some of the Renaissance paintings.

About thirty seconds after we arrived at the exhibit, Albert's phone started chiming. I almost wanted to chuckle at the pained expression on his face. It was obvious he wanted to check his messages, but that he was pretty sure it was going to lose him points with me.

"Go ahead, Albert. I don't expect your life to stop just because we're at the museum together."

"Thanks. I normally would just ignore them, but this is John's first time setting up without Danny or I being there. If he's got a question, that probably means he's only a couple of minutes away from plugging two things into each other that were never meant to be hooked up."

I laughed and waved for him to proceed. My phone had vibrated on the walk to the museum, so I figured it was fair for me to check my texts, too. They were both from my mom. Now that I had a cell phone she usually checked in with me a couple of times a day whether she was in the country or not.

Hope your date goes well. This Albert sounds like my kind of guy. Text me when he drops you off at home.

I shook my head at Mom's first message, but her second text made my stomach do flip-flops.

Russ wants to do Christmas together, just the three of us. I'm telling you now so you don't feel like I'm springing stuff on you at the last minute, but I'd really like this to happen.

I debated what to say for several seconds before finally inputting a response into my phone.

Albert is really nice, you'd like him. Not sure about the Russ thing, but I guess it won't be all bad if it means you'll be around for a few days.

I knew I was heaping on an extra-large helping of guilt there, but honestly, it felt like I needed to do something at this point. Mom was around less and less. I'd thought it was bad back when we'd been in Sanctuary, but I saw her even less now than I had back then.

Albert's phone chimed again. He sighed and put it away. "Okay, I think he's got the right pieces all hooked together now. You'd think a guy who does all of the electronic bits of our stuff would be a bit more technically savvy than he is. Sometimes it's like things don't exist for him if he can't see them on his computer screen. I know I'm a geek, but he's a whole level beyond me."

I smiled at the thought of Albert-the-math-tutor calling *anyone* a geek, but then again he looked even more the rock star today than he had last time I'd seen him. There weren't any new piercings or anything, but his level of confidence seemed to be growing by leaps and bounds.

"I'm glad you got him straightened out without anything blowing up."

"We'll see. He probably wouldn't even notice a small explosion. You got your text taken care of?"

I sighed and nodded. "Yeah, it was my mom. She thinks I'm going out with Albert-the-tutor today. I haven't told her about Albert-the-rock-star yet."

He looked at me oddly. "Is that a problem?"

"No, that's all fine. It's this new guy she's dating. She keeps wanting me to meet him, but I really, really don't want to get involved in my mom's dating life. Plus, I'm having a hard time not being jealous of him. Right now I think he gets to see my mom more than I do."

Albert nodded, seemingly relieved by the direction the conversation had turned. "I can see how that would be hard. Your mom works a lot then?"

"Yeah. We moved to New York so she'd be closer to the center of things, but all it's really meant is that she shaved five hours off her commute to Europe."

I needed to dial back the bitterness, but I was finding it really hard to do so. Mom had helped convince me that I needed to walk away from Alec, and then she'd abandoned me to deal with the aftermath all by myself.

"Maybe you should meet this guy, Adri. If he really likes your mom and she really likes him, then he's probably not any happier about how much she's gone than you are. Maybe the two of you can double-team her."

I wasn't convinced, but I nodded anyway. It was better than any of the ideas I'd managed to come up with on my own so far. The conversation turned back to lighter subjects and I actually found myself having fun.

Albert swore he'd told Danny that Dom had a boyfriend, but it looked to me like Dom's date had already forgotten that fact. I couldn't blame him though. Even with her scar, she was so pretty and exotic that any guy would have done a double-take if he'd walked by her on the street. The fact that she was a genuinely good person just magnified her appeal.

It was obvious though that Dom's frustration was starting to pile up. Danny kept trying to lead her off so they could be by themselves. Even if James hadn't been in the picture, Dom still wouldn't have gone off with him. She was 'working' right now and I could tell she was starting to get frazzled from the effort of keeping Daniel at bay while still keeping Albert and me in sight.

We were in the middle of some kind of rebuilt Egyptian temple when I finally nudged Albert and pointed at Dom. "Can we head to dinner a little early? I think Dom needs a rescue."

"Sure thing. I'll see if I can redirect his focus a little, too. He's usually a pretty good guy, but the fame is starting to go to his head a little."

Albert grabbed my hand and tugged me forward as he called out to Danny. A few minutes later we were all bundled back up and headed back outside. The restaurant the boys had chosen was a twenty-minute walk from the museum, but Albert kept Dom and me entertained with stories about the band's misadventures.

"...so I looked back to see what was going on and I couldn't see Danny anymore. We'd tested the mist machines out on either end of the stage, but Danny had decided it would be a lot cooler if we stuck them in the middle of the stage, right behind him."

Danny nodded and smiled wryly. "Yeah, I was trying to upstage everyone a little. I probably would have been okay if I hadn't thrown in a new mixture without testing it. The stage hand turned them both on and it was working pretty well for a couple of minutes until all of a sudden I couldn't see my drums anymore. It turns out I wouldn't make a very good blind drummer."

We all laughed and then Albert was grabbing the door for us. We'd arrived and it was the kind of charming hole-in-the-wall you'd have expected a New York native to take you to. The menu had a little bit of everything on it, but the prices were a lot more than I remembered back from the couple of times I'd eaten out in Sanctuary. Albert saw my look of concern and waved away my worries.

"Don't worry; the band isn't starving or anything. We actually sold out of our T-shirts earlier than expected, so even after ordering replacement inventory we still have some cash left over. My share will cover a meal with you and still allow me to eat for the rest of the week."

Danny nodded in agreement so I figured I was safe and ordered lasagna. Dom ordered rice and beans while the boys both ordered pizza. A few minutes before the food arrived, Albert's phone started vibrating. He ignored it for the first couple of times, but then Danny's phone started chirping too.

"Sorry, Adri. It's probably John again."

"It's really fine. Go ahead."

Albert flipped his phone out and then sighed. "This is probably going to go faster if I just give him a call. I'll be back in a second."

There was silence at our table for a couple of seconds before Danny cleared his throat. "Sorry, you would think that the other guys would be able to set up on their own once in a while, but Albert is pretty much the organizational brain behind the band. John is the idiot savant when it comes to the music, but Albert is the one who makes sure we make it to our gigs and get paid."

I shrugged again. "It's no big deal for me. I'm still having fun, and I understand that he's got commitments. Actually, I'm surprised he was able to get away like this only a few hours before you guys are supposed to play. That's not normal, is it?"

Danny shook his head and took another bite of pizza. "Nope. I don't think anybody else would have gotten away with it, but everybody owes Albert for having taken down almost by himself at the last two shows."

The way that Danny trailed off would have told me all by itself that he'd just realized he was touching on something he shouldn't have, but Dom leaned forward with a look of innocent curiosity on her face as soon as he finished talking.

"Why did he have to clean up by himself?"

Danny shifted a little in his seat and took another bite of pizza to buy himself some time. "Well, he didn't have to take down completely by himself. John was there, but John tends to get lost inside of his own head after a show. The other three of us kind of went to parties after the last couple of shows."

Dom looked at me and raised an eyebrow. Her confirmation was nice, but I would probably have figured out that these weren't just 'parties' all on my own. Albert hadn't been kidding when he'd said Danny was letting his newfound fame go to his head. It wasn't particularly surprising, but I still lost some respect for him. More interesting was the fact that Albert hadn't been joining in the fun.

I was still rolling that bit of information around in my mind when my phone vibrated with another incoming text.

Adri, please just leave me alone. I know u guys are worried, but I'm fine.

It wasn't a number I recognized, but they obviously knew who I was. I dashed off a quick response.

Who is this?

What do u mean? It's Ben. u know, the guy you've been bothering for the last half an hour...

Hi, Ben. It's nice to talk to you, but I don't know what you're talking about. I've been with Albert for the last half hour.

Albert had finished up his call and was headed back to our table. I was still trying to puzzle out Ben's cryptic texts when my phone popped up with an incoming call. It was Ben.

"You're really there with Albert?"

"Yes, why? Do you want to talk to him?"

"Yes, can you hand the phone to him?"

I passed my phone over to Albert, mouthed 'it's Ben' in response to his questioning look, and then shrugged to indicate that I didn't know what was going on. Right about then I was wishing my hearing was as good as Dom's. All I could hear was Albert's side of the conversation.

"Hey, man. What's up...yeah, she's been with me for the last couple of hours. Texts? No, there was one an hour or so ago to her mom, but nothing since then. How come?"

Now it was Albert's turn to look confused as he handed me my phone. I shot Dom a questioning glance, but her headshake seemed to indicate that she didn't know anything more than I did.

"Ben, what's going on? You're acting kind of crazy."

"I got a text twenty-eight minutes ago. It was a list of names and dates, and it came from your phone number. Do you swear to me that you didn't send it to me?"

A chill ran through me. "Ben, I didn't have your phone number before now. I haven't sent you anything other than the couple of texts before you called just now."

I could just make out the sound of Ben breathing on the other end of the line. Each breath was fast and shallow.

"I recognize some of the names. They are customers, people we did work for. I never had last names before now, but there were pictures online. They are the same people."

My breathing was speeding up. This was X-Files weird. "What does that mean, Ben?"

His response came fast and almost a little hysterical. "I'm not sure, but if you didn't send them, then someone else is trying to tell me the same thing that Dominic told me the last time I saw you guys. Every single one of those customers is dead, and they were all gunned down doing something illegal. Not just like smoking weed illegal, like seriously messed-up stuff."

Dominic caught my eye and mouthed 'give me the phone.' I nodded and jumped in as soon as he paused.

"Ben, Dom needs to talk to you."

She snatched the phone out of my hand, like I wasn't moving fast enough. She pulled out her own phone and started typing as she put mine up to her ear.

"Ben, you need to get out of there immediately. Don't go back to work, don't go to anyone they know is your friend. Grab whatever money you have there with you and get on a bus or a train. Walk if you have to, but you need to get out of there. Leave your cell phone. When you make it into Manhattan, get on a payphone and ask them to look up Allen Anders in Pinedale, Wyoming. When he answers, tell him the cat sends her regards."

There was a pause in the conversation as Ben tried to process everything Dom had just said. Dom passed her phone over to me face down and then shook her head at whatever Ben had just said.

"Ben, there isn't time for that. Allen Anders in Pinedale, Wyoming, the cat sends her regards. Repeat it back to me. Okay, hang up and get moving."

I flipped Dom's phone over and saw the message she'd typed in. *Lose the boys. Now!*

There probably wasn't anyone else on the planet more unsuited for spy stuff than me. I panicked and just showed the phone to Albert. His eyes were already pretty big after hearing Dom's instructions to Ben, but they got a little wider. He nodded and pulled Danny to his feet.

"Come on, Danny. You're going to need to go back and help John finish setting up."

Dom shook her head at me and then took her phone back and dialed another number as Danny started to protest.

"No way, man. Things were going really well."

"No, Danny, they're going really, really badly. You owe me, and I'm cashing in right now."

Dom stood up and walked away from us as she talked very quietly into her phone. For a second I thought Danny would argue, but he finally nodded and grabbed his coat as Albert walked him to the door.

Dominic had my phone partially disassembled and was reading something off to whoever it was she'd called. I was still sitting there more or less in shock when Albert came back to our table and waved for the check.

Dom had put my phone back together and was powering it off. She gave Albert a frustrated look when she saw that he hadn't left yet, but he held up his hands.

"Look, I don't know what the crap just happened, but Ben and Adri are both my friends, too. I'm not just walking out the door and pretending like nothing is wrong."

"Fine, you can come, but only because I can't waste time arguing with you."

Dom pulled out a wad of bills, waved them at the waitress, and then slapped them down on the table. She was herding both Albert and me out the door while Albert was still trying to tell her that he'd been planning on paying.

"Albert, you're a nice boy, but we just don't have time, and I can't risk you paying with plastic. Cash is fast and safe. Now move."

We set out at a fast pace. It was nothing compared to what Dom could have managed if she were by herself, but it had Albert and me both breathing heavily in short order.

"If the first text came through less than an hour ago, then it's unlikely that they've had a chance to make it here, but it's not outside the realm of possibility. We need to make sure we're not being followed. I need both of you to keep up for the next few minutes and then we can get a cab."

I didn't know that Alec's pack knew this kind of stuff. I'd known they knew how to fight, but I hadn't realized they were super spies as well. We jumped in a cab twenty minutes later, and Dom told the driver to get on FDR Drive headed north.

"Dom, where did you learn all of this stuff?"

"We had a recent addition to the...extended family. He's been bringing us up to speed on all kinds of stuff that we'd never had the time or incentive to learn before. Hopefully he's taught me enough."

Dom looked around, seeming to be checking our location against a mental map, and then nodded and leaned forward so she could whisper to us.

"Okay, we're making pretty good time. There's a block of road up ahead that is obscured from overhead view by the trains. We're going to jump out of the cab as soon as we make it there and then I'm going to steal us a car. With any luck we can make the change fast enough that they won't be able to track us."

Albert's eyes got a little wider at the calm way that Dom had told us we were just about to be accessories to grand theft auto, but he just nodded and sat back in his seat. Dom watched our surroundings and then suddenly reached up and hammered on the glass separating us from the driver.

"Turn left here!"

As the elevated part of the tracks came into view, Dom pulled out two hundred-dollar bills.

"If you can stop directly under the tracks, and then keep driving across the island after we are out you can have both of these."

The cabbie nodded like he'd had similar requests in the past and then brought the car to a sudden stop exactly where Dom had instructed. All three of us barreled out of the vehicle and he was back on his way only a couple of seconds later.

"Follow me, and make sure you stay under the tracks."

We walked for nearly ten minutes before Dom found a car she was happy with. She pulled a metal probe out of a pocket and then stabbed it through one of the front headlights. She waited only a second to make sure the electrical system was really shorted out and then took off her jacket and wrapped it around her arm.

The windshield shattered with a rain of glass and then she was waving us both over as she did something to the steering column.

"Albert, have you ever driven stick?"

"Yeah. The van's a stick."

"Okay, get into the driver's seat and put it into gear. When I get it moving, pop the clutch and give it some gas."

I'd only thought Albert's eyes were wide before. When Dom proceeded to get the car moving more than five miles an hour pushing all by herself, I thought they'd pop right out of his head. Despite his shock, Albert got the car running, and a few seconds after that, Dom had moved him over to the passenger seat and we were off.

The next hour was a crazy blur as we went from the car to the subway and then ditched our coats and walked the last little way to Dom's apartment in the cold. Albert's T-shirt left him even more exposed to the cold than our sweaters, but he didn't complain. Once we were up to the top floor of Dom's building, she pointed the two of us to one of the sofas in the living room and told us to sit down.

She already had her phone out again. She'd pulled it out from time to time as we'd been running, but now she seemed to mean business. I watched as she disappeared into the hall and then turned and looked at Albert. He looked a bit like he'd just stepped into a world that failed to fit almost every facet of his definition of reality.

"Are you okay?"

He started a little and then nodded. "Yeah, I guess so. I just wasn't expecting any of this. I mean, Dom's like frickin' Jason Bourne. Not only that, she pushed that car like it didn't weigh anything."

I found myself sighing. Albert was the last person I would have wanted to drag into the craziness of pack life. He was just so painfully normal. Even as a rock star, he was just so completely down to earth.

"Sorry, but you're probably not going to want to talk to anyone about any of that. If Danny says anything about the phone call he overheard just tell him Dom's a little loopy."

"Are you going to be okay? I mean, they've got your number and some of what I overheard Dom say sounded like she was telling someone to make sure nobody could link your number back to your address."

I nodded. I'd actually never even seriously considered that I wouldn't be okay. Dom and the pack always made sure that everything worked out okay.

"I should be fine. Dom will let me know for sure, but if Plan A to protect me doesn't work then she and Alec will have a Plan B and a Plan C lined up already."

Albert nodded absently but I could tell he was already thinking about something else. Several more seconds of silence passed and then he looked back up at me and smiled.

"You know, before we picked you guys up tonight, I thought the worst thing that would happen was that you might turn me down when I invited you to come see Les Misérables with me over Christmas."

"You didn't ask me to go see Les Mis with you."

He shrugged. "I was planning on doing it towards the end of the date, but I didn't count on Danny being quite so obnoxious or on Ben dragging us into some kind of CIA op. I guess I'm asking you now."

Mention of Danny reminded me of the 'parties' that the rest of the band had gone to, but which Albert had sat out.

"Can I ask you something first?"

"Sure, just don't sell my answer to the tabloids."

I rolled my eyes at him and then just jumped right in. "You've had to take down the last couple of shows pretty much by yourself..."

Albert shook his head and then stared at the ceiling for a moment. "Danny really is an idiot. No wonder Dom didn't like him. I didn't expect anything to happen there, not with James in the picture, but how stupid do you have to be to talk about other girls when you're on a date?"

"So why didn't you go with the rest of the guys? Don't get me wrong—I think that's admirable—but that's hardly the kind of thing you expect a guy our age to abstain from."

I'd made him uncomfortable, but he gamely hung in there and gave me an answer.

"I could tell you that I figured you wouldn't approve, and that would mostly be true, but that's not all. I guess I've always been a romantic. Someday, I'd like to find that one person who makes me excited to get out of bed in the morning. Joining in with the rest of the band would have just been going through the motions. I'd rather wait and have the real thing."

He was practically perfect. We had a history and he made me laugh, but what I felt for him wasn't the feeling he was describing. Even if he thought he felt that way about me right now, it still wouldn't be right. That kind of feeling couldn't be sustained unless it was mutual.

"Albert, what I'm about to say isn't easy. In fact, it's a lot harder than I expected it to be. I can't go to Les Misérables with you because I'm not that person. I really wish I could be, but I'm not."

He met my gaze fearlessly and then nodded. "You knew that before we went out tonight."

"I didn't know for sure, but I suspected. It was hard for me to separate everything out from the friendship I feel for you, so it took a little while to really decide."

"Fair enough. Why did you ask me about the 'parties' then? You'd already made your decision by then."

"I guess I just wanted to know how good of a guy you are. It…well, it seemed only fair to know what it was I was saying no to. It made it harder, but it was the right thing to do. I respect you even more than I did before. I hope us not working out doesn't make you change your views there."

Albert's shoulders dropped a little but he shook his head. "Just because you're 'not that girl' doesn't mean anything else has changed. Can I ask you a question now?"

"Yeah. I'll try to answer whatever you want to know."

"Is it Graves? Is he the reason?"

I would have been less shocked if he'd reached over and slapped me. Not just because of the question, but because of the way every fiber of my being yelled that it was indeed Alec who was the reason Albert and I couldn't be together.

"I…I guess it is. If you'd asked me that a week ago, I probably would have said no, but I think Alec is part of the reason that I'm not the one for you."

"I thought the two of you were over. I've heard that he's dating someone else now."

My nod was jerky, but I managed to keep the tears at bay.

"We are. We're through, but that doesn't mean that I don't still love him. I left him, but I still love him desperately. I'm sorry, Albert. I didn't mean to lead you on; I've just been in denial this whole time. It's stupid. I should move on, but I can't. I can't go back and I can't move on. I'm just stuck here with no way out."

Albert reached out and wiped a tear off of my left cheek. "You'll figure it out, Adri. You're special somehow. Every guy in school could see it almost from the first day you arrived in Sanctuary, it was just that only Brandon and Alec had the guts to go for it. I'd better go. I know I'm absolutely no help in the crazy world that you, Ben and Dom seem to live in, but if you need something, just call me and I'll do whatever I can to help you. Always."

Chapter 11

Dominic Sanchez
Upper East Side
Manhattan, New York

I'd felt bad eavesdropping on Albert and Adri, but they hadn't activated their privacy generator and after everything that had happened over the last couple of hours, I hadn't been able to justify turning mine on while I still wasn't sure whether or not we'd managed a clean getaway. It had been obvious that Albert was head over heels for Adri, but it was harder than I'd expected to hear him admit it and then hear her turn him down. They were both such nice people. I kept wishing that there was a way for me to help them find happiness, Adri especially.

I'd quietly called a car service as their conversation had wound down. A motorcycle would have gotten Albert to his show faster, but that wasn't a particularly smart way to go during the winter, so there wasn't anything to do but get a car and hope the driver would be able to get him there on time. I walked Albert downstairs, told him a car was on the way, and reiterated the need for secrecy about everything that had happened.

He despondently affirmed that he'd be discreet, and then seemed to want to be alone so I returned upstairs and found Adri crying in her room with the door shut. I debated going in there to try and comfort her, but then my phone started ringing.

It was Ash. "Okay, I think we've got all the loose ends tied up. My guy has deleted the entry for Adri's sim card. You'll have to pick up another one for her. I'd recommend a prepaid sim. He confirmed that nobody had accessed her information in the last eight hours as well. Have you heard anything from your guy in Wyoming?"

"No, nothing. I'm starting to worry that Ben didn't make it out."

"Are you going to tell her?"

I sighed. That was the question, but I'd been avoiding making a decision. "I'm not sure. Definitely not tonight. Probably not ever unless she asks. She's going through a lot right now."

Ash seemed to chew on my response for a few seconds and then he sighed, too. "We're probably okay unless they pull the information straight out of Ben's mind. How does Adri keep getting involved in this kind of stuff?"

"I don't know. I'm just glad Alec wants us to keep an eye on her. She's not ready to survive in our world without some kind of help."

"Okay, you headed to bed pretty soon?"

"No...I have somewhere I need to be. I was considering breaking the appointment, but it's important, so if you're comfortable that we got away clean then I'd like to try and make it still."

"It wouldn't be my first choice, but I'll try to avoid spilling the beans to Alec."

"Thanks, Ash. Tell Kristin hi for me."

"Sure thing. Have a good night."

The crying from inside of Adri's room had died down. I tiptoed down the hall until I got close enough to confirm that she was sleeping and then went back to my room and wrote her a note.

Adri, I had to leave. I'm sorry—call me with the burner phone in the study if you need anything, but hopefully I'm back before you wake up. Please don't leave the apartment.

I hung the note in the hall across from Adri's bedroom and then left. The trip to where Mrs. Valencia had asked me to meet her went quickly, almost too quickly. I really hadn't liked Danny, but in all fairness, some of my frustration tonight had been driven by my nervousness about the meeting I was headed to right now.

I'd debated for days before finally calling and arranging to meet her. I was having second thoughts, especially about the fact that nobody knew where I was or who I was meeting, but I was still headed towards the agreed upon location so apparently my worries weren't strong enough to overcome the lure of spending more time with her.

An hour later I stepped inside an old, but well-maintained, building and made my way up to the fourth floor. Mrs. Valencia answered on my first knock and smiled when she saw that it was me.

"Dominic, please come inside."

I paused halfway inside the apartment. "How do you know my name?"

Her smile this time was a little wistful. "We have...I guess you couldn't say that we have a mutual friend. Let's say that I have a friend who has kept a watchful eye over you for a number of years. He's told me a lot about you. That's part of why I extended an invitation to you to come here. You're his grand experiment."

"Who are you talking about?" The question was reflexive. I already suspected that I knew who she was talking about, but it was a memory I didn't particularly like revisiting. I had almost no decent memories from the time before Alec's pack, but the one she was referring to was more disturbing than most.

She looked at me for several seconds. "Do you really not remember? Think of a time when you thought you were surely going to die and that is your first clue."

"The Hunter."

"Yes, that is as good a name for him as any. He's very proud that you've proved him right so far, but that isn't why you are here."

Words couldn't possibly have served to convey the level of shock I was feeling, but I found myself stepping the rest of the way inside the room so she could shut the door.

"Why *am* I here, Mrs. Valencia?"

"Please call me Vanessa. You're here because you have a role to play in the events that are about to unfold. I suppose in the larger view you'd have to say that everyone has a role to play, but your role is special. Rachel and Jasmin couldn't have done it all by themselves, but I suppose I'm speaking out of turn."

"Rachel and Jasmin couldn't have done what?"

Vanessa shook her head. "I really shouldn't have said anything. Suffice it to say that you're important in ways you don't yet understand, Dominic."

She paused for a second and then gave me a searching look. "Why do you think you're here? What was it that made you accept my invitation?"

I debated lying, but it just wasn't part of my nature. "I'm here because you did something to me the last time I saw you. I've been tired and weak for weeks now, but the night I saw you all of that went away. I was strong again, maybe even stronger than I'd been before I started getting so tired."

There was a hint of a smile to her face now, but it was overshadowed by seriousness. "Being strong is important to you?"

"Yes. I don't expect to be able to stand toe to toe with a hybrid, not generally speaking, but I need to be able to carry my own weight inside of the pack. I need to know what you did so I can repeat it in case I start getting sick again."

"I thought your kind couldn't get sick, Dominic."

"We're not supposed to be able to, at least not for long, not really, but somehow I'm sick. So are Rachel and Jasmin."

The hint of a smile was a little more pronounced. "An apparent contradiction."

"Yes, I guess so."

"Dominic, I've lived a very long time. I no longer believe in contradictions. One of your premises is wrong."

My respect for her work was starting to be overshadowed by frustration at the vagueness of her answers.

"Which premise is wrong?"

Another headshake. "It's not for me to tell you, not right now. If it makes you feel any better, it should become apparent to you before too much longer."

I sighed and turned to go, but she stopped me with a gentle hand on my arm.

"Where are you going, Dominic?"

"You said that you could heal me. You pointed at my scar, but then I was strong again. Tonight you tell me that the exhaustion can't be healed. That was the only kind of healing that could really help me. The scar doesn't matter, not really."

"I can see why you made it out of that snake pit your father left you in. You're incredibly stubborn. Very well, I can see that I'll have to tell you some things in order to help you fulfill your purpose. Please follow me."

I put my hands on my hips and waited for several seconds before finally going into the room she'd just entered. It was small but warm with a massage table in the center of the room and bottles of oil in a warmer off to one side.

"You have the ability to heal, but right now it's locked away inside you, Dominic. I would like to help you unlock that ability. It isn't going to help with what you, Rachel and Jasmin are going through right now, but it will help with other things you'll face in the next little while. It will also allow me to help restore your beautiful face."

Her explanation wasn't much more enlightening than what she'd been saying before, but I pushed the frustration aside and focused on the important thing she'd finally let slip.

"Why do you think I have the ability to become a healer? That goes against thousands of years of history. Southern shape shifters don't develop extra powers, at least nothing beyond the ability to track. Surely you mean that you're going to heal me."

Vanessa shook her head. "No, Dominic. I have certain gifts, but healing is not among them. I can however help you unlock your potential. I'll step out of the room so you can undress. There's a sheet on the table that you can cover yourself with for modesty's sake."

She walked out of the room, and I was left looking at the table by myself. After a little while, I took a deep breath, pulled off all of my clothes and then piled them in a corner of the room. Once I was safely under the sheet, I called her in.

"Very good. I'm going to start with the soles of your feet and work up. The key to all of this isn't for you to *try* and heal yourself; it's for you to relax as completely as possible. Once you relax sufficiently, the healing will happen on its own. You are the thing that is currently standing in the way of your power."

It initially felt odd to have a near stranger rubbing my feet, but I found myself starting to relax into the firm, smooth pressure of her hands. "What are you?"

"How do you know I'm not a shape shifter like you?"

I tried to think back over our conversations, but I couldn't remember if she'd ever told me that she wasn't a shape shifter.

"I don't know. You might have told me so, but I'm not sure. For whatever reason, I feel like you're different than me. You...you don't feel like a shape shifter."

"I'm not, but why do I have to *be* anything? Can't I just be another human?"

That one was easier. "No, there is a sense of power around you that is too great for a human."

I could hear another smile in her voice as she switched to the other foot. "You're still very young, Dominic. You might be surprised at how powerful some of the 'normal' humans out there are. Still, you're right; I'm not a normal human. So if I'm not a normal human or a shape shifter what does that leave?"

"You're not a vampire. I'd have been able to smell it on you if you were. You can't be a werewolf because werewolves attack shape shifters without provocation."

"Do all werewolves attack without provocation, Dominic?"

That was an easy answer. "The Southerners only have fragments of oral histories and rumors, but the wolves have thousands of years of written history. I've read through some of Alec's family journals, and they all seemed to take it as a given that werewolves attacked for no reason. Shape shifters and vampires especially, but humans sometimes too."

She paused for a second as if debating something, but her next question distracted me from thoughts of what it was she'd been trying to decide.

"You've eliminated four different species. What's left?"

I tried to sort through rumors and legends. I was pretty sure there were other things out there that were even rarer than shape shifters, but nothing seemed to explain anything I'd seen out of her yet.

"I don't know. You must be something rare though for me to have never run into another...I mean for me to have run into only two of you. The Hunter has been a dark legend in my country for hundreds of years at least, so you must be long-lived."

She'd just changed over to my other calf and I could feel the muscles relaxing almost against my will.

"Very good. I think that is as much as I can answer for you right now, but you're correct in your supposition so far. You know, I'm surprised you haven't asked me the question I get from almost every one of my fans."

"Why you haven't written more books?"

"Exactly. I wrote three books in less than a year, and while they have never sold millions of copies, they've been extremely well-received in some circles. Almost everywhere I go, I get asked when I'll be writing another book."

I was feeling whipsawed. The change back to something as mundane as her job wasn't where I'd expected her to jump next.

"What do you tell the people who ask you that?"

"I lie to them. I tell them I've exhausted my store of creativity, that I'm not sure I have another novel in me. The truth though is that I've continued to write. I'm almost compelled to write, but I've never allowed anyone else to read my later work, and I have no plans of submitting it to a publisher."

Nothing I'd ever read about her, none of the interviews she'd given over the years, had even hinted at anything like this.

"But why?"

The question had popped out of me without conscious thought on my part, but it was the question I wanted answered more than anything else at that point.

"I don't write for other people. I write to help me remember the really special people I come across. Normally I wouldn't have even published those three books, but someone I respect very much, someone I trust almost implicitly, told me there was a very important reason to publish those particular books."

She'd moved up to my thighs now. Her efforts were so amazing that I was having a hard time staying awake. A part of me worried that this was all a trick, that it wasn't natural for me to be relaxing this quickly, especially not with someone I didn't know. Most of me just couldn't be bothered.

I managed to get another question past my lassitude though.

"Why?"

This time she laughed out loud. "Those three books were written for the purpose of bringing today about. I'm sure they had other benefits. He…well, he doesn't do anything for just one purpose. I like to think they have helped the world at large in some small way, but they were written with you in mind."

I felt like maybe I'd missed something there. She was working my neck over, but I couldn't remember how she'd gotten there. Everything from my shoulders down felt like a puddle though, so she hadn't skipped anything.

I managed one last 'why' and I heard her sigh in sadness this time.

"What would you do if you knew a future was coming in which the world would be torn asunder? You don't have to answer because I already know; I've seen it. You would fight with everything you had to try and save the innocents who would be endangered. I'm doing the same thing. I was faced with two paths, two ways of bringing about a future where humanity has a chance of surviving. All I can hope is that I chose correctly."

Vanessa turned me over and started on the front of my legs. Being flipped over should have pulled me out of my near coma, but I just couldn't manage anything more than passive assistance. I tried to get another question out but my whole body felt light and energized and my mind seemed to be shutting down.

I thought I remembered her touching my face, softly rubbing the scar that Raphael had given me, but it might have just been my imagination. When I finally opened my eyes it was nearly morning and the only evidence that it all hadn't just been a dream was staring back at me in the mirror.

My scar was gone, and the apartment was empty.

Chapter 12

Alec Graves
Graves Estate
Sanctuary, Utah

Kristin found me in the middle of a picnic of all things. Tasha had barged into my studio an hour before lunch with a teasing look in her eye and cajoled me into agreeing to show her more of the estate.

I suspected she'd already ranged through the entire estate on her own, but she was right that it would do me good to get out of the house. I hadn't been painting, not really. I'd actually put my brush to the canvas, but it hadn't been like before, I hadn't had any vision of what I wanted to create. I was just playing with shapes and colors.

I agreed mostly because Tasha had been right. I needed to get away from the house and spend some time outside. We'd just laid the food out when Kristin showed up.

"Alec, we need to talk. Right now."

She obviously didn't want Tasha in on the discussion, but I'd already considered leaking knowledge of Kristin's dreams to the rest of the world. It shouldn't hurt as long as we kept her close by and it might even make one or two of the challengers reconsider.

"If it's about your dreams you can tell me now. Tasha may as well know about that, too."

Kristin didn't look happy at the order. I felt my beast test its bonds with a surge of power, but I kept control of it. My beast was harder to control lately, but that didn't matter. I was a dominant. I controlled my beast; it didn't control me. It had become my personal mantra lately, and sometimes it even worked.

This turned out to be one of those times. I managed to just wait expectantly until Kristin finally nodded.

"Okay, yeah. I had another of my precognitive dreams. It was another challenge match, but this time was different."

Tasha sat up and leaned forward. She was either doing a very good job of acting surprised, or we'd actually managed to keep Kristin's abilities a secret so far. I was betting on the latter. Even Addison seemed to have finally realized that leaking information to the world at large was asking for serious trouble.

"How was it different?"

She shot me another frustrated look, like she wasn't happy that I was rushing her, but she waved her hand and shrugged.

"It's hard to describe. It was like I was dreaming and then suddenly I was watching two time streams at once. We're going to have a challenger, a big guy with red fur. You send Ash in first and he gets off a couple of shots, but they bounce off of something. It was kind of like an air shield or something."

I looked over at Tasha, but she shook her head. "That doesn't ring any bells. When we get back to the house I can pull up a list of known dispossessed with red fur in their hybrid forms, but I've memorized every hybrid with known abilities and an 'air shield' doesn't ring any bells."

I frowned. I didn't like unknowns generally, but they were becoming more and more frequent lately.

"So someone who just manifested a new power?"

"Possibly, but my money would be on someone who's had a power for a while but has kept it quiet so far. It occasionally happens and isn't a bad idea. If your power isn't strong enough to serve as a deterrent then you're better off holding it in reserve as a surprise. If he were to challenge and win while displaying a new power, it would probably buy him some time before the stream of new challengers started back up. Nobody would be eager to go up against a complete unknown like that."

I sighed and turned back to Kristin. "Okay, there's nothing else we can do about that right now. What happened next?"

"I think Jasmin and Isaac were still hurt. I think I saw them there with us, but they weren't moving like normal and you didn't send them into the fight."

"Okay, so the challenger is going to arrive sometime in the next day or two. It makes sense; your visions haven't ever predicted more than a day or so in advance."

"Right, that's what I figured, too. Anyways, Ash took a couple of shots at this guy and then when the bullets ricocheted off, James jumped in. James got his butt kicked. It was almost like having to fight a guy with three arms. James would find an opening and go for it but the air shield would pop back up right where he was going to attack and deflect the blow."

I wasn't liking the sound of anything she was telling me, but I started making a list of questions to ask once she was done. I needed to know whether or not the 'air shield' could be used offensively, too.

"So James was trying really, really hard, but he kept getting blocked and then the other guy tore into him. That's when the future kind of diverged. In one future, you jumped in and attacked the challenger right after he sank his claws into the left side of James' chest. In the other timeline, you just sat there and let James keep fighting."

I nodded, trying very hard to keep my frustration in check. It was obvious Kristin was having a hard time processing everything she'd seen in her dream. It was understandable; I doubted that the human mind was meant to be able to see two things at once like that.

"What happened after that, Kristin?"

"In the first one, the one where you jumped into the fight, you...you died. It happened too fast for me to see all of it, but it seemed like he blocked you so hard that you missed a step. He...he got around behind you a split second later and killed you within a couple of minutes."

A chill washed through me. It wasn't every day you had someone predict your death in quite such specific detail.

"What...what happened in the other timeline?"

Kristin stared at me blankly for a couple of seconds and then shook herself slightly. "The blow to James' chest missed his heart, assuming you guys actually have a heart. He fell backwards, but the other hybrid didn't follow up, almost like he was expecting you to attack. James pulled himself up to his feet and kind of looked at you for a second like he was expecting you to jump in, too. You told him to get back in there or Dom would suffer."

My beast tried to break free again. It wasn't the kind of thing we would have done, and my other half wanted to challenge Kristin's version of the future. Again, I managed to keep it in check despite the torrents of power running off of me. Tasha unobtrusively slid back slightly, putting a little distance between us, but Kristin was too deep into her memories to notice my internal battle.

"James got angry then and attacked again. He clinched with the challenger, and they tore at each other for a couple of seconds and then I saw James lose control of the challenger's left hand. He took another pretty bad wound to his chest, but then you joined the fight. You did something with your foot, it was like you trapped his foot and then flipped him around. You killed him a few minutes later."

I took a couple of deep, calming breaths as my beast finally backed down fully and then nodded to Kristin.

"Okay, thanks, Kristin. You can go now. I appreciate your warning."

Tasha held up a hand and shook her head. "You should keep her around, Alec. We still need to plan how you're going to handle the challenge when it shows up."

"No, there isn't anything else she can tell us. I know about both of those time streams, which means I should be able to avoid them when the actual fight happens. Her dreams interfere with the future she sees just by their very nature. I'll tell James what to expect from this guy, and he'll do a better job in the fight than he otherwise would have."

I got the feeling Tasha was just giving me enough rope to hang myself with, but she gestured for me to go on.

"Once James has worked this other hybrid over a bit then I'll jump in and use the technique Kristin just described to end the fight."

Tasha gave me a look like I'd just failed some kind of verbal exam and then she turned to Kristin and started asking questions.

"In the first vision Alec died, but James was okay because the blow didn't get his heart. Did James die in the second vision?"

Kristin shook her head, but the motion didn't communicate very much certainty to go along with her answer.

"I don't think so. At least, he wasn't dead when the dream ended. There was a lot of blood, but the last injury was to his right side."

Tasha nodded. "And the challenger, in the second version was his leg injured? The one that Alec used to knock him down?"

Kristin shrugged. "I don't remember. There was a lot of blood, some of it his, some of it James'. James might have injured his leg, I just can't be sure."

"Okay, last question for now. In the second version, the one where Alec survived, how injured was he?"

Kristin started to answer and then stopped and looked at me. I nodded for her to proceed, which earned me a frown.

"He was pretty hurt. Again, it was hard to tell how much of the blood was his and how much was the challenger's, but he was hurt pretty bad."

"Thank you, Kristin. You can go now."

She shot me another unhappy look as she left, but she left. Tasha waited until she was out of hearing range and then turned back to me.

"Don't tell James anything. Right now you need to try and avoid changing the future any more than you already have. The best scenario is for you to do exactly as Kristin described in the second timeline. Send Ash in, then send James in, and keep him in there until he takes the second serious injury to his chest."

My beast was back, and he wasn't happy with what she was proposing. "You're asking me to send James in blind, and then to leave him in the fight longer than I should and risk him dying."

"Kristin just told you he'd be fine. What I'm asking you to do is to follow the timeline you know will let you survive this fight. You recognize that Isaac and Jasmin still aren't at one hundred percent yet, but you seem to have forgotten that you're still not quite back to normal either."

"I haven't forgotten, but I'm not willing to just let Kristin's dream play itself out and take that kind of pyrrhic victory, not when we can chart a third course, one that is better than either of the two she saw."

Tasha didn't get mad very often, but I could see she was headed that way right now.

"You might achieve that third option, but you also might come up with a fourth option where you still die and James dies, too. James' place is securing your victory. You can tell Donovan to have an extra batch of medical supplies nearby. If James' heart isn't pierced then all you have to worry about is blood loss and possibly re-inflating a lung. Donovan is more than capable of dealing with both of those, especially with some advance warning."

"And what do I do after the victory? James will be down for at least a week, Isaac and Jasmin will still be a day or two away from being back to full strength, and I'll be in bad enough shape that a strong wind would blow me over."

"I'll call my mother and she'll come up and stand off any challengers for a week or so until you're back on your feet."

I shook my head. "If I do that I may as well tell the whole world that she's dominant to me."

"But she is, Alec. Even hurt like she is right now she could wipe the floor with you on your best day. You're good, but without your power you're simply not in her league."

My beast surged up with enough force that I lost control of my hands and they both shifted into hairless replicas of my hybrid form.

"You don't understand, Tasha. You've always been submissive to her. I can admit that she's a better fighter than me, but that doesn't mean I want her to come in and protect me like I'm some kind of child who got in over my head."

"That's the point though. You are in over your head. Your whole pack is. You can see that as well as I can."

"I will not roll over. If I decide to marry you and join the packs, that will be one thing. Then it will be my decision. What you're proposing would be nothing more than me giving up. I will *not* give up."

"What if I stood in for the next challenge? What would you think of that? Guest right would permit that, wouldn't it?"

"Yes, you could stand in, but that's different. I'm dominant to you and we both know it."

"Fine. I'll call Mom on the way back to the house and she can send Alexei and one of the others out here with orders to do whatever I tell them. They'll stand between you and whoever shows up for however long it takes for you to either get back in fighting trim or to agree to the alliance. I'm dominant to them and you're dominant to me. That would mean you'd be dominant to them as well."

"That's a hell of a risk to run for you and your mom."

"You're not leaving me any other choice. I need you to survive and marry me or I'll end up somebody's whipping girl. It will be even worse for me than it is right now for Jess. Whoever takes over my pack will always be after my family's money. That would be bad enough, but even worse will be the fact that I know what it's like to rule. If you won't just bend your stiff neck and let my mom come make all of this go away then this is the only option that guarantees that you'll make it through this fight and still gives us all a chance to survive the next one too."

"What do I do about James? If I make that kind of threat against Dom, he'll never forgive me."

"After the fight is over I'll tell him the truth, that it was all my idea. We'll tell him Kristin had a dream and that this was the only way to make sure the pack survived the fight. Kristin will back us up and confirm that you never actually planned on delivering on your threat, that it was just a mechanism to make sure the fight went down like her dream told us it needed to."

I didn't particularly like it, but I found myself nodding. We cut the picnic short and headed back to the house so she could call her mom and I could talk to Donovan.

The challenger arrived only half an hour after we got back to the house and all too soon I found myself standing on the edge of the sand again. The challenger had said his name was Richard, which didn't ring any bells for Tasha or me, but when he shifted he had red fur and Kristin nodded at me, confirming that it was the hybrid from her dream.

I looked around as the pack huddled up and saw exactly what I'd expected to. Isaac and Jasmin were up and walking around, but they were both still moving gingerly from our recent run-in with the werewolves. Jess was a little better off, but she was still the next best thing to worthless in a fight.

That just left James and Ash, both of whom looked willing, but James had no idea what he was up against and Ash probably already knew he was going to come out of this fight okay. I sighed, flipped open my app, and moved Ash's name at the top of the list, then James, then me.

The fight opened exactly like Kristin had foretold. Ash opened up with three or four shots, all of which were deflected by some kind of plane of force that materialized just in front of Richard.

A ripple of stillness swept through the pack at the unexpected development and then James charged into the ring. The fight moved at incredible speeds, even for an engagement between two hybrids. James was in rare form. He almost seemed to be in more than one place at a time, but it was obvious he was getting frustrated. Time and time again, his attacks were blocked by the momentary appearance of Richard's invisible shield.

James wasn't a very patient fighter at the best of times. I saw the mistake coming several seconds before he actually made it. Richard left a bigger than usual hole in his defenses and James stepped in with both hands, presumably in an effort to make sure that one of them made it through.

The shield flashed into existence again, but this time it was at an odd angle that knocked James' right hand into his left hand. Neither blow connected solidly, and Richard calmly sank his right hand into James' chest.

James dropped to the ground as Richard stepped back and looked at me. Every single part of me wanted to rush into the fight, but instead I fixed James with my best poker face.

"Get back in there and actually do some damage or Dominic is going to pay for your failure once I finally let her come back home."

It was like I'd flipped a switch. A wave of power roared out of James, and for the briefest of seconds I almost thought he was going to turn and charge me, but instead he rushed Richard with all of the subtlety of a battering ram. They went down in a blur of limbs and for a moment James had the better position, but then Richard's gift kicked in again and suddenly James was taking four hits for every three he managed to inflict on Richard.

My beast was prowling at the edge of my control, unhappy that I was letting this slow demolition derby proceed. The tide was turning inexorably against James and then suddenly he lost control of Richard's left hand and it flashed forward and tore into the other side of James' chest.

I transformed between steps as I charged into the ring, yelling for Isaac to get James out and into Donovan's care. My first strike was blocked by the oddly yielding surface of Richard's shield, but my second got through and connected with his left arm.

James had worked him over enough that he was slowing down, but I wasn't at my best either. I had an edge in speed, and probably endurance too, but in a protracted fight his ability to deflect a significant percentage of my blows would go a long ways towards balancing things out.

I hit him again with a combination of blows, consciously choosing not to get my feet involved yet, and again was stopped, but this time it felt like the barrier gave more than before. Under other circumstances I would have assumed he was reaching his limits of being able to use his power and attacked with more force to try and break through, but given Kristin's dream, I had to assume the give to his barrier was just a ploy. It was the best explanation for what Kristin had seen in the first timeline.

I continued to use fast, mobile attacks to try and slip something around his defenses. It was a valid strategy, but mostly I just wanted to keep him moving. A minute later I was bleeding from more than a dozen minor wounds and a couple that would be serious if the fight went on for much longer. I was starting to worry that I'd somehow changed Kristin's version of the future to something worse, and then suddenly I saw the opening I needed.

Richard ducked backwards, but he left his right foot a little too far ahead of him in the process. I seized the opportunity, lunging forward and sinking one set of talons into his foot as I pushed.

He twisted as he fell, ensuring that he'd be able to get right back up, but that exposed his back to me and I latched on with everything I had. He was strong. Not as strong as the werewolf had been, but stronger than I was expecting. He spun around with tremendous speed and I nearly lost my grip on him. I let go with one hand, looking for another hold, but when I tried to sink my claws back into his shoulder, the plane of force was there again, stopping me from getting a new hold.

Richard twisted away and only the fact that I had a good hold on his legs with my talons enabled me to not lose control of the situation. He still tore free of my feet, but the effort brought him to his knees, and I rode him to the ground, slashing and clawing the entire way down. A few seconds later I got all five of the major arteries running through his neck, but not before he managed to spin around and slice open my stomach from one hip to the opposite set of ribs.

I rolled away from him, confident he was only seconds away from death and wanting nothing more than to put some space between us until he wasn't dangerous anymore. I took a couple of stumbling steps before I realized that somewhere along the way I'd shifted back into my human form.

It wasn't a safe thing to have done. Not yet, not while Richard was still a threat. I reached for my beast, trying to force myself back into my hybrid body, but my beast weakly pushed me away.

Darkness closed in around me as I fell to the ground. Strangely enough, it was Jess who made it to me first.

"Make sure James knows that I wasn't going to hurt Dom. Tasha knows."

Chapter 13

Adriana Paige
Upper East Side
Manhattan, New York

"I'm not mad."

"Adri, honey, just tell me the truth. I know you're mad. You're hurt and you're disappointed, too. It's okay to just come right out and say so."

I was in an untenable position. If I said I wasn't mad or even disappointed, then my mom would be hurt and claim I hadn't even wanted to spend Christmas with her. If I blew up and threw a royal hissy fit because she'd just upended our plans at the last possible moment, then she'd claim I was selfish and that I didn't appreciate how hard she worked to put a roof over my head and food on the table.

Things weren't made any easier by the fact that I didn't really know how I felt about the change in plans. I'd been looking forward to some time with Mom, but I hadn't been very excited about finally meeting Russ. Honestly, I'd pretty much figured something like this would happen, and the more Mom had assured me that it wouldn't, the more I'd been positive that it would.

She'd gotten the call on Christmas Eve. There was a huge show the day after Christmas in Italy, and the photographer they'd lined up had canceled at the last minute. It was a new show, so they needed the legitimacy of a big-name photographer to help make sure it didn't flop.

I didn't think that justified loading my mom up on one of the latest Gulfstream jets and flying her over at the drop of a hat, but apparently the show's backers didn't agree with me. Mom hadn't even waited five minutes before she'd called them back and accepted the job. She'd been on the plane less than two hours later.

Today was Christmas, and I was suffering through a call that was part apology, part self-justification, and mostly just about her trying to stay awake long enough to avoid the worst of the jet lag. She was already starting to bob a little, so I figured I didn't have much longer. Certainly by noon my time, she'd decide to throw in the towel and just go to bed.

I checked the clock on my iPad and nodded to myself. I'd been on the Skype call for nearly an hour so far and shouldn't have much more than half an hour left.

"I don't know what to tell you, Mom. I wanted to spend the day together, but I'm not mad. It would have been nice, but you already know that I'm not super keen to meet Russ. How did he take the change in plans?"

It was a last-minute stroke of brilliance. In hindsight I actually couldn't believe I hadn't thought of it sooner. Mom frowned and shrugged.

"He wasn't very happy last night when I called him, but he said he would find another way to spend the evening. I think maybe I went a step too far this time with him. Honestly, I didn't even think of him when I took the job. He's such a great catch. I hope I haven't chased him off."

"Maybe you should give him a call and apologize again."

"You're right, honey. I don't know where my mind is lately. I guess I'm more tired than I realized. I'll talk to you later...not tomorrow or the next day. I have to work the show. I guess I'll see you when I'm back there in New York."

"Okay, Mom. That sounds good. I'll see you then."

I hung up the call and then stood and stretched. Christmas by yourself was pretty depressing. The only thing I could think of that might be worse was maybe New Year's Eve by yourself. The odds were pretty good that I'd get to experience both this year, so I guessed that meant I'd be able to settle that question once and for all.

Dom had flown back to Utah early in the day yesterday. Apparently James had been in some kind of big dustup. Rachel had been the one to call and tell her that things weren't looking very good for James. Dom had made me promise not to wander the city by myself and then she'd left for the airport.

Ben still hadn't called Dom's guy in Wyoming. I'd gone to sleep each night half-worried that some vampire mafia type guys were going to come find me, and now I was spending the next few days all by myself.

I considered texting Albert, but that would have just been cruel. I couldn't do that to him. I considered my options for a few minutes and then bundled up, grabbed my tablet, and headed downstairs. Dom's place was bigger and emptier than my place, but it had the benefit of not being a place where my mom was *supposed* to be. I was going to order an entire pizza just for myself and see if Dom had stocked the fridge with any ice cream. She had a sweet tooth so there was a pretty good chance there'd be something in the house that would make me feel better.

The journey over to Dom's building was thankfully uneventful. I wished the doorman and the desk clerk both a merry Christmas, and a couple of minutes later, I was curled up in a blanket on one of the huge leather couches in the living room dialing a pizza place.

It took me a while to find something to watch on the gigantic TV, but I finally narrowed it down to two options. One option was a movie that was ironically about werewolves and vampires. The other was a romantic comedy that included a bunch of actors I'd never heard of. My own life had plenty of potential for sudden violence, so as I ran back downstairs to get the pizza, I decided on the romantic comedy.

I made it through almost the entire three-hour movie before I broke down and started crying. I might have even made it all day if the movie hadn't included a heart-wrenching subplot. By the time the movie ended, I couldn't even see the screen. I just closed my eyes and let the tears wash over me. At some point the crying ran its course and I dropped off to sleep.

Interlude

It had been so long since I'd visited this particular dreamscape that for a second I almost couldn't believe I was back. It simultaneously made up for the crappiness of my day so far and made it worse.

I couldn't remember whether I'd had one of these vivid, perfect dreams without Alec being present, but it was kind of irrelevant either way. When I thought of landscapes where trees were softly glowing tendrils reaching up to the sky, I thought of Alec.

The ten thousand scents the air was carrying past me just made me remember how divine he'd smelled here. I did a slow turn, taking in my surroundings, and saw him almost immediately behind me. He was kneeling down, a few steps away from a large, flat rock that had some kind of rosebush planted on the other side of it.

He looked up as I walked hesitantly towards him, and it took me a couple of seconds to realize that he'd been crying. My vision suddenly switched and the soft, golden light coming from the living things around us dimmed slightly so that I could see Alec's features better.

"It's been a long time since I shared a dream with you, Adri."

"I know. I'd almost forgotten what it was like, just how much beauty you see on a daily basis. Is this a real dream? Are we really both here, or are you just a dream?"

He shrugged. "I don't know. I thought about asking you the same thing, but ultimately it doesn't matter. We're probably not going to get a chance to compare notes in real life later on."

It was like being doused in ice water. I'd entered the dream unhappy because I'd known it was going to bring back memories of Alec, but once I'd seen him that had all vanished. For a second there everything had felt almost exactly like it had before I'd left. It was like a part of me had been missing, and for a brief few moments that part had been reunited with the rest of me.

His words reminded me once again of just what I'd walked away from. It hurt more than I'd expected. Maybe time had done more to dull the pain than I'd realized.

"No, I guess you're right; we probably aren't going to see each other again. I may not even remember this when I wake up."

Alec took a deep breath and nodded. "There is that. Is it sad that I'm hoping that's the case? It just seems easier that way. I've even started sleeping at odd times to try and make sure we wouldn't overlap and have a chance to share dreams again."

"No, I understand. I guess I feel the same way."

I looked back at him and saw that the tears had disappeared, but there was still evidence that they'd been there. It hadn't just been my imagination. I walked to almost within arm's reach of him and knelt down beside him.

"Where are we?"

Alec gestured with his hand, taking in the low rise we were kneeling on. "This is the pack's cemetery. All of the people who just disappear as far as the normal world is concerned are buried out here. Brandon, Vincent, Alison, Jack, they are all buried over there. This is where my dad is buried. We couldn't risk a real headstone, so Donovan put that rock there. We planted the rosebush a little while after you left."

I looked back at the rose bush and realized it wasn't just any regular flower, it was Lagrimas. It was fitting. It was one of the few things that connected Alec and the father he'd never really known. A shared passion that had finally come to fruition nearly two decades after his father's death.

"It's beautiful. I'm sorry; I wish I could have been there to help you plant it."

Alec shrugged, but I knew him too well for the motion to fully conceal the pain he was feeling.

"I'd planned on having you come out here with Donovan, Rachel and me. After you left there didn't seem to be much point in making a big production out of it. I slipped out here and planted it myself one evening."

He looked around again, seemingly searching for something. After a couple of seconds he nodded, stood, and walked over to a low mound of dirt.

"I was wondering whether or not this would be here. I added another grave yest...actually I don't know when it was that I killed him. What is today?"

"It's Christmas, Alec."

"It was a couple of days ago then. We had another challenger show up. He almost killed James. I guess maybe that is why I came here. I was checking to see whether or not they'd buried James, too. Hopefully this means he survived."

"It sounds like things are getting bad. Dom doesn't say much; she knows how much it hurts me to think about you, but I can tell that the pack is struggling."

Alec's laugh had more bitterness to it than I remembered. He smiled, but it didn't reach his eyes. "I've told each and every member of the pack that I'll kill them if they say your name out loud where I can hear it. I should hear absolutely nothing about what's going on with your life, but they've just come up with a bunch of circumlocutions to get around the rule. It was working okay right up until I sent Isaac out to play bodyguard. With all of the craziness you've been experiencing lately, there wasn't any way to avoid learning at least a little bit about what's happening in your life."

There was a crude stone bench facing the cemetery. Alec walked over, sat down and then patted the stone next to him.

"It was harder than I expected to hear that you'd started dating. I wanted to hunt Albert down and kill him, but I was also glad in a way that it was him. Albert is a good guy. I really hope things work out between the two of you."

I nodded. "You're right; Albert is a good guy, but nothing can happen between us. What about you? I hear some new girl in town has caught your eye."

Alec shook his head. "It's more like a political alliance. Tasha and her mom have a solution that would save the pack. It's perfect in almost every way, but I can't bring myself to throw my lot in with them."

"How come?"

This was like it had been before I'd left. I missed being able to talk to him. He'd spent so much time worried that I was becoming addicted to his touch, and it had turned out that it was talking I missed the most.

"I…well, I guess there are two reasons. Tasha is more practical than I am. You could say she's what you were worried I'd become. It's possible I might be able to get around that. I've already set my foot on a path that will make me like her eventually. Even so, I always thought that when I married it would be for love, not for political expediency."

There were things there that he wasn't telling me, but I didn't have the right to pry anymore. We sat in silence for several seconds before Alec chuckled again. It still didn't have any joy in it.

"We have a new girl in the pack. She can see the future, or at least a version of it. Sometimes I think that you could see the future too. That's why you left me; you saw what I'd become, and you knew it wasn't worth staying around for."

I opened my mouth to protest, but he stood and pointed to his father's grave. "I've spent my entire life trying to figure out where he went wrong. It seemed so easy. He could have just let Agony kill Donovan. Maybe a few other people would have been sacrificed before it was all said and done, but he could have kept his pack together, he could have preserved the greatest number and lived to challenge the Coun'hij later on."

He looked up at me with a kind of naked need for me to understand that made me reach out to him.

"I couldn't sit by and let the same thing happen to Jasmin and Isaac and the rest. It wasn't about me; it was never about me. I wanted to save the people who were most important to me."

I took his hand and nodded. "I can understand why you did what you did. I've thought back to what I said a dozen times. I...I know I can't go back, that those things can't be unsaid, but I'm not convinced anymore that I was right."

Alec shook his head and the look of sadness on his face tore at my heart. "No, Adri. You were right, you and my father both. The pack is falling apart, and all that I'm sure of anymore is that it would have been better if I'd died rather than being forced to watch the pack slowly disintegrate around me."

Chapter 14

Adriana Paige
Upper East Side
Manhattan, New York

Dom had been acting oddly ever since she'd returned from Utah. At first, I'd been worried that Alec had punished her, but that turned out not to be the case.

When you got right down to it, I didn't have much room to be pointing fingers though. I'd been acting a little strange myself ever since I'd woken up from my Christmas nap with a roaring headache and the sense that I'd dreamed about something important, but I had no recollection of what it might have been.

Rather than focusing on the crazy bits of my life, I decided to worry about Dominic. It took me a while to tease all of the information out of her, but I was relentless—in a nice, subtle way.

The real breakthrough came when we were shopping for the stuff we'd need to help my mom make dinner.

I turned to ask her where she thought the ricotta would be, and suddenly realized that her scar was missing. I steadied myself against the cart for a second and then grabbed her arm.

"Dom, your scar is healed! I can't believe I didn't notice it before now. I guess your face just looks so right the way it is now that I didn't think anything of it."

Dom put a hand up to her cheek as if remembering what the scar had felt like and then nodded. "It...well, it was gone before I went back to Utah."

"How is that even possible? You told me it wouldn't ever heal, that the guy that had done it to you was like Agony."

That last part had been said in a quiet hiss, but Dom still looked around like she was worried someone would overhear us. I checked too, but there wasn't anyone around.

"I can't explain it all. Someone told me that I had it within me to heal the scar, that I could become a powerful healer and that A...the pack would need me. The next day, the scar was gone. That is part of why I went back to Utah. I thought maybe I could heal James."

"Is that why James was okay?"

Dom shook her head. "I don't think so. He was really hurt, but Donovan had stabilized him by the time I got there. I tried to relax and tap into whatever it was that had allowed me to heal myself, but I couldn't seem to do it. Right there at the first it felt like I was close, but the longer I was in Sanctuary, the more tired I got. It was really odd. I went from feeling fine to wanting to curl up under a blanket and never move again in the space of maybe an hour."

It was one of the most amazing things I'd heard yet, but in other ways it didn't surprise me at all. Dom had been helping Donovan patch the pack up for years now. Her disposition was perfect for helping people get better.

"I thought that wasn't possible, Dom. You said that cats don't gain abilities like hybrids can."

"You're right. There hasn't ever been any kind of record of a cat being able to do anything like this. I can't explain it."

We both sat there in silence for a few seconds, she because she was uncomfortable, me because I was shocked. Dom finally shook herself and pointed down the aisle.

"We need to get moving or we're not going to be done shopping in time to get the food ready."

I grimaced. I'd agreed to a second, no, a third attempt at dinner with Russ, but that didn't necessarily mean I was excited about it. The shopping trip had served as a distraction from the thought of meeting someone who was currently auditioning to replace my dad, but the distraction had run its course. I was going to have to start mentally preparing myself for dinner.

Dom accidentally bumped a floor display with the cart and muttered something under her breath that I was pretty sure was a profanity in Spanish. Even if she hadn't sworn, I still would have known she was angry. Power arced off her in unpredictable waves, sometimes lashing out with enough force that I found myself unconsciously rubbing my arms and other times subsiding to a background hum that wasn't any worse than the fluorescent lighting above us.

"Are you okay, Dom?"

"I think so. I just haven't felt right since before I came back."

I shook my head, worried about her again. Dom was here to take care of me, but there wasn't anyone to take care of her.

"Let's finish the shopping and get you back home. Maybe you should sit this dinner out."

Dom's power flared up again and for a minute I thought she was angry with me.

"No. I'm not sitting anything out. My job is to make sure you're safe."

It wasn't the kind of argument I was going to win while standing in line waiting to pay for our food. I shrugged and decided that once Mom got home, I'd have better odds. Even Dom would have a hard time arguing both my mom and me to a standstill.

I started to exit the store and then had to stop abruptly as a guy about our age hurried past with a woman a couple of years older tagging along behind him.

Dom's power pulsed out again as she almost ran into me.

"Adri, what just happened?"

Dom's smooth voice momentarily took on an even deeper accent than normal as her frustration peaked.

The guy who had just walked in front of us stopped and looked back. What had begun as curiosity suddenly turned to anger as he took Dom and me in. He moved towards us aggressively, and Dom was suddenly between him and me.

A split second later, the woman that had been trailing the guy was between him and Dom.

"What's going on, Shawn?"

"She's a southerner. I felt her power as I walked by and then I heard her talk."

It was the one disaster I hadn't even considered. Dom had been clear that shape shifters weren't allowed east of the Mississippi. I'd expected vampires or mermaids, not another shape shifter, but there was no denying the power lashing out from both him and the girl that I was realizing was his bodyguard.

I tried to pull Dom backward into the store, but she was on high alert. I would have had better luck moving a bronze statue.

"Listen, 'Shawn,' I don't have any quarrel with you. I'm not what you think. Just back away and we can all go our separate ways."

There was absolutely zero give in Dom right now, but I knew she couldn't win a fight against two wolves. If one or both of the pair in front of us was a hybrid, then she had even less chance of surviving. There was only one thing I could think of to do. Dominic was screening the right side of my body from their view, so I pulled my phone out and dialed Rachel's number. It went through to voicemail but that was okay; I didn't actually need to talk to her. I cleared my throat and then held up the phone.

"I don't know who you are, Shawn, but you need to calm down. Dominic isn't your enemy, but more importantly, if you hurt either of us then our friends will hunt you down and kill you. I promise you that."

The girl let out a low growl that was only barely audible to me, but suddenly Shawn was pulling her back with confusion once again flashing across his face.

"Dominic, like Dominic from Sanctuary?"

"Yes, that's right. Who are you?"

"Shawn Bishop."

Dom bit off another curse. She was in rare form today. She looked back at me for a second. "Shawn is the heir apparent to the Chicago pack."

Shawn nodded and pointed to his companion. "This is Vicki. What are you two doing in New

York? Alec is already on thin ice with the Coun'hij. The last thing he should be doing is letting his people run wild like this."

It was said with a smile, but Dom didn't return the gesture. "Where Alec sends us is his business. Your pack may be the largest in North America, but your father is hardly the kind to court problems with the Coun'hij. He doesn't know where you are right now, does he, Shawn?"

It was Shawn's turn to go all frigid. "That's our business."

I held up a placating hand. "Okay, so we all have things we're doing here that we're not anxious to have the rest of the world know about. Let's just agree to keep each other's secret and part ways without trying to kill each other."

Shawn shook his head and pointed at me. "You haven't told us who you are."

"My name is Adri."

"Okay, Adri. We'll leave you to go about your business and we'll go about ours. If, however, you tell anyone, it will eventually make its way back to me and then there will be an accounting."

"That's fine. I've kept bigger secrets than this."

It wasn't until we were almost back to my house that Dominic finally seemed to get control of her beast. The flashes of power suddenly died out and then she turned to me with a look of amazement.

"Adri, your ploy shouldn't have worked. Shawn is about as dominant as they come. Forcing his hand like that really should have had the opposite effect. Who did you call?"

"Rachel. Which reminds me, I need to text her and tell her not to do anything about that message."

Dom nodded absently, but it was obvious she was only half listening. "Something very odd just happened, Adri. I just can't figure out why Shawn would have been in New York or why he would have backed down so quickly."

I shrugged and hit the elevator call button with the hand that wasn't carrying the food. She was probably right, but I couldn't think of anything that was less important. What Shawn did or didn't do wasn't going to have the slightest impact on my life.

Walking into my house and finding out that Mom still wasn't back, however, was the kind of thing that was going to have a very immediate impact on my night. She was late, not just the 'not-here-when-she-said-she-would-be-here late.' No, she was later than even the hour leeway I normally gave her past her stated arrival time. I had a very bad feeling about this, and it only got worse when she picked up my call on the first ring.

"Adri, honey. I'm sorry—I know I'm late, but I just can't get away right now."

I'd barely seen her for the last couple of months, and now she'd canceled our New Year's

Eve dinner. It was disappointing, but it was also something I could live with because it meant I could put off meeting Russ for another couple of months.

"It's okay, Mom. I'll just put the ingredients away, and Dom and I will order some takeout."

"Actually, that's what I wanted to talk to you about. What would you think about you and Dom having dinner with Russ still?"

I hated it. Mom already knew that without asking me. Unfortunately, that meant she didn't really care how much I didn't want to have dinner with Russ.

"I'd rather not, Mom."

"I know, honey. It's just that this is the second time I'd be canceling on him at the last minute. I don't really think he's going to take this well, but I don't want to drive him away. I...well, I thought if you guys still had dinner together that maybe it would help soften the blow and give me another shot at making things right in a couple of weeks after everything slows back down."

Somehow I didn't think things would ever slow down, not really. My bet was that Russ was smart enough to realize that. Mom took my pause as a sign that I was weakening.

"It would really mean a lot to me, Adri. I've tried to give you your freedom and not ask very much of you lately. I know how hard it was for you to decide to leave Sanctuary, but I think it showed that you are ready to be an adult. Can you please do this for me?"

I knew my mom was using guilt on me but that didn't necessarily stop her ploy from being effective. Ultimately, I didn't really have a choice. If I told her no and then Russ walked out, she'd always blame me. If I helped her the best I could and he still walked out, then it wouldn't be my fault.

"Okay, I'll do it. Dom hasn't been feeling very well lately, but I think she can make it for a few more hours. I'll cook dinner and then I'll play nice with Russ."

"Thanks, sweetie; that means a lot. I'll call Russ now and make sure he's okay with the change in plans."

I'd told Mom that Dom wasn't feeling well because I'd wanted to dish out a helping of guilt the other way—not that it had done any good—but when I looked over at Dom it seemed like she really wasn't doing very well.

"Dom, the door is locked and nobody is getting in here without you being able to hear it from the other room. Why don't you go lie down and get some rest? You look like you really need it."

"Okay, but just for a few minutes. If you need something just yell. I won't be going to sleep."

The fact that she'd agreed actually made me more worried about her. Dom wasn't the kind to give in so easily, not unless she was in really,

really bad shape. I already knew that trying to convince her to go home wasn't going to work, so I just crept over and shut the bedroom door before getting started on the lasagna.

Cooking wasn't my favorite thing to do, but occasionally it served as a good distraction. For the half hour or so that it took to put everything together and preheat the oven, I managed to leave aside worries about Dom, Russ, or what might be happening with the pack back in Sanctuary.

Once the lasagna was in the oven, the table was set, and everything was more or less ready to go, I went into the living room, set the alarm on my iPad, and put one of my new favorite songs on repeat as I stuck the headphones in my ears.

I figured the heavy drop to the music would stop me from falling asleep, but it turned out that I was more tired than I'd realized. The next thing I knew, the doorman was buzzing to ask if he could let Russ come up.

"Yes, please, Vince. Thank you."

I rolled off the couch and headed to the kitchen, where Dominic met me looking like she'd just woken up and was more than a little disoriented. A quick look confirmed that everything was ready to go so we both stumbled into the bathroom and ran fingers through our hair.

A few seconds later, Russ was knocking on our door. Dom answered it while I grabbed juice from the fridge. I turned around from putting it on the table and had a hard time pulling my eyes away from Russ.

He was tall, but not tall and lanky, tall with the kind of shoulders you'd see on a rodeo cowboy. He looked like someone who spent a lot of time outside working for a living, who'd then been stuffed into designer jeans and a charcoal polo that did incredible things for his gray eyes.

It took me a second to realize he was waiting to shake my hand.

"It's nice to finally get a chance to meet you, Adri. Honestly, I almost told your mom no when she called tonight to rearrange plans. Spending the evening with two underage girls didn't sound like the smartest thing I could be doing, but I couldn't resist the chance to finally see what Nicole's daughter was like."

It was an abrupt reminder that he was the enemy. The fact that he was gorgeous as well as rich didn't change anything other than to make him a little bit more dangerous.

"Yeah, well, I'm afraid I'm not much like Mom. The lasagna's almost done though, so I guess you'll at least get to compare our culinary efforts."

He smiled—even his smile was amazing—and held up a bottle of wine. "I didn't have a chance to make it back home and drop this off after your mom told me she wasn't going to be here. Can I leave it here without the two of you drinking it?"

I took the bottle and looked at him oddly. "If I'm the kind of girl who would drink it, wouldn't I also be the kind of girl who would lie about it?"

He shook his head. "I don't think so. Not if you're anything at all like your mom. I think you probably break rules, but I don't think you like lying about it. Your mom breaks plenty of rules, but she doesn't do it out of some kind of immature need to prove she can break them. She breaks them because she sees something on the other side of the rules that she thinks is important enough to justify breaking them. Does that sound familiar?"

"Yeah, I guess that does sound familiar. I didn't realize my mom was like that too though."

Russ shrugged. "I don't have kids of my own, but I've noticed that parents are often slightly different with their kids than they are when their kids aren't around. That's one of the reasons why I was actually willing to have dinner with you and your mom so soon after I met her. At some point, I'd like to see what she's like when you are around."

He'd given me plenty to think about already. I was starting to feel like I'd come to a gun fight with a knife. If I wasn't careful I'd find myself liking him despite my best efforts. I held up the bottle of wine and then put it on the counter. "Dom and I won't drink this, and we won't give it to any of the lame kids from my school. It will be right here waiting for my mom whenever she gets back."

I got a serious nod from Russ in response to my promise and then my iPad started beeping at me. Pulling the food out of the oven gave me a chance to gather my wits about me again. By the time the food was on the table and we were sitting down to eat, I felt ready to do battle again.

"So tell us a little bit about yourself, Russ. How did you get involved in fashion? Is that where you made your money?"

Dom shot me a warning look. She obviously thought I was being too confrontational, but I had the final call when it came to all things involving Russ and my mom, so she didn't actually say anything.

"Actually, I got involved in fashion almost by accident. It's pretty much the last thing I thought I'd end up spending two months a year on. I joined the army as soon as I graduated from high school and then spent three years in Iraq. I ended up leaving at the end of my second tour despite the fact that I didn't have any idea what I was going to do with myself."

Russ took a second bite of his lasagna and smiled at me. "This is really good by the way. It's not quite the same recipe as your mom cooked, is it?"

"No, not quite. We were out of nutmeg when she made it."

Russ nodded and took a drink of juice. "Who knows what would have happened after that, but my grandfather died a couple of weeks after I got back to the States. He...well, he left me a lot of money. He didn't approve of my parents. He didn't approve of any of my family really, but I guess he respected me for having entered the military, despite him telling me not to."

"So what happened next?"

Russ did a half snort, half laugh thing that somehow didn't look unnatural coming from someone who was probably a billionaire.

"I nearly self-destructed. Booze, parties, you name it. I surfaced two months later just because I'd gotten so stoned that I'd lost my wallet. I got another set of credit cards ordered and realized I had a choice to make. I could either become the kind of man who was worthy of the fortune my grandfather had left me, or I could let it destroy me. There wasn't any kind of halfway measure there."

"So you decided to own the money rather than letting it own you."

"Yeah, that's as good a way of saying it as any. So I took a crash course in finances, put my money to work and then started looking for causes that were worthy but needed a little push."

I looked over at Dom, wondering if he'd been telling the truth or not, and she nodded. Interesting.

I turned back to Russ and raised an eyebrow. "And the fashion show?"

"It's one of the few shows that actually mixes pro designs in with designs from high school and college students. They do it without attributing the designs to anyone until weeks after the show. By the time anyone knows a given design was done by a student rather than a big name, the student in question is usually sitting on a quarter of a million in orders for their new design."

"That's a good cause as causes go, but there are those who would argue that there are better ways to spend your money, other things you could support that would be better causes..."

Russ shrugged. "It actually pays back, so it helps me preserve my working capital, but honestly, I still have more money than I know what to do with. I support Alicia's show because it fosters talent. I'm not interested in just giving people handouts. I've seen what that does. It could have destroyed me, and I'm not going to do that to other people. I'll foster talent almost wherever I find it, because I think that ultimately it will help make the world a better place."

I checked with Dom again and got another nod, this one more emphatic than the last one. He believed what he was telling me, and strongly. I took another bite of my lasagna and shrugged.

"I can't argue with your aim. What did you do in Iraq?"

Russ looked a little like he wished I hadn't asked the question, but I was realizing that he wasn't going to lie to me. It was impossible to know for sure if he was just that honest with everyone, or if he felt like he needed to make a good impression with me because of my mom, but I was prepared to take shameful advantage either way.

"I was a sniper, Adri. I killed people from incredible distances without any kind of warning. I saw things I hope you never have to see, but the point I kept coming back to was that war was about destroying investments. Roads and bridges, factories and refineries, but even more than that, it was about destroying human capital. I think that's part of what brought me back after I inherited all that money. An incredible, almost incalculable, amount of time, money and effort goes into raising a child. They are tiny little universes of possibility, and I extinguished them one after another."

Russ looked up at me almost like he was surfacing from a deep hole and shrugged. "I don't regret what I did, not really. I was killing according to clear rules of engagement, rules the people there knew, but it still seemed like a senseless loss on both sides. I now have the ability to help people realize that potential. I'm going to do that to the best of my ability."

"How do you decide who gets help and who doesn't?"

"I'm a pretty good judge of character. It's not that hard once you know what to look for; it's all about observation. I learned that while I was in the armed forces. It took a while to learn a new theater of operation, but I expected that when I started this."

There was a challenging glint to his eye, but it was a challenge I was willing to pick up. I didn't want to like Russ. If he couldn't back up what he'd just said then I'd be able to write him off as a lame poser.

"Fine, read Dom and me then."

Russ leaned back in his chair with a satisfied smile. He knew he was in the middle of an audition and seemed to welcome my stubbornness.

"I can do that, but before I do you, I need a promise from you, Adri, that you won't react negatively to what I'm about to say."

"You don't need a promise from Dom? Are you only going to say mean things about me?"

"No, but the promise from you is the most important. It will actually bind her better than her own promise."

A wave of alarm washed through me, but I tried very hard to keep it off of my face. "Do you have any idea how ludicrous that sounds?"

"Probably, but that doesn't change the fact that it's true. Do I have your promise, Adri?"

"Okay, you have my promise. Let's hear it."

Dom let out a hiss of frustration but I held a hand up, silencing her.

Russ nodded and pointed at Dom. "Your friend, Dominic, is one of the more dangerous people I've met recently. I can't explain it, but it's the truth. From a thousand yards away with a high-powered rifle I could take her down in a heartbeat, even as rusty as I am right now. In close quarters, I suspect she'd tear through me before I could even blink."

My mouth dropped open. "How can you possibly know that?"

I got a shrug in response, but after several seconds of silence he decided to humor me. "She moves like she's dangerous. She's got the kind of situational awareness I usually only see inside a combat zone. What's more, she seems to feel like she needs to defer...no, to protect you. Generally that would mean someone like her would be packing all kinds of hardware, but I'm pretty sure she doesn't have anything bigger than a two-inch knife on her. That could just mean she has something secreted nearby, but I suspect it means she's just that good with her hands."

I sat back in my chair and shook my head like I was trying to clear it.

"Am I wrong?"

"No, you're mostly right. Dom is dangerous, and she's here to keep an eye on me."

"Are you going to fill me in on the parts where I'm wrong?"

I looked at Dom for half a second and then shook my head. "No, you're just going to have to live with not knowing. It's not my secret to tell. It's not even just Dom's secret to tell. Okay, what have you observed about me?"

Russ tapped his fingers on the table for a couple of seconds before continuing. "You're both harder and easier to understand. I came here expecting to ask you what your passion is, what it is that you want to pursue. With your mom it's blindingly obvious. She wants to be a world-class photographer. She'd love for it to be in a different area than fashion, but she'll take fashion if that's all she can get. You're different."

"How so?"

"You don't have a passion. Only that's not quite right. You had a passion but now it's gone. There's a listlessness to you that isn't the way you would normally move. I think your passion is to find someone you can believe in more than anything else and then to back their passion."

It didn't seem very flattering, especially not from someone who was in the business of finding stuff people were passionate about and then helping them develop their gifts. In his world there probably wasn't a worse insult to apply to someone.

Russ held his hand up, stopping me before I could take off on my rant. "That's not a bad thing, Adri. In some ways, you're more like me than you realize. You're what I think of as an enabler, but not in a bad way. If you believed in your mom with everything you had, then she'd be Anne Geddes famous in a matter of years. Don't feel guilty that you haven't gotten behind her and pushed though. That's a huge sacrifice, and you should never feel guilty for not pouring yourself into someone else's dreams. When you find the right person, it will flow naturally. The key is to either find someone who won't use you up and discard you, or to learn to limit just how far you go for people."

It was like he'd held a mirror up for me and I'd seen myself for the first time. It was more disturbing than I'd expected it to be. I'd just opened my mouth, I think to thank him for his insights, when the phone rang. Nobody ever used our landline. I was pretty sure Mom had gotten it more out of habit than anything else. I let it ring a couple more times and then the machine picked up.

"Adri, it's Ben. I need you to pick up if you're there!"

Dom moved even faster than I did. She made it to the phone and tossed it my way while Russ and I were still turning towards it, him in curiosity, me in shock.

"I'm here, Ben. What's going on?"

"I can't leave. My boss showed up a couple of seconds after I finished talking to Dominic and he did something to me. I physically can't make myself leave, and they've been really careful not to leave a telephone around since then. I was going to call Dominic's guy, but I can't remember his name. I can't remember anything. It's like they wiped the memories away."

I made it over to the answering machine and managed to kill it. Dom was back at my side with her hand out for the phone.

"Ben, I'm going to give Dom the phone."

"No! I...I can't seem to talk to her. Every time I think of calling her, something odd happens. Adri, I don't know what they did to my mind, but it's not right anymore."

I looked at Dom, completely at a loss for what to do next. She bit her lip for a second, looked at Russ, and then nodded.

"Put it on speaker, Adri, and ask Ben if he gets the same kind of panicked feeling at the thought of overhearing me talk to you."

"Ben, what about if you listen to Dom talk to me, and you only talk to me? How does that feel?"

"I...I think I can do that."

I knew there was a chance this would all come back to bite me, that Russ might turn me in, but I still hit the speaker button. Ben probably didn't have much time, and this was the only way to get him and Dom talking.

"Okay, go."

Dom took a deep breath and began talking very quickly. "It would be very useful to know

Ben's address. The shop, and anywhere else he thinks they might take him."

I looked around for a notepad and a pencil, but Russ had already grabbed one off of the kitchen counter, and he started quickly writing as Ben started telling 'me' where the shop was.

"They haven't taken me anywhere else so far. I just work the shop during the day and then sleep in the apartment in the back at night. Can you guys get me out?"

Dom was chewing on her lip again. She looked more worried than I'd seen her in a long while.

"I don't think I could get him out by myself. It's at least a two-person job and he's just undone all the work we did to try and keep you safe from his…bosses."

"What about James?"

Another headshake. "Alec will never allow both James and me in the city. He'll be worried that we'll leave and never come back. James might really do it, too. He's mostly recovered from the last fight, but he's really, really mad at Alec right now."

I bit my lip and then told Ben what I knew was the last thing he wanted to hear. "Ben, we might be able to get you out, but Jasmin is going to have to be involved."

There was a hitch in his breathing. "I don't want to see her again."

"I know, but I don't have any other way to get you out. If Jasmin flies out and brings Isaac, then they might be able to do it. Alec might be willing to come help, but I'm not sure he can just disappear like that right now. If I can come up with another option then I'll take it, but I think you need to start adjusting to the idea that the cavalry might include Jasmin."

Ben sighed and then he cleared his throat. "Okay, do what you have to do. I believe Dom now. Every word. If I don't get out soon, I'm worried that I won't make it much longer."

Dom already had her phone out, but she paused for just a second to reassure Ben. "We'll work as fast as we can. You should hang up now. We can't risk someone walking in and seeing him talking to you."

"I heard. Bye, Adri. If I don't...well, just tell Jasmin I'm sorry I didn't wait around so that we could've talked things through."

Ben hung up, and I sat there for a couple of seconds holding the phone while Dom dialed Ash. "Yeah, it's me again. Look, we've got a problem."

Dom disappeared into my room talking quietly enough that I couldn't catch more than a word here or there. There wasn't anything left to do but face the music. I turned and met Russ' eyes as he held out the notepad with the piece of paper on it.

"That sounds like some pretty dangerous stuff that you're involved in, Adri."

"Yeah, it is. I actually thought I'd left it all behind in Utah, but I guess you can't really go back. Once you know the world is a certain way, you're always going to notice the bits that don't add up, even if nobody else notices them."

Russ nodded. "And the very act of noticing can sometimes drag you back into that world. I understand, at least a little. That still leaves me in a bit of a difficult position, Adri. Your mom would be pretty pissed at me if she found out all of this and then realized I knew and didn't tell her. More importantly, I'm not sure you're ready to be doing the things that I suspect you're about to go do."

I almost laughed. He seemed to think I was going to mount up as part of the supernatural SWAT team Dom was busy organizing. His powers of observation had obviously failed him there.

"I'm not going to go charging into the middle of a rescue mission, Russ. I'll stay safely on the sidelines. Dom and the rest of the...group will take care of things. Normally, I wouldn't worry too much about them, but they are under a lot of pressure right now. It would be bad if they went in unprepared and understrength."

Russ considered my statement for several seconds before sighing. "I might be able to help out. I know a couple of guys who turned mercenary after they finished up their tours. They might be able to put something together, but it would have to be discreet. We can't launch a full-scale firefight in Brooklyn."

"We can ask Dom when she gets back out, but I expect that the Sanctuary crew will want to deal with it themselves. The guys you know might do the trick, but this is the kind of thing Dom and the rest have been doing their entire lives. They have...advantages that your friends aren't going to have."

I got another very considering look. "What have you gotten yourself into, Adri?"

"To be honest, some days I'm not really sure. I'll stay out of the direct line of danger, though, if at all possible. Is that enough for you to agree not to tell my mom?"

Russ nodded, and I realized what it was that I liked about him so much. He treated me like an adult.

"Just try not to make me regret it, Adri. I really do like your mom."

Chapter 15

Alec Graves
Graves Estate
Sanctuary, Utah

Tasha found me in my studio again, but this time she came with a different kind of proposition.

We'd more or less recovered from the challenger who had almost killed James and me. James was still pissed at me, but Jaclyn had agreed to leave her people here for another few days to give me time to try and bring James around. Dominic was actively trying to calm him down too, but unfortunately even that was backfiring this time around. Because she'd been the leverage I'd used against him, her efforts to smooth things out were just making him angrier.

Isaac was fully healed and seemed resigned to the fact that we were going to have to deal with another challenger fairly soon. He seemed to have bought into Ash's philosophy with a vengeance. As a dominant, Isaac's life would be better in another pack than Ash's life would be, but it would still represent a rough, potentially fatal, transition period while he worked his way into the pecking order of the new pack.

Jess was still pretty much a non-asset when it came to a fight, but it seemed like she was trying harder than before. She'd started out scared of fighting, but after dealing with first the batch of vampires and then the werewolves, she seemed to have realized that being scared and ignorant wasn't any kind of protection when something bigger and meaner than you came calling.

Jasmin was a bigger concern than she'd been before. Whatever had gone after her, Dominic and Rachel seemed to have gone at least slightly into remission, but she hardly even looked at me these days. I'd been trying to catch her alone and figure out what was going on, but she'd been doing a masterful job of avoiding me so far. I could always force the issue, but that wasn't likely to help her open up once I finally had her in front of me. I second-guessed the decision on a regular basis, but she couldn't avoid me forever. Eventually I'd get a chance to talk to her, and it would be less confrontational this way than the alternative.

All in all, I was just glad to have made it to the end of another week. Getting everyone back to school would go a long ways towards alleviating some of the pressures inside the pack. It was a Friday afternoon, and even sitting in my studio pretending to paint was better than dealing with everyone's issues.

"So when are you going to paint me, Alec?"

She'd caught me woolgathering again. "Sorry, Tasha. You've never evidenced any kind of interest in painting before now. What changed?"

"I never asked before because I'm not interested in painting, I'm interested in you. Now that I've been here a few weeks though, I'm realizing that this is where you spend most of your time. This seems like a good compromise. I'll sit for you, you'll paint me, and we'll get to spend some more time together."

I started to shake my head, but she looked up at me with such earnestness that I couldn't bring myself to say no. I'd kept her here for weeks, cooling her heels while she waited for me to work through my issues and either say 'yes' or 'no' to her marriage proposal.

"Okay. If you want to sit for me then I'll try to paint you. No promises that what comes out the other end will be even half decent, but I'm willing to try."

"Here, or somewhere else?"

I considered for a second or two, but there was really only one answer if I wanted to preserve at least a shred of the privacy I'd come to crave so badly over the last few weeks.

"Let's do it here. I can arrange you on a stool and then come back and put the background in after the fact."

She lifted up the bottom of her tank top and raised an eyebrow questioningly. It wasn't a very long tank top, so even that minute action left a long expanse of firm, tan stomach exposed. The invitation was perfectly clear, and I couldn't deny her substantial beauty. I'd already gotten some pretty extended glimpses both before and after the fight with the four werewolves, but I found myself shaking my head almost before I'd had a chance to consider the suggestion.

It would have felt wrong on several levels, but it wasn't just that I was old-fashioned. I knew Adri wasn't coming back. I knew I'd already lost her respect, but there was a tiny part of me that was screaming not to do something that would further disappoint her.

It was a dangerous thing to be courting. A hopeless kind of hope that was threatening not just the pack, but also any future chance I might have of being happy. It was ludicrous. I probably wasn't going to have much of a future if I didn't seal the alliance with Tasha and her mother soon, but I just couldn't seem to let go of that last sliver of hope. My mind knew better, but I was finally seeing just how much stronger my heart was than my head.

"No, let's keep your clothes on. There's no telling how frequently we'll get interrupted."

She nodded, but I could tell she wasn't completely happy with my excuse. I thought about potential poses and backgrounds for a moment before hitting on one that *felt* right. It took only a couple of minutes to get her arranged how I wanted her. She was sitting so that the painting perspective would be looking down at her from a couple of feet higher as she looked off into the distance. It wasn't quite a profile shot, but it was close.

I adjusted the lighting inside the studio, making it brighter and adding in more yellow, and then started mixing paints.

"I know I ask this every day, Alec, but how are you feeling? Are you back to full strength?"

"Yeah. I'm a little stiff still in a couple of directions, but I'm good enough. Is your mom coming under pressure? Does she need the boys back in Tucson sooner than we'd discussed?"

"No. In some ways, it would be ideal if we were able to send them back before the next challenger arrived, but she's still willing to leave them here through the end of the weekend. Believe it or not, I asked just because I don't like to see you injured. So much depends on you. You're carrying a pretty heavy load. It's got to be hard enough to deal with when you're healthy. I can only imagine that it's a lot worse when you're unable to get out of bed."

There it was again. Every time I was tempted to dismiss Tasha as some kind of cold-hearted manipulator, she turned around and said something like that. There was a kinder, more vulnerable person lurking under the armor that pack life had forced on her. I needed to find a way to strip the armor off and get a clear view of the person beneath it if I was ever going to have a prayer of moving forward with this alliance, with this marriage. I knew it. I'd known it for weeks now, and yet I still hadn't acted upon the knowledge.

I deftly sidestepped the opportunity she'd just provided, and instead of taking the conversation into deeper things, I guided it back to the stuff that wasn't important. Safe stuff like finances, rumors about the dispossessed, and the Coun'hij. We covered a variety of topics for several hours until Jasmin burst into my studio with power arcing off of her like an electrical storm.

"Alec, I need the plane and I need Isaac. I'd really appreciate it if you didn't ask questions."

I took a deep breath and wished for a second that Tasha wasn't here. Jasmin was hard to reason with at the best of times. When there was someone else around, getting her to see sense became even harder. I couldn't just send Tasha packing though, not without giving Jasmin too much control of the situation. I had to keep the upper hand or I risked her beast making her even more stubborn than normal.

"I'm sorry, Jasmin. This isn't a refusal, but I need to know what you're up to before I say yes."

Jasmin's eyes flickered over to Tasha, wordlessly asking, but I slowly shook my head.

"Out with it, please."

"Dom and...well, Dom's found Ben. He's in New York. They actually found him a couple of weeks ago, but he didn't want anything to do with me, so they've been keeping it a secret. I need to go to him right now."

"Jas, what's changed? He didn't want to see you before, why would he want to see you now?"

I hadn't meant the reminder to be cruel, but she still flinched. I suddenly wondered just how much of the crazy erratic behavior I'd seen out of Jasmin could be traced back to Ben in some form or fashion. I'd been guilty of some pretty irrational things when Adri and I had been dating. I should have keyed into the possibility that Ben was the reason Jasmin had been so difficult, but I'd been so wrapped up with my own issues that I hadn't even considered it.

Jasmin took a deep breath and then told me the piece she'd been hoping to keep a secret.

"He's gotten involved with some vampires. It sounds like they've got their hooks in pretty deep. One of them must be a mentalist because they've made it so he physically can't make himself run away. I need Isaac so I can go in and get Ben out."

It was exactly the kind of thing the Coun'hij had been trying to stop when they'd issued their prohibition against anyone traveling east of the Mississippi. There were several thousand shape shifters in North America, but the last time I'd seen any estimates on projected vampire populations, it had put it at between five hundred and a thousand of the blood suckers just in New York City alone. That would have been bad enough all by itself, but the bit about them being able to make more vampires by biting humans was at least partially true. It meant that if they ever felt really threatened, they could grow at a nearly exponential rate.

"How many vampires are you going to be up against, Jas?"

"I don't know, Alec. I wish I did, but I don't. It doesn't really matter though. I'd go if it was a hundred and just hope I could find a way to sneak in and out without running into problems."

"Okay, here's the plan. You can have the plane, but get the one in New York headed back this way so I've got options if I need to get somewhere quickly. Leave Dominic out there to help you guys. You do surveillance until you have a way in and out with a minimal body count, and Ash decides what's minimal and what's not. I don't want to lose any of you."

"Thanks, Alec. Can I ask for one modification to the plan?"

"You can ask, but I may not be able to give it to you."

She didn't look like she wanted to ask, but something compelled her to do it. "Can you call Dom back? It gives you a little more cover while we're gone, but more importantly, I might need James to make this work. I know you won't agree to both him and Dom, and I'd rather have him than Dom. She's still pretty wobbly. Besides, Ben might have accidentally created some extra visibility for...the person Dom is there watching. Ash is saying that he could use some help back here managing the damage control efforts to keep...a certain individual off the vampires' radar."

My beast ripped free in a shower of clothes. I grabbed Jasmin by the throat with one clawed hand and slammed her into a wall. "This isn't the first time, is it? She's been in extra danger and none of you have said a damn thing to me."

Jasmin grabbed my hand with both of hers, but she wasn't trying to get free, she was just trying to make sure I didn't choke her.

"I'm sorry, Alec. I just found out myself. I know you're pissed, and probably worried, but I'm not the one to take it out on, and you don't want to be jostling Ash or Dom's elbows right now."

She was right. Even my beast knew it. I forced my hand open and let her drop to the floor. It took a couple of seconds of deep breathing to force my beast back into its metaphysical cage, but when I looked over at her again, I was back to the 'me' I wore most of the time.

"Okay, take the plane. Send Dom back here, and then look for a way for you and Isaac to get Ben out. If you have to, you can add in a couple of Ash's hired guns. It's not very likely that I'll be able to send James though, not with current circumstances."

"Thanks, Alec."

Her mouth said thanks, but her eyes said that I could do more. It would only take one small word to change the status of the pack and put us in a place where it wouldn't be risky to send James along. The only problem with that scenario was that it would require me to give up on my hopes. She didn't have the right to ask that, not just to save her hopes, and she knew it.

I started gathering up scraps of clothing and then saw Tasha still sitting on the stool exactly where I'd arranged her. I'd nearly forgotten about her.

"I need to get some pants on. Do you want to call it a night?"

She let her gaze dance across my bare chest and then smiled. "No, I'm perfectly happy for us to continue."

I slipped some pants on over my ha'bit and then went back into the studio and picked my brush back up. The banter from just a few seconds ago seemed to have evaporated, and apparently neither of us was really in the mood for the shallow conversation we'd been having before that.

I worked in near silence for another couple of hours. Tasha was a good subject. She held very still, and I only occasionally had to adjust her back to the original position I'd put her in. I knew something was up though when I looked back over and saw her staring at me rather than looking off to the side like I'd posed her.

"Alec, you know you could have guaranteed that you'd be able to send James with her. All it would take is for you to agree to the alliance. Mom could be up here a few hours later and drop any and all challengers until we got the rest of the logistics sorted out."

"I know."

"So why won't you do it? I saw the way you looked at Mom the night we went hunting. You've seen that she's able to keep the pack headed in the same direction without the constant infighting that exists in most other packs. She can guarantee your people won't get roughed up too badly in the transition as the new power structure gets worked through."

I didn't have a good answer, not one I was willing to give her. The silence stretched out for several seconds, and then she pulled her knees up under her chin. She looked the most vulnerable I'd ever seen her.

"It's okay, I already know the answer. You're impressed with what my mom has put together, so it has to be me that's the problem."

I shook my head. "It's still bigger than that, Tasha. It's not just about you. It's still a big risk for my people. Maybe not physically, but we're talking about upending everything they know. Your mom will impose an artificial power structure. It's one of the things I admire about her, but who's to say Peter won't come out above James because Peter has the experience tracking werewolves? Your mom can enforce that kind of artificial dominance, but that doesn't mean it's going to make James very happy."

Tasha shrugged. "It's not necessarily about any one person being happy, Alec. If that's what's best for the pack, then that's what Mom will do. If James, for instance, ends up in a position he hates then he's always free to leave."

"He'd be dispossessed. It's rare for one of the dispossessed to find another pack, at least not without challenging."

"My original statement still stands. If it's what's best for the pack then it's the right thing to do."

I was still skirting around the issue, but I needed to buy some time.

"So if I were to say yes, how would I know that I'd still be able to send James to New York to help? Once your mom is top dog there isn't anything to stop her from recalling Jas and Isaac and refusing to send James anywhere."

I got another confused shrug. "Put it in the negotiations with Mom before you agree. She wants you on board in a big way. She'll give on a lot of points to make that happen."

I shook my head. "It's not about tomorrow or the day after, Tasha. It's about the fact that I won't have the ability to chart the course I think is best for my people. At some point, we'll be up against a situation that isn't covered by the terms of my agreement with your mother and then I'll just have to do whatever she wants done."

"She's not an ogre, Alec. She'll listen to reason."

"Eventually we'll disagree, Tasha. It's inevitable. I know that I'm risking my people by leaving us out here exposed to additional challengers, but I can't get around the fact that handing off my responsibility to your mother feels wrong."

The vulnerability was gone, and the fire was back.

"I think that's just ego talking, Alec, but I think we should park all of that for a minute and talk about me. Don't think I didn't notice your very careful evasion a couple of minutes back. This is as much or more about me than it is about my mom."

She was forcing my hand. I opened my mouth to respond, but I didn't know what to say. The silence stretched into several seconds and then Kristin burst into the studio.

"I just had another dream, Alec!"

As both of us turned to look at Kristin, I caught a look from Tasha that said this wasn't over.

"Calm down, Kristin. Just tell us what happened and we'll come up with options that we like better than whatever you saw."

She nodded, but I could see the panic still lurking behind her eyes. "You were somewhere else, somewhere I'd never seen before, and you were fighting another hybrid. You were hurting him and he was hurting you, but your wounds were bleeding more than they should have. He...he killed you, Alec."

It wasn't a very promising view of the future, but I tried to keep my voice even and coax more details out of her.

"What else can you tell me? Other people that were there, details of the surroundings? Anything might help."

Kristin shrugged. "Mostly they were just people that I'd never seen before. Big guys with lots of tattoos and piercings. I think I saw James and Dominic there. Ash was there, but I'm not sure about anyone else. The focus of the dream was on the fight."

"No split timelines showing us a way to win?"

Kristin shook her head. "No, just a sense of inevitability. I don't know how we got there or what led up to the fight, but whoever that is, he's going to kill you, Alec."

"You're positive I was dead? I wasn't just unconscious?"

"Yes. You...you weren't breathing. That and your opponent made sure you were dead."

I looked back at Tasha and I could tell she was thinking the same thing I was.

"Thank you, Kristin. You can go back to sleep now."

After it was just Tasha and me in the studio again, I found myself cleaning my brushes. The silence grew uncomfortable after a couple of minutes, and Tasha was the first one to crack.

"It had to have been Agony, and he had a full complement of Coun'hij thugs with him."

"Yeah. The wounds bleeding like she said they were would match up with Agony's power."

"What are we going to do about it?"

I found myself shrugging. It wasn't that I didn't care; I just couldn't imagine a world where there was anything I could do about the future that Kristin had just seen.

"We aren't going to do anything, Tasha. If Agony finds a way to maneuver me into a fight then I'll die just like Kristin says. My dad wasn't a match for him and I'm not as good of a fighter as my dad was. With Agony, it's always a question of fighting him or sacrificing something you care about. It's just the way he works. If he asks for something I can't give up then I won't have any choice."

Tasha shook her head violently. "No, there are other options. Get Mom up here and have her shadow you. Agony can't take her. If he pushes the issue, she can step in and stand in your place."

I was suddenly tired. Tasha was older than me, but she didn't understand what it was to be dominant. She understood intellectually, but she didn't really know. Not deep down inside where the beast made decisions and the man had no choice but to try and shape things to an outcome that was acceptable to both.

"Nothing has changed, Tasha. Your mom isn't going to want to buck the Coun'hij, not unless we've agreed to merge the packs. Even if she were willing, I don't think I could let her bring that kind of penalty down on her pack, not unless I was willing to stand shoulder to shoulder with her and help weather the storm."

Tasha had been slowly walking towards me while I was speaking. As I finished, she reached up and slapped me. Not hard enough to rile my beast up, not hard enough to injure me, just hard enough to tell me she wasn't happy. She walked out of the studio without saying a word.

I finished cleaning up and then closed my bedroom door and stumbled to my bed. It was too early for me to go to sleep. There was a decent chance that Adri was still asleep, but I couldn't bring myself to care. We hadn't shared a dream yet and surely we'd had some overlap over the last few weeks.

Interlude

I knew I was dreaming almost instantly. Given the state of things right now, I couldn't imagine any other circumstance where I'd waste time with a stroll through our estate. I recognized my surroundings, and I found myself shaping my course through the hedge maze so that I'd end up at the pond.

It was another of my refuges that I hadn't visited since Adri had left. Just like so many other things, it had been poisoned slightly by the knowledge that I wouldn't be able to go there with her ever again. The pain had lessened a lot lately though. Kristin's news from earlier had pretty much put the final nail in the agony.

It didn't matter so much anymore that she had left. I didn't have much time remaining to me. I could either spend it hiding from my past, or I could embrace it and try to squeeze whatever enjoyment out of it that I could.

The pond was just like I remembered it, a lush sandy beach with freshwater fish darting back and forth in the warm water. I stepped up to the edge of the water stripped down to my ha'bit. A few minutes later I was floating on my back in almost perfect stillness.

I heard Adri approaching from within the hedge maze for several minutes before she actually arrived. I knew it was her even before I could see or smell her. There was no explanation for how I knew, I just knew. I used a flick of my wrist to move me around so I could turn my head and see her as she walked onto the sand. She stood on the sand for nearly a minute watching me float, watching me watch her.

I was still wondering how long we'd stay there without speaking, when she stepped forward into the water and suddenly wasn't wearing jeans and a white top. Her street clothes had been replaced with a lovely, light green two-piece. I watched as the water crept up her beautiful white legs and swallowed her firm stomach. A couple of seconds later she was floating on her back only a couple of feet away from me.

"Have we done this before, Alec?"

"Floated here together or shared a dream?"

"Both...neither. I'm not sure. I guess this just feels familiar. Kind of comfortable—like I've done it before."

It seemed the threat hanging over my head was going to cut through my normal defenses. I opened my mouth to 'talk about the weather' and instead found myself turning so I could look her in the eye.

"How have you been, Adri? I mean, how have you really been? I've missed you. I knew I would miss you after you left, but I didn't realize it would leave this kind of gaping hole inside me. It seems like I no longer have the will to do what needs to be done."

Adri held my gaze, and for a second it was like she sucked me into her eyes. There wasn't anything else but the two of us, and that felt like it was how things should be.

"It's been hard for me too. I...I guess I'm kind of stuck. It's like I made the wrong choice, and now I can't get past it."

I shook my head gently, sending tiny waves out from my face to touch her. "No, more and more I think you were right. I just can't seem to find a way to get back on the path I was on before Agony visited us. I want to, but I'm just not sure how to do it."

Adri got a faraway look on her face. "Have we had this conversation before? It feels familiar too."

"Maybe. I don't remember, but I know I've had it inside my own head countless times since you left."

"How do we know this is for real?"

I shrugged, sending out more ripples. "I'm not sure it is. Ultimately, it doesn't really matter. I don't have much time left, Adri."

She abruptly stood, pulling me around so I had to stand and look at her. "What is going on, Alec?"

"I'm not sure. The new girl in the pack had a vision. Agony killed me in it. She's never predicted anything more than a day or so in advance though, so I can't have long until it comes to pass."

I'd started looking away from her as I'd talked, unable to bear seeing what I was about to lose, but she put her hands on either side of my face and brought it back around so I had to meet her eyes.

"We have to stop it from happening."

"There's no way, Adri. Agony always charges too high a price for survival. My father knew that, but it's taken me longer than it should have to understand that."

I could see the tears starting to form at the corners of her eyes, but I gave her my best smile as I pulled her hands down to my chest and then reached up and wiped her tears away. Adri buried her head in my chest, I think more to save me from having to watch her cry than out of any weakness. She was so much stronger than I'd realized back when we'd been dating.

"I don't care whether or not this is just a dream, Alec. If I remember this when I wake up, then I'm coming straight out to Utah. I'll swallow my pride and beg for your forgiveness. I'll plead for you to love me again and then I'll do whatever I have to do to earn my way back into your heart."

It was my turn to gently pull her face up so I could see her eyes.

"You don't need to ask for forgiveness, Adri. I haven't stopped loving you, and my heart has been yours almost from the first day we met. I forgave you a long time ago."

I could feel my voice getting rougher as tears started threatening to undo my composure.

"I'm...glad we had our time together. I'm thankful that I got to tell you how I felt one last time, Adri. I guess I hope that this is real, that you aren't a figment of my imagination, but I hope you don't remember any of this when you wake up. Seeing you again would just make it harder to do what I'm going to have to do."

The dream started to dissolve around me, but I locked gazes with Adri until the very last of the dream was gone. My memories of the last few minutes started disappearing only a few moments after the blackness came for me. I couldn't have come up with a better last request myself. Not if I'd had weeks to think of it rather than just a few hours.

Chapter 16

Adriana Paige
Upper East Side
Manhattan, New York

We'd seen Russ out and then Dom had escorted me back to her place. It had been obvious that I was just in the way, so I'd gone back to my bedroom in the hopes that once I was out of sight that she'd be able to just get on with the business of saving Ben and making sure Mom and I didn't end up with some kind of vampire hit squad knocking on our door at some point in the next few weeks.

I fell asleep a few minutes after I flopped onto my bed and didn't wake up until Jasmin barged into my room.

"Sorry, Adri. I know you're tired, but can we talk? I've heard Dom's version of things, but I'd really like to hear your side of things while it's still fresh in your mind."

As I looked up at Jasmin I saw her expression change and then realized a few seconds later that I was crying.

"What's wrong, Adri?"

I wiped my tears away and tried to get control of myself, but I was finding it surprisingly hard to stop new tears from replacing the ones I'd wiped away.

"I don't know. I thought maybe I was just really glad to finally see you again, but I don't think that's it. It almost feels like something really sad happened in my dream, but I can't remember anything about it."

"Nothing?"

"I think maybe I was happy and I felt really safe before the bad thing."

An idea floated up from the deepest recesses of my psyche and I almost couldn't bring myself to ask the question.

"Jasmin, is Alec okay? I can't explain it, but I feel like something bad happened to him."

The snort I got in response was hardly the kind of thing you'd expect out of someone who looked like a supermodel, but Jasmin pulled it off.

"Alec is the best he's ever been. I saw him only a few hours ago with that slut Tasha. He's got two of the bruisers from her pack standing by to pummel any challenger who might show up, and right now the biggest danger he's in is that he might stumble into Tasha and bruise his lips against her face."

I let out a gasp. I almost attributed it to my normal difficulty hearing Alec's name, but there was something else there, something that didn't feel right. I was blindly reaching for the answer but Jasmin was my only clue.

"That's not like you, Jasmin. What's really going on?"

She looked at me for a second and for the first time in ages, I could see the frustration at her core. Her incredible beauty was so blinding that sometimes it was hard to see past it to the person underneath everything.

Jasmin put her head in her hands for a couple of seconds and then stood up and closed the door.

"Do you have a privacy box in here?"

"I think that's it over on the dresser."

Dom would have sat down next to me on the bed. Jasmin turned the white noise generator on and then paced the full length of the room as she was talking.

"You know how I've been able to beat James and even Isaac sometimes? Well, that shouldn't be possible. The only reason I even had a chance against them is because one of my ancestors cheated."

"What do you mean?"

"Thanatas was the second king over the northern shape shifters. His father, Jaldul, created the monarchy through little more than brute force of personality. He created a web of alliances that ultimately united every pack under his rule and then broke the back of the southern invasion. What the histories tend to gloss over is that the war took decades. Thanatas grew up knowing nothing but war."

My eyes were as wide as they'd ever been. This was exactly the kind of information I'd wanted to know when I'd been in Sanctuary, but which Alec had been reluctant to tell me.

"Thanatas seemed to think of peace as some kind of mythical thing. He made some very bad decisions that ultimately cost him the monarchy, but before that happened, he had four sons and he passed on a measure of his gift to them."

"What does that mean?"

Jasmin smiled bitterly. "It means his descendants have an unfair advantage. Thanatas' power was the ability to make small, gradual changes to his body that made him faster and stronger than even any hybrid should have been. Some of those changes apparently were dominant genetic traits. Any descendant of the royal line has a chance to manifest a kind of juiced-up version of the normal wolf or hybrid form. Think faster, stronger, harder to kill."

Bits of information were starting to click into place for me. "That's how Alec was able to be so clearly dominant to Isaac and James."

"Bingo. The thing is, you only get one souped-up form, either wolf or hybrid. I manifested my 'royal' hybrid form back before anyone else in either pack had become hybrids, so for a little while there, Alec and I traded off on who was top dog. Once Alec became a hybrid then he got all of the royal goodies. I think Donovan suspects some of the truth. He spends too much time fixing Alec and me up to not get at least a clue here and there when Alec's circulatory system doesn't look right, even for a hybrid, but as far as I know you're the first person outside of the royal line to have ever been told that we get extra advantages the rest of the shape shifters don't get."

Jasmin was still pacing, but if anything, she was more worked up now rather than less. My hope that the movement would burn off the edge of whatever was bothering her was obviously vain.

"I've lost my royal traits, Adri. I'm not better than any other wolf, in fact in some ways I'm worse. I keep acting like I still have extra speed that just isn't there. It almost got me killed a little while ago."

"Are you sure? It's not just the effects of whatever has been bothering you, Dom and Rachel?"

"I'm sure. It all just fits too nicely together."

Her words didn't match with her expression or tone. My chest went tight as I realized that, for Jasmin at least, losing the extra vitality that had seen her through so much danger somehow wasn't the worst part of what she had to tell me.

"It's Alec. He's the reason. Who are the three members of the pack who are the most loyal to him? Rachel would lie across a railroad track and wait for a train to hit her if Alec told her to. Dom's nearly as bad, and I'm obviously worse than I thought."

"What do you mean?"

"I know that he's feeding on me somehow. His power is actually working, it just works all the time rather than in a sudden burst like what took Brandon's pack down. I know it, but I haven't left yet. I've dropped all kinds of hints, but he's never reacted in the slightest. He can lie when he needs to, but not like this. He's consuming all three of us, and I still can't bring myself to just leave him to die all by himself."

A couple more pieces dropped in place inside my head. "That's why Dom has been feeling better when she's all the way out here. His power must not work when the...victims aren't close by."

Jasmin nodded and finally collapsed onto the bed next to me. "Yeah. That was the bit that finally put it all together for me. That and the fact that I think Alec is getting physically stronger. I saw him do something the other day that shouldn't have been possible. He's turned into some kind of metaphysical vampire."

I wrapped my arms around Jasmin and put my head on her shoulder. "We'll figure something out."

"I hope so, Adri, but I just can't see any options. We're getting ringed in at every turn and I just can't see a way out of this. Not one that I'd be able to take and then still live with myself after it was all over."

Chapter 17

Jasmin Bianchi
Outside of Up Town Customs
Brooklyn, New York

I looked out the van window at the mostly darkened street and found myself tapping my fingers on the dashboard. We weren't far enough out for Brooklyn to have turned into something very rural, but at least there weren't as many neon signs around.

Adri had been fighting a severe headache ever since the night Ben called. It wasn't bad enough to go to a doctor over, but I was starting to worry about her.

She'd told me everything she could remember about Ben's call, the night they'd seen him at the book signing, and the time he'd texted while she'd been on a date with Albert. I'd filed everything she'd said away and then left so she could go back to sleep. I was pretty sure she'd spent at least the next few hours worrying about my latest set of Alec revelations, but there wasn't anything I could do to take it all back now.

Usually I was smarter than that. Adri wasn't the kind of person you could drop a bomb like that on and then expect them to shrug it off like nothing had happened. It was one of the reasons she was so likable.

She hadn't been sleeping well the last couple of days. There was a definite pattern where the headaches were their worst early in the morning, and then they seemed to taper off in the evening. Assuming Isaac and I made it through the next couple of hours, I was going to suggest we give her something to really knock her out tonight and see if that made things better. Alec could have Dr. Samuels call a prescription out here pretty much on the drop of a hat.

Isaac snapped his fingers to get my attention and I nodded. He was right. A few minutes before we launched an operation that could get us killed wasn't the time to be woolgathering.

"You still sure you want to do this tonight, Jas? Even another couple of days of surveillance could make a big difference."

"Unless you tell me that you won't go in tonight, I want to do it now. I don't trust those parasites. If they've realized that Ben called us, they may have already done something drastic to him. Even if they haven't, he has to be getting antsy. I don't want him doing something stupid because he thinks we're not coming for him."

Isaac nodded and I worried again at how morose he was getting. Isaac and I weren't close enough for girl talk, but it was obvious he still hadn't worked through his crap where Alec and the rest of the pack were concerned. There was a lot of that going around.

"Okay, tonight it is. It looks like three a.m. is the best time from what we've seen so far. You want to get some sleep before we roll?"

"No, I slept before I came out here to relieve you. Why don't you go ahead and crash in the back of the van. I'll just run through the building blueprints again."

"Sounds good. Just don't get too fixated on them. A place like that could have all kinds of modifications to the floor plan since it was built."

"Yeah, I know. Dealing with mind readers makes everything tougher. If this were just a regular bunch of drug runners, we could at least get someone inside to look around and tell us what the public areas look like."

"Woulda, coulda, shoulda. We'll just have to do the best we can. In and out quick and hope they left Ben there by himself."

"You think we'll actually get that lucky?"

"Everything points that way, but no, I don't. Nothing's gone our way since Agony showed up in town the last time. We'll end up having to fight our way in."

"You're turning into a pessimist."

"School of hard knocks and all that."

Isaac worked his way to the back of the van and then lay down in the aisle between the two banks of equipment. He dropped off to sleep almost instantly, and I was left to face the next couple of hours of waiting by myself.

The shop where they were holding Ben had been quiet since about ten, and nothing particularly exciting happened while I waited except for a recurring feeling that I was being watched. Under other circumstances, it would have been enough to make me call off the op, but I wasn't leaving Ben in there for any longer than I absolutely had to. I woke Isaac up twenty minutes before go time and we stripped down to our ha'bits.

I gave the word to Ash's hacker over an encrypted messaging line, and thirty seconds later, every light for three city blocks went out. We were less conspicuous on two legs, so we jogged up the street toward the shop. My shoulders itched the whole way.

The yard where they stored the vehicles they'd been paid to modify was secured with a giant chain and a padlock. Isaac transformed his hand to the wicked, semi-retractable claws of his hybrid form and sheared through the lock without breaking stride.

The phone relay for the alarm system had taken some work to track down, but it turned out that some idiot had run it from the roof up to the nearest telephone pole. Apparently your garden-variety vampires weren't very good with technology, and their contractor had pulled a fast one on them.

I positioned myself against the exterior wall of the building and braced myself as Isaac ran toward me. I made a stirrup out of my hands and launched him as high as I could. Just as I'd expected, the impact pretty much leveled me. Isaac was a big boy, but I managed to help get him an extra six or seven feet of vertical. He sank both clawed hands into the side of the building and then reached up and grabbed the eaves of the second story that his jump hadn't quite made it to. A few seconds later, he'd cut through the security phone line and he was sliding back down.

Odds were decent that whoever was inside had heard something, but hopefully they thought it was some kind of big rat or something. We sprinted around the corner of the building and then Isaac dropped his shoulder and hit the door so hard that it didn't even slow him down.

I followed him through the door expecting to find one of the big, open bays where they worked on vehicles. I didn't expect to find half a dozen individuals, none of whom looked happy to see us.

Isaac dodged left as I dodged right. We almost weren't fast enough; I actually felt the first couple of bullets whistle past me as four of the six opened up with handguns. Unlike recently, my beast didn't need any coaxing to complete a transformation. She ripped up out of me with a fury that took my breath away.

There were plenty of tools and equipment scattered around the outside edge of the room. I ghosted along behind the clutter as I heard two of our opponents moving slowly toward the door Isaac and I had used to enter the building.

The smart thing would have been for Isaac and me to beat a hasty retreat, but I wasn't interested in smart right now. I waited until the one on my side was almost to the door and then I sailed over a large tool chest and hit him with all the force my nearly two hundred pound wolf body could muster.

The jump was a thing of beauty. I knocked him over and sent both of us rolling behind another set of machinery. He was still trying to figure out what had happened when I killed him.

If his scent hadn't confirmed that he was just a human, his reflexes would have. It smelled like there were seven or eight different vampires who regularly came through here, but we were only facing two vampires. The other three were humans.

Something went spinning through the air with a buzz and then a meaty thunk told me Isaac hadn't shifted yet. He was using improvised tools for now. Not a bad idea. He'd have an even harder time keeping his hybrid body concealed than he was going to have with his normal form.

"You two work your way towards them. We'll be right behind you."

That had to be one of the vampires. They weren't likely to be taking orders from humans, and I couldn't see very many circumstances where a vampire would be willing to let an armed human get behind them.

The humans were at a disadvantage. The shop was too dark for them to see very well. The vampires were probably in better shape though. The smart money would be on them trying to use the humans to flush us out.

I listened to the sound of footsteps as I quietly circled back around the way I'd come. Isaac apparently had the same idea. I felt a rush of power as he shifted and then his wolf form came ghosting towards me. Our prey was less than five feet away from us when we moved almost as one, springing out from around our cover once again.

These humans were more prepared than their fellows had been. They each got a shot off before we hit them. My beast snarled as a bullet creased my flank. It hurt, but it wouldn't impair my effectiveness. I ripped the throat out of my target and then rolled away as a sword came slicing through the volume of space I'd been occupying just a split second before.

I sprang again, trying to put space between me and the vampire who was so intent on skewering me. As I whirled around and set for another jump I got a glimpse of Isaac. He'd taken a shot to the chest. It didn't look like it had hit anything serious, but he was losing a lot of blood. He'd reverted back to his hybrid form now and seemed to be pressing his vampire pretty hard despite the wound.

I dodged to the side, just avoiding a thrust from my opponent, and then I danced back towards the center of the space. I really hated fighting vampires. They always had a sword or some kind of weapon on them, and it gave them a reach that was even better than some hybrids. My best chance was to move the fight somewhere with some room to maneuver and then see if I could coax this idiot into a mistake.

The next stab was even closer than the last, but I darted in and got a piece of his upper arm before spinning away again. If I'd managed something lower down I might have chosen to hold on, but with the upper arm there was too much chance he'd still be able to stick me. At least now he was bleeding. If nothing else, that could eventually shift the fight my direction as his weapon started to get harder to hold on to.

I dodged another stab, but this one was a feint, and I had to throw myself to the side at the last second to avoid a slashing attack. I still took a respectable gash on my right side, but that was better than dead, which was what I'd almost ended up being.

I caught another glimpse of Isaac as I rolled back to my feet and put more distance between me and the sword. Isaac had ripped a length of chain out of a piece of equipment and was using it to keep his vampire on the defensive.

I saw an opportunity develop and the next time my guy came in with a stab I didn't just dodge sideways, I lunged forward. The angle sucked. There was no way I could have used it to attack him, but I hit him hard enough to send him sideways as I streaked past and launched myself at Isaac's opponent.

My vampire called out a warning but he was a split second too late, and then my jaws fastened on the back of Isaac's guy's neck.

I hadn't had this much fun in a fight for ages. Isaac kept my guy backed off for the couple of seconds that it took me to finish off his guy, and then we were spreading out, flanking my guy. If you had to choose between keeping eyes on a seven-foot hybrid wielding six feet of chain or a slightly larger than normal wolf, you'd almost always choose the hybrid.

This guy tried pretty hard to split his attention evenly, but eventually he took his eyes off me for a second too long and my kill count went up to four. I changed back to two legs as I followed the most recent Ben scent trail back to a tiny room on the other side of the building.

Ben was sitting on his bed in a tiny sliver of light that made its way in through his window. He looked like he was debating whether or not he should be investigating the ruckus we were causing.

"Jasmin, I can't believe you guys really came. I was starting to think you'd abandoned me."

"No way in hell, Ben. You and I still have a lot to work out."

He took in the tattered condition of my ha'bit and started to offer me his jacket, but I waved him off.

"It's really cold out there. You'll need it more than I will. Let's get out of here."

I pulled his hand up to my shoulder to compensate for the darkness back in the main part of the building and then started leading him back to Isaac.

"How did you guys beat everyone? I mean, there must have been nearly two dozen of them between the crews of both dealers."

My blood ran cold.

"Isaac, we're out of time! There's another batch of drug dealers on their way. We must have arrived just before the meet."

He muttered a swearword under his breath. "There's gas in here. I've already taken care of the garage. You get Ben back to the van, and I'll splash some gas on the side of the building I chewed up on my way up to cut the security alarm."

"Can do."

I had Ben almost to the door outside when he suddenly went crazy, kicking and punching as he tried to break away. It had to be some kind of programming from the vampires, so I did the only thing I could think of.

"Sorry, Ben."

I hit him hard enough to drop him without needing a follow-up blow, and then picked him up and slung him over my shoulder. Isaac was already on his way back with a couple of incendiary devices we'd gotten courtesy of Ash's contacts.

I popped open the back of the van and slid Ben inside. Isaac was back a couple of seconds later.

"They are on three-minute timers. Let's go before the rest of the vampires show up."

Chapter 18

Adriana Paige
Upper East Side
Manhattan, New York

Mom had left on another trip, down to somewhere in the Caribbean this time, so there wasn't any reason for me to spend the night in our house. Instead, I'd crashed at the penthouse while I waited for the results of Jasmin and Isaac's attempt to rescue Ben.

Before she'd left, Jasmin had suggested I get some sleep, but I'd known that wasn't going to happen. The headaches always seemed worse when I woke up. Besides, I was too anxious about Ben. He'd been through so much already. Hopefully the rescue went off without any hitches.

I knew Isaac was worried. He'd said even less than normal around me, but he always seemed to be asking Jasmin for more time to do surveillance. Jasmin was relentless though, and I was pretty sure they were going to go ahead and attempt the rescue tonight.

Instead of sleeping, I spent the night pacing across the living room while reruns of some sitcom I'd never seen before blared from the TV. At about five in the morning, Jasmin called my phone.

"Are you guys okay? Did you get Ben out?"

"We got Ben out, but there have been some complications. We're just inside of the park, can you come downstairs and meet us? We're just off 86th. There's a kind of mini playground here."

"You guys can't come up?"

"I'm sorry, Adri. I know we're not supposed to let you wander around outside by yourself, but I can't come up and get you."

"I'll be right down."

Honestly, wandering around Manhattan, even the nicer parts of Manhattan, at night didn't necessarily top my list of things I was comfortable doing, but if Jasmin was asking me to come downstairs then something serious had happened. I'd just hurry and hope that if something happened, they'd be close enough to hear me scream.

There wasn't time to change, so I just pulled a coat on over what I was already wearing, slipped into my tennis shoes, and ran for the elevator. It was too cold to run, so I settled for a quick walk that wouldn't burn my lungs and tried to ignore the way the cold wind knifed right through the thin pants I was wearing.

I kept getting the feeling I was being watched. It got so intense that I started looking around, trying to find whoever it was that was following me, but no matter how fast I turned my head, there wasn't anyone there when I looked.

I told myself I was just being paranoid and tried to hurry a little faster. Ten minutes later 86th came into view and I relaxed slightly. Jasmin and Isaac were just barely inside the park. They were both bloody, but Jasmin was pacing while Isaac just leaned against the fence like he was trying to conserve his strength. As I got closer, I realized the entire side of his chest was soaked in blood.

Jasmin walked forward to meet me. "Thanks for coming down, Adri. I couldn't just walk into the building covered in blood like this. We need to go; the van is right there. We can be in the air in half an hour, and land in Sanctuary a few hours after that."

"Wait a second; you didn't say anything about leaving. I've got school tomorrow. I can't just leave. My mom will freak out when the school calls and tells her I didn't show up."

"I'm sorry, Adri, but this is the only option. Isaac will be okay until we get back to where Donovan can pull the bullet out, but I've got to get him back to Alec and the others, and I'm not leaving you here by yourself. Alec would go ballistic when he found out."

"So fly Donovan out here instead. That won't take any more time, and it will allow me to stay here. I can't just disappear again. The last time I got sucked into pack business, it caused major problems with my mom. I don't want Isaac to die or anything, but it will be just as fast to get Donovan as it would be for us to fly out there."

I could feel tendrils of power reaching out towards me as Jasmin tried to keep her beast under control. Whatever she might have said was preempted by every single light within sight suddenly flickering off.

Jasmin muttered an oath and looked at Isaac. "Do you think we can make it to the van?"

"Doubtful, but it's our best chance. We don't have many options at this point."

Jasmin grabbed my arm and started pulling me towards the street. We'd only made it a couple of feet when something out of a nightmare jumped over the wall between the park and the street.

I felt a push as Jasmin tried to get me out of the way, and then twin waves of power washed over me as both Isaac and Jasmin transformed. As I sprawled out on the pavement, I saw Jasmin dart in towards the creature that was attacking us, but it swept a huge, clawed hand towards her almost faster than I could follow, and she was forced to duck away.

There was just enough moonlight for me to make out some of the beast's features. It was big, like a clay hybrid that had been left out in the rain. Its features sort of ran together in a kind of unfinished look, but I noticed all of that more as an afterthought. Mostly, I just couldn't believe how big it was.

Isaac seemed to be trying to work around to its side, but it spun around and attacked with a blur of swipes I didn't even have a hope of following. Isaac seemed to dodge away from most of them, but something got through, and he went flying backwards through the air as the creature turned on Jasmin.

She was fast, faster even than I remembered her being, but the creature seemed even faster still. For a second or two Jasmin gave ground, retreating in an effort to keep it from getting ahold of her, but then I heard a yelp and saw it pick her up by her stomach and slam her into the fence hard enough that she went immediately limp.

Blood was pouring out of her stomach wound, but Isaac was back in the fight before the creature could finish off Jasmin. There was another blurred exchange of blows but it was obvious that Isaac was on the defensive. Isaac backed away, but the creature was faster and suddenly he was dangling by one shoulder from its jaws as incredibly sharp claws raked down his body.

I stepped towards Isaac, wanting to save him but knowing full well that there wasn't anything that I could do. All three of us were going to die in the next few seconds. Time slowed down as the creature tore into Isaac, and then suddenly, a slender figure stepped out of the shadows. There was some kind of sword in the new arrival's hands and it licked out, scoring a deep hit in the creature's arm.

The beast dropped Isaac and spun towards the man with the sword. My breath caught in my throat, but our rescuer ducked the blow and managed another strike with his weapon as the creature's other hand passed overhead. It was like nothing I'd ever seen before. The man wasn't much bigger than I was, but he'd just crippled both of the beast's arms in a matter of seconds.

One moment it was only heartbeats away from killing Isaac, the next it was fleeing away before the man with the sword could kill it.

"Come help me, child. We need to get both of them into their van quickly before it brings help."

"You mean there are more of them?"

I asked the question as I moved towards him and helped pick up Isaac, who'd already shrunk back down to his slightly more manageable human form. For a minute I thought the man wasn't going to answer, but once he had his sword sheathed and was positioned under Isaac's other arm, he finally looked over at me and nodded.

"There are more of them than you can possibly imagine. Someday soon, unless we do things just right, they are going to carpet the earth and bring about the end of everything."

We were almost to the van by the time my brain was able to gloss over enough of what he'd said to resume processing events, albeit in a halting manner.

"What was it?"

"It was one of the earthborn. Your friends would call it a werewolf."

I opened my mouth to ask another question, not because I had one in mind, but because I got the feeling it was important to get as much information out of this man as I could. He pulled the van door open before I could find my voice again, and then we were laying Isaac down in the back of the van.

"There should be a first-aid kit somewhere inside. Grab it and start bandaging Isaac. I'll be back in a second."

I'd seen the results of Donovan's handiwork enough to have an idea how to go about it. I found the first-aid kit and started taping the worst of the gashes closed without worrying about gauze. Hopefully Isaac's natural healing ability would do the rest.

A few seconds later the man was back, carrying Jasmin this time, and I got my first good look at him. He was dressed all in black with an odd-looking collar that I couldn't quite place.

"Take this and get to the front of the van. You drive while I finish up with Isaac, and then I'll start on Dominic."

I took the small electronic device from him and then stopped partway through climbing over Ben. "That's not Dominic. It's Jasmin."

I didn't realize just how calm the man was until I saw him really rattled.

"It's not possible. It was supposed to be Dominic here, not Jasmin. Where is Dominic?"

"She's back in Sanctuary with Alec and the rest."

The man stared blankly at me for several seconds before shaking himself and pointing at the steering wheel. "Please get us started moving, Adri. We don't have much time before they'll be back. We're off script now, so please drive fast. The GPS unit will guide you."

"I don't understand. How do you know my name?"

He looked up at me with a kind of terrible majesty I'd never seen out of anyone else before. He didn't raise his voice, but he pointed at my friends.

"I don't have time to answer any more questions for you right now, Adri. If you don't get this van moving towards the airport, you and your friends will all die. Not just Isaac and Jasmin, but Dominic, Alec and Rachel too. By the love of everything you hold dear in the world, please sit down and start driving."

Every rebellious bone in my teenage body wanted to take offense at the way he was ordering me around without an explanation, but I found myself sitting down and turning the key that Jasmin had left in the ignition. I couldn't have said how I knew he was telling the truth, but I was absolutely convinced that every word was painfully accurate.

The GPS mounted to the windshield and turned on without any problems. I could hear the man muttering as he worked on Isaac. Most of it was too quiet for me to pick out, but I caught an occasional phrase here and there. I got the feeling he didn't realize he was talking to himself.

"...inconceivable...talk to her? ...no, too dangerous...never meet...but she can't keep on like this...to go blind now...so many years..."

I drove as fast as I dared, considering that I didn't want to try and explain away three unconscious, mostly bloody passengers to a cop if I got pulled over for speeding. The muttering got too faint for me to make anything out, but that didn't stop me from trying. It seemed like forever, but it couldn't have been more than twenty minutes before we drove under a train. The sound of the cars rumbling overhead worked some kind of transformation on the man. It was like someone had flipped a switch inside of him and changed him back to the confident fighter who had driven off the werewolf. He climbed over Ben, Isaac and Jasmin and seated himself in the passenger chair.

"We don't have much time left. When you get to the gate, enter the code that will flash up on the GPS. That will get you inside the airfield. You need to get these three onto Alec's jet and into the air as quickly as possible. Dom, I mean Jasmin, should have called ahead and gotten the pilot up and ready to go. I left six syringes in a case resting on Isaac's chest. Inject one syringe into each of the shape shifters every half hour. That should keep them unconscious enough for you to make it to Shawn. As soon as you are inside the plane, you need to call Alec and tell him what happened."

"I don't understand. Where are you going?"

"I can't be there with you. Things need to unfold in a certain way, and if I'm there they won't go like they need to."

"Are you sure?"

The calm, unruffled man who'd fought off a monster, the one who'd reappeared as I'd driven under the train tracks, cracked a little again and I saw worry and uncertainty in his eyes.

"I...I'm sure of less now than I expected to be, child, but I can't go with you. There...there are things that I need to do still with whatever time I might have left to me."

He was quiet for several seconds as though trying to decide how much to tell me, and I suddenly remembered his comment earlier about being off script. I got the feeling he'd been following his script for a very long time.

"It is absolutely vital that you get Alec to meet you in Chicago. Isaac and Jasmin won't make it long enough to fly all the way back to Utah. If...if Alec tries to suggest an alternate meeting point, you have to convince him that Shawn needs to be involved. I can't explain why, but it's important. Also, it's important that you, Rachel and Dominic are all there when it happens. Make sure he brings Dominic and Rachel."

"When what happens?"

"I can't tell you that either. I can only ask you if you love Alec."

It was crazy, but it was somehow easier to tell him, a complete stranger, the truth that I'd been unable to fully admit to anyone else I knew. Alec wasn't just an ex that I had fond feelings for, he was the one person who I'd risk everything to save even if he never wanted to see me again. "Yes, I love Alec. Now tell me what is going to happen so I can save him."

He looked worried again. "What makes you think Alec needs saving? It's Dom...Jasmin and Isaac who are hurt."

"I don't know. It's just a feeling, I guess."

He muttered something else that sounded like 'more meddling' and then looked up and fixed me with a gaze that pinned me to my chair.

"I don't have any more time. All I can tell you is that your love for Alec is vitally important right now. You need to hold onto that love. Wrap yourself in it. Wrap him in it. Don't tell Alec this, but it's the only chance he has against Agony."

We were at the gate. The GPS flashed a string of numbers at me, and when I looked back at the man, he'd already slipped out the passenger door and was walking away from the van.

Chapter 19

Alec Graves
Graves Estate
Sanctuary, Utah

I was tempted to ignore my phone. It had woken me out of the first night of restful sleep I'd had since Kristin's latest dream warning.

"This is Alec."

"Alec, it's Adri."

A wave of emotion washed through me that was even stronger than I'd expected it to be. All of these weeks and months that I'd been waiting, hoping she'd change her mind, and now she'd actually called.

"I'm sorry, Alec. I wouldn't have called, but Jasmin and Isaac are hurt. We're taxiing down the runway right now, but I don't think they can make it all the way to Sanctuary."

Of course. She'd only called because her friends were hurt. The hope I'd felt just seconds before crashed, leaving nothing but duty, duty to my friends and my family. I rolled out of bed and pulled my pants on with one hand while the other hand held the phone. I was walking down the hall, shoes in hand, almost before the echo of her voice had died away.

"What happened?"

"I'm not completely sure. They got Ben—he's here in the plane with me—but Isaac got shot in the process. We were down in the park and then something attacked us. I think it was a werewolf; it was huge and it almost killed Jasmin and Isaac."

"Jasmin and Isaac wouldn't have been a match for a werewolf. Are you sure it wasn't another hybrid?"

"No, but they weren't a match for it. It knocked Jasmin unconscious and was about to kill Isaac when an old man with a sword showed up and drove it off. Then he got us all in a van and driving towards the airport. I've got syringes I'm supposed to administer every half hour, but he didn't say if I was supposed to start now or wait half an hour before the first dose."

"Give it to them now. The risk of an overdose from whatever it is isn't as severe as the risk that Isaac will regain consciousness and kill everyone on the plane."

I waited while she administered the sedative, my mind spinning the entire time. An hour and a half wasn't very much flight time. I needed a friendly pack with dominants who were strong enough to contain Isaac if he lost control of his beast. There was only one option. I burst into Donovan's office and felt my mouth drop when I saw Rachel standing under her own power for the first time in over a month.

Rachel gave me a sad smile, but I couldn't have said why she was sad. She looked healthier than she had in weeks.

"Hi, Alec. Donovan has just ordered the plane prepped for takeoff. It will be ready to go by the time we get to the airport. I've called Dom already. She's waiting for us in the garage."

I shook my head. "I don't know how you knew Adri was going to call me, but you're not coming with me, Rachel."

"I just knew, Alec. Call it a feeling."

Adri was back. "What's going on Alec?"

"I'm not sure, but Rachel has taken the liberty of getting the flight crew started. She's going to turn around now and go back to bed."

That last bit was said for the benefit of Rachel, but she just gave me another of those sad smiles and pointed to my phone. I didn't understand what she was trying to say until Adri cleared her throat.

"Actually, I think you should let her come, Alec. I can't explain why, but she needs to be there. Dominic, too."

My beast growled with suspicion. "What aren't you telling me, Adri?"

"The old man who saved us, he said you needed the people who loved you there when you stood up to Agony."

It was a moment I'd been anticipating for more than two days, but it was still harder than I'd expected to hear the location of my death confirmed. I took a couple of deep breaths and nodded to myself. It was only right that those who loved me should be present to see me finally atone for all of my mistakes over the last couple of months.

"Okay. Rachel can come. Get to the garage, sis. Donovan and I need to talk for a second once I'm done with Adri."

Rachel nodded, but just before she turned around the corner, she looked back at me with a look of disappointment. "Donovan loves you too, Alec."

I looked over at the man who had raised me and registered for the first time just how tired and old he looked. Somewhere along the line, while I'd been sulking like a thwarted teenager, he'd started showing some of the signs of whatever had been eating away at Rachel and the others.

"Would you like to come with us, Donovan?"

He knew about Kristin's dream. There was no way he should have been able to find out, but I was sure that he somehow knew. I got a short, choppy nod and a half bow. "Indeed, Master Alec. I would give anything in my power to avert it. Nothing short of a direct command from you will keep me from being there by your side."

I clasped Donovan's forearm with my free hand, nodded and then gently pushed him towards the door. All of the friction we'd been experiencing over the last few weeks was nothing compared to the bond we had. It was sad that it required things to get this bad before I saw that.

"Please get the rest of the pack up. Addison stays here with Mother, but anyone else who wants to come is welcome. It's not mandatory though."

Adri hadn't said anything while our little drama had played out in Donovan's office, but I hadn't forgotten her.

"Adri, where are you headed?"

"Chicago. I hope that's okay."

"It's perfect. I'm starting to feel like someone has attached strings to us all though. Nothing to do but dance to the music until it stops. I'm going to do everything I can to make sure someone is waiting for you when you land. His name is Shawn Bishop. If he's there, he'll get you somewhere safe until I can get there with the rest of the pack. If he's not there, then I'll try and have someone else waiting. Hopefully with more drugs and some medical experience."

"Okay, I guess I'll see you in a couple of hours then?"

"Yes. We shouldn't be much more than an hour behind you."

I hung up and almost ran over Kristin, who'd been standing in the hall.

"I just had the same dream again, Alec. It cut off sooner, but I think I know where it takes place now."

I managed a smile. Kristin went to such efforts to present a hard exterior to the world, but that was all undermined by just how hard she tried to keep everyone around her safe.

"Thanks, Kristin. It takes place in Chicago, I already know. I'm about to get on a plane, but I expect Agony will show up just a little while after I arrive."

"Why would you be headed to Chicago right now? You'll die!"

"I suspect you're right, but the price of not going to Chicago is too high. Go find Ash and tell him that I release him from his promise. The two of you are free to disappear into the woodwork again."

I dialed Shawn's number before I was even out of sight of Kristin.

"Hey, Shawn. It's Alec."

"Hey, Alec. What's up?"

I took a deep breath and then just launched into it.

"I've had a couple of people in New York for the last little while. They both got hurt and are flying back west, but I need somewhere to put them until I can join up with them and make sure Isaac doesn't lose control of his beast."

"You're thinking we could take them in?"

"Yeah. The people with them have enough sedatives to keep them under control for about an hour and a half, but it will take me longer than that to even get to you."

Shawn was quiet for several seconds. I covered a quarter of the length of the house by the time he responded.

"You don't ever ask for any small favors, Alec. You know how the Coun'hij will react to all of this. If they find out you've been screwing around back East, they are going to come after you. If they find out we helped you break the rules then they'll come after us too."

I stopped walking for a second so I could concentrate.

"Before you answer, you need to know that the odds are very good that Agony is going to show up within the next three or four hours. I'm telling you that because I want you to take care of my people, and then when Agony shows up, you're going to throw me under the bus. He won't come after you and your dad because he's going to be positively giddy that he's finally got me dead to rights."

"That's still a big favor."

"I know it is, Shawn, but you can either agree, and then live up to your word, or I'll hunt you down and kill you. It may be the last thing I ever do, but I will avenge my people if anything happens that you could have prevented."

Shawn sounded tired all of a sudden. "Okay, Alec. I'll meet your plane on the tarmac and then I'll keep Isaac under control and get him some medical attention until you can come and claim him."

"Thanks, Shawn. I'll see you in a few hours."

Tasha wasn't in the Lilac Room. I followed her scent trail back through the house, and it led me back to my bedroom and into my studio. She was looking at the portrait of her that I'd been working on. The work had captured me with a force I hadn't expected. It meant I'd spent my last couple of days painting again. It was nearly done, even the background.

She stepped to the side and I took in the last painting I would ever work on. The viewpoint was exactly as I remembered it. I'd painted her up on the top of the mountain at the far end of the estate. She was sitting down on the edge of the drop-off and seemed to be looking off into the distance.

"This isn't me, Alec."

"Of course it is, Tasha. You were the one who sat for me when I painted it."

"No, it's not. The outside is me, but everything else isn't me. It's someone else, someone more compliant and weak than I'd ever want to be."

"I don't see someone weak when I look at that painting, Tasha. That doesn't really matter though. I've come to tell you that I'm flying to Chicago."

"To fight Agony. I know already. You do realize that you're throwing everything away, don't you? You'd be better off disavowing Jasmin and Isaac and then accepting my proposal."

I shook my head. I needed to be in the air already, but Tasha deserved an answer.

"I can't disavow Isaac and Jasmin. Agony will kill them and never look back. We've been through too much together for me to do something like that to them. Please tell your mother that I'm sorry things didn't work out differently."

"You've decided against me, but you've never even bothered to tell me why."

I took a deep breath and then pointed at the picture. "It has a little bit to do with that. You see weakness; I see a strength that is on the inside rather than on the outside, a strength that sacrifices self rather than sacrificing others. That's what has always bothered me about the thought of marrying you, Tasha. There may be times when it's okay to sacrifice people, but that seems to be your default response to everything. If I marry you, then I'll be giving the darker, more practical parts of me the lead, and I'm not sure I'd like where that would end up taking me."

"Death? You think death is preferable to marrying me?"

"No, Tasha. It doesn't always have to be about avoiding one thing. Sometimes, it's about what you're choosing rather than what you're trying to avoid. The truth is that this was all decided before you even arrived here. It's just taken me a long time to realize it. You can have the picture, but I understand if you don't want it. You should probably take your people and leave though. It would be best to limit any connection with me. I expect Agony will be looking for a reason to make some hay out of what he's about to do to me."

Tasha stormed out of the room without another word. A part of me wanted to sit in my studio and give the moment the significance it deserved but there simply wasn't time.

The group waiting for me in the garage was bigger than I'd had any right to expect after the hell we'd all been through since Agony's last visit. Rachel and Dom were there. Donovan, too, of course. I hadn't expected Ash, but he gave me a wry smile that told me Kristin had delivered my message. She had ahold of Ash's arm, and while she didn't look happy, it was obvious that she wasn't going to let him go anywhere without her.

James was there. He gave me a nod that seemed to say he might not have come if Dom hadn't been so determined to come, but that she wasn't the only reason he was present.

Jess had already loaded Andrew and his wheelchair into her Escalade. I knew Andrew's primary concern was Isaac, but I suspected Jess was more concerned about Isaac than she was ready to admit, even to herself.

It was a tiny group to be throwing into the limitless maw of the Coun'hij, but if I played my part correctly then maybe Agony would only require one sacrifice today.

Chapter 20

Adriana Paige
Chicago Executive Airport
Wheeling, IL

The flight from New York had been nerve-racking for me. The pilot was a solid, no-nonsense guy in his early forties who'd pulled out all the stops to get us to Chicago as fast as he could, but I still worried the entire time that something would go wrong.

I injected both Jasmin and Isaac every half hour religiously and spent the rest of my time wishing I had the knowledge and equipment to do more than just sit there while Jasmin and Isaac slowly bled to death.

Ben never stirred, which just made things worse. I couldn't go up and bother the pilot just because I needed somebody to hold my hand and tell me everything would be okay, so I was left with nothing but the company of my own thoughts.

I was up and out of my seat as soon as we touched down. I checked both sides of the plane, but I couldn't see any sign of the welcoming party Alec had promised us, until we finally pulled into an airplane hangar that was set off a little distance from the rest of the buildings.

My knees nearly collapsed when I saw Shawn leaning against the side of a large, black SUV. He waved a couple of tough-looking guys forward as soon as the plane came to a stop. They were inside the plane a few seconds later, and I followed them as they carried Isaac out.

Shawn nodded to me as I walked down the stairs. "I should have known that you'd be mixed up in all of this."

"Me? You talk like I'm some kind of magnet for trouble."

"You are. Every time I see you things get worse than they were before."

I looked at him oddly. There was something about his tone that I didn't understand. "What happened after the last time I saw you?"

Shawn sprang forward and put a hand over my mouth as he hustled me back up inside the plane. He motioned the pilot out and then pulled the door closed and flipped on one of the ubiquitous white noise generators.

"You promised not to say anything about seeing Vicki and me. I don't care what kind of hell you can bring down on me. If you tell any of the people out there that you saw me in New York, I will kill you."

I should have been terrified. A part of me was, but the rest of me was calmly analyzing his words, trying to fit them together in a way that made sense.

"What exactly is your power, Shawn?"

"I've never developed a power, Adri."

He was lying. There was no way for me to know it, but somehow I *knew* he was lying.

"I think you just lied to me. You have a power, and it has something to do with knowing how much of a threat Alec is."

"You're delusional."

"No, I'm not. There is no reason in the world to think Alec could execute on any kind of threat to you. He's got a tiny little pack that is a baby step away from disintegrating. You, on the other hand, are the 'heir apparent' for the largest pack in North America. I know he's dangerous, but you shouldn't. Not like you seem to."

Shawn grabbed me by the throat as a wave of power hit me, but the calm portion of my mind choked out one final point.

"I'm not going to tell anyone as long as you come clean. You're the only liar here, Shawn."

He released me and then put one hand up on the side of his head. "I don't know how Alec puts up with you. You're like fifty tons of loose brick suspended from a crane. A stiff wind could bury anything around you in a heartbeat."

"Alec doesn't really tolerate me these days. Now 'fess up. You can always kill me, but that would just make Alec deliver on his threats."

"I do have a power, but my dad and I have kept it a secret for years. I can sense the...potential around people. When someone makes a promise or delivers a threat, I can tell whether or not they mean it. More importantly, I can tell whether or not they can deliver on it. I sensed it when you threatened Vicki and me back in New York, and I sensed it a couple of hours ago when Alec told me he'd kill me if I let any harm befall any of you. He didn't used to act this erratically. Needless to say, my dad is pissed."

I rubbed my throat and then nodded. "I won't say anything. What's next?"

"We go back out there and watch while my people get blood transfusions going for Jasmin and Isaac. Then we just wait for Alec to arrive or for the bricks to come crashing down. No telling which will happen first."

I checked on Isaac and Jasmin, but Shawn was right. They'd each been hooked up to an IV and strapped into cages. I protested their treatment, but I couldn't deny that they were moving around too much now that the drugs were wearing off for anything else to keep the IVs in. Apparently the cages were standard issue for dealing with severely injured shape shifters.

We'd been waiting in the hangar for almost forty minutes before Shawn's phone rang. I wasn't close enough to overhear any of the conversation, but he didn't look happy when he hung up.

"Agony arrived twenty minutes ago. Dad tried to keep a lid on things but apparently we had a leak. Six of the Coun'hij bully boys are on their way out here already. We've got maybe five minutes before they arrive."

"Your people leaked?"

"Of course they did, Adri. No pack the size of ours could possibly hope to keep everything a secret. We keep whatever we can on a need-to-know basis, but this little expedition was put together too quickly for me to keep it out of the pack grapevine."

My throat went dry. I still had nightmares about the last time Agony had shown up.

"What do we do?"

"We wait for them to arrive and then we go back to the compound with them. If I try to get any of you away before they arrive, they'll know and it'll be my people who suffer."

I opened my mouth to argue with him, but he turned on me with a flare of power that rivaled anything I'd ever seen out of Alec. I was a slow learner sometimes, but I could tell that Shawn had been pushed as far as he was prepared to go.

Two white SUVs pulled up a few minutes later, and half a dozen tattooed and heavily pierced men got out. I thought at first that Abaddon was running the show. He'd been with Agony last time, and he'd been one of the top dogs then, but when Oblivion stepped out of the second vehicle, I knew who was really in charge.

Abaddon might run his mouth the most, but it was Oblivion who made any resistance futile. He was one of those relatively rare hybrids who had manifested a power and his, at the very least, included the ability to strip memories out of a person's mind with a simple touch. He was the one who had wiped Jess's mind clean, and in some ways, it was every bit as bad as Agony's scarring power.

The Jess we all knew was long dead. The person walking around inside her body was someone else, someone who wasn't sure whether or not she could trust any of us.

Abaddon walked over to Shawn and then looked us all over.

"What brings you out to the airport on this cold frickin' day?"

Shawn shook his head. "I don't have to tell you that. I've just been informed that Agony has arrived, so I do have to return back to the compound with you, but nothing says that I have to tell you jack."

"Agony isn't going to accept that kind of answer."

"That's his prerogative, but you're not Agony."

They were working themselves up to a full-blown dominance fight. I'd seen it a dozen times before, but I was starting to see just how much sense it made. Shawn was dominant to his people and Abaddon was dominant to everyone but Oblivion. Rather than having everyone present kick the crap out of each other, it was faster and easier to have the two top dogs fight it out.

I didn't have a lot of hope that Shawn would come out on top. Abaddon had wiped the floor with Isaac, and Isaac had several inches and twenty or thirty pounds on Shawn.

Oblivion stepped between the two of them, and suddenly, neither Shawn nor Abaddon could back up fast enough. Oblivion was the only person from the Coun'hij without extensive body art. He didn't need it to intimidate people because his reputation was plenty scary all on its own.

That should have made his expression easier to read, but when he looked at me, his face was a perfect mask. He was at least as good as Alec when it came to his poker face, but I got the sense that Oblivion was tired. Not physically tired, more like emotionally and morally tired.

Oblivion gestured for Shawn and the rest of us to mount up and then gave Abaddon a look that seemed to say it was time for the other hybrid to get back to business. I could feel an incredible, almost inconceivable amount of power roll off of Abaddon. It was obvious he didn't like being pulled up short in front of us peasants, but after several seconds of locked gazes with Oblivion, he finally nodded.

"Did anyone important leave yet?"

Shawn shook his head. "A pilot who doesn't know anything. Everyone else is here."

"All right. Mount up, and no funny business or Agony will kill dear old dad for your sins."

Shawn pulled his phone out and started texting as soon as the vehicles were in motion. "I can't do much to head things off at this point, but I can at least make sure Alec knows what he's about to step in."

"Will it help?"

"Probably not, but I can't just sit around and do nothing."

The drive to 'the compound' was about half an hour, and the sun was just starting to send weak beams of light over the horizon as we pulled up to a massive gate.

A couple of minutes later we were tromping through the snow up to a manor house that was even older than the Graves Estate. Shawn had gestured for his guys to pick up the cages holding Jasmin and Isaac and he'd picked up Ben himself. I followed along behind them and hoped somebody would clue me in before things got too serious.

We filed through a house that had obviously been built with entertaining in mind. A grand central staircase dominated most of the entryway, but that wasn't where we were headed. Instead, we walked down a hall you could have driven a car through and then turned off into a much less ornate staircase. This staircase led down to a basement that was nothing more than bare concrete and sparse fluorescent light bulbs.

The gathering of people waiting down there was bigger than I'd expected. On one side of the room stood Agony along with another six or seven of the Coun'hij enforcers. The other side of the room was filled with a large group of men and women who all gave off a noticeable vibe of power. When everyone had said that the Chicago pack was the biggest I'd thought that meant the pack consisted of a dozen people, or maybe twenty at the outside. I'd been way off though because there were at least seventy people here.

Even if only a quarter of Shawn's pack were hybrids they still should have been able to easily crush Agony and the rest. The fact that they were going to allow Agony to dictate to them finally drove home for me just how much power the Coun'hij wielded.

Agony stepped into the center of the gigantic room and waited for us to reach him.

"I'm very disappointed that you weren't here to greet me, young Bishop."

Shawn shrugged nonchalantly. "When you choose to drop by without announcing yourself, you can't expect everyone to be here. Dad's perfectly capable of working through whatever you need to talk about. I don't need to be around for any of this."

"Oh, but you do. You see, some concerning rumors have reached me. I was reluctant to believe them at first, but I just can't seem to dismiss them no matter how hard I try."

All I could figure was that Shawn had ice water in his veins. He didn't even blink despite the fact that Agony was easily within arm's reach of him. The silence stretched out for several seconds before Agony turned and looked at the rest of us who had just driven in from the airport.

"I think my little rumor can wait for another day though. I'm much more interested in learning why it was that a significant portion of the Sanctuary pack has arrived on your doorstep looking like they've been through a war."

Shawn's cool cracked slightly. "That's not my business. I got a call requesting that I provide assistance for the Sanctuary wolves, so I helped. I've broken no rules by doing so."

"A call from young Mr. Graves?"

"Yes."

I could tell Shawn was going to make Agony drag the information out a word at a time, but Agony didn't seem to mind the game.

"Are you offering the hospitality of your pack to these four individuals? Do you stand ready to answer for their sins?"

"I have no right to extend that kind of offer on behalf of my pack. That decision lies with my father."

Agony smiled like he had just received the answer he'd been looking for.

"What say you, Ulrich? Are the Sanctuary wolves under your protection?"

I turned to look at Shawn's dad and was amazed at just how big he was. If you'd given Brandon an extra inch and forty more pounds of muscle, you would have had a younger version of Ulrich. The grizzled alpha stared at Agony for several seconds before shaking his head.

"They aren't under my protection. What are you going to do with them?"

"I'm merely going to let our laws run their proper course. If there is no one here who is willing to offer them their protection, then any individual with unresolved business towards either of them is free to...resolve that business."

Abaddon stepped forward almost like he'd been waiting for a cue. "The boy challenged my dominance the last time I was in Sanctuary, and the fight was never properly finished. I demand satisfaction for the slight I suffered at his hands."

Agony stepped back as if to give Abaddon room to work in. I looked around at the gathered shape shifters, but nobody looked like they were going to interfere. Shawn's jaw was clenched, but he was just as motionless as the rest. I stepped forward and felt every eye in the room fix on me.

Abaddon grinned like a child about to pull the wings off a butterfly. "Are you really foolish enough to challenge me, girl?"

"No, I'm no match for you, but I think that somebody wants to talk to you."

Confusion flittered about the room until I held up my phone and pushed the speaker button.

"One of Agony's thugs is here, Alec, and he's going to kill Isaac."

Alec's voice came out smooth and confident. "Agony, everyone there knows this isn't about Isaac or Jasmin. This is about me. The Coun'hij has been looking for a reason to kill me for years now."

I could tell that Agony didn't like this development. If Alec couldn't come up with a way to save us all then I was going to pay for having interfered with Agony's macabre theater, but I wouldn't have done anything different. I couldn't have lived with myself if I'd just sat there and watched my friends die.

"Alec, I'm very disappointed that you would level that kind of accusation at the august body that watches out for the interests of our people as a whole."

"Yes, I expect you probably *are* disappointed. Disappointed and angry, but that doesn't change the fact that it's true. Your careful evasions aren't going to convince anyone that this is anything other than a lucky break that allowed the Coun'hij to finally execute on the assassination they've been wanting to wrap up for ages now."

Agony shifted slightly and then leaned forward. "What are you saying, Alec?"

"I'm saying exactly what you think I'm saying. Leave the four members of my pack currently in your power alone and I'll give you the chance to do to me what you did to my father."

There was an almost inaudible intake of breath from the gathered shape shifters. Faces that had been grimly stoic looked almost on the point of protesting.

"I hardly think you're framing things in the proper manner, Alec, but there is precedent for what you're describing. If you want to stand in the place of your pack members then I'm not going to stop you."

There was no hesitation in Alec's response. "Good. They'd better be alive when I get there, Agony, or I'll hunt you down, regardless of how long it takes me."

"Your people will be fine. If you're standing in their place, then tradition prohibits them from being harmed."

Shawn stepped forward and faced the phone I was holding.

"I'll witness the promise, Alec. Your people will be held harmless."

There was a general murmur of approval and then Ulrich stood from the throne-like chair where he'd been sitting. "We all witness it."

It was obvious to me that Agony didn't like the way the Chicago pack was prepared to get behind Alec, but he didn't really have many options, at least not in the short term.

Alec and the others arrived less than half an hour later. I wondered what they'd driven, but it wasn't important. All that was important was the fact that everyone was there.

The entire pack moved towards me, and Shawn's people shifted over closer to the rest of the Chicago pack so that there were now three clearly defined power blocs in the room. Jess and Andrew were in the lead with Donovan limping along behind them. Then came a guy and a girl I didn't recognize, but I figured they had to be Ash and his girlfriend. They were unique in that they were the only people in the room who were armed. They each had one visible pistol hanging from a shoulder harness, and Ash had several knives where he could get at them quickly.

Dominic and James were next with Rachel close behind. Dom and Rachel came and stood next to me, each grabbing ahold of one of my hands, but my return squeeze was an absentminded thing. My attention was completely captured by Alec's appearance.

He looked like he'd dressed in a rush. He hadn't even taken the time to get a shirt, just jeans and boots, but that just made him more perfect. A light snow must have started while we were downstairs. Snowflakes dotted his perfect, muscular shoulders and chest but they were already melting and trickling down his body.

His presence hit me almost like a physical blow and my knees went weak. I managed to remain standing, but it was a close thing. Rachel hissed and I looked down to find that I was squeezing her hand much too tightly. I loosened my grip, but she didn't look very good. I hadn't realized it when she'd walked into the room, but now that I'd had time to look at her more closely, I could see that she belonged in a bed somewhere, not standing in a cold basement watching her brother prepare to fight to the death.

Agony started clapping sardonically, but Alec answered with a rush of power that literally took my breath away. It was possibly the only thing he could have done to shut Agony up so abruptly. Shawn's surge of power back in the plane had matched anything I'd felt out of Alec previously, but it was a pale shadow of the display Alec had just completed.

"I will fight you, Agony, but I will not allow you to turn this into anything but what it is. I'm fighting you because I refuse to be party to a system where our rulers manipulate the rules required by our nature so that they can kill innocents. The Coun'hij has all but turned its back on our duty to defend humans. The werewolves run rampant, and rather than helping organize hunts to trim their numbers back, you kill any pack caught policing its borders. I'm fighting you because the last time we crossed paths I sacrificed part of my pack to preserve the rest of my friends and family. I've realized that the only person I can rightfully sacrifice is myself."

Agony shook his head and then turned and looked at the gathered shape shifters. "You see before you the spoiled heir to a system we as a people rejected centuries ago. The rules we have are in place to keep us safe as a society, but he expects to be able to flout them and avoid the consequences. He is the one who hopes to use brute strength to twist our laws into protecting those they were never meant to protect. I take no joy in what I'm about to do, but when you find a cancer you cut it out before it can spread. The Graves family line is a cancer, nothing more, nothing less."

Agony fell back a couple of steps and transformed into his hybrid shape with a dramatic flare of power. Alec took a deep breath and shifted forms with hardly a ripple on the metaphysical plane. I knew Alec wasn't a match for Agony. I knew he was probably going to die for his conviction, but none of that mattered. I was proud of him.

The man with the sword had said that I needed to send Alec all my love, and in a very real way, it felt like that was what I was doing right now. I needed him to know how much I loved and respected him, but I wouldn't shame him with some kind of outburst just before this fight. I sent my love to him because it was the only option I had left.

Alec and Agony were still with a completeness I'd never seen before. They were like twin statues set to face each other through the ages. One moment they were motionless. The next they exploded into a violence I'd never seen matched before.

The fight was just getting started. An uneducated observer might have thought we were going after each other with everything we had, but they would have been wrong. Isaac wasn't the only one who had been toying with Abaddon's fighting style. I'd spent more than a few hours trying to tie it back to some form of human martial art that I already understood.

The breakthrough came for me when I realized that, for Abaddon, there was no defense. He didn't block; he attacked his opponent's limbs as a way of countering their attacks. It was a bit analogous to the stop-hit in fencing, but it relied less on that instant between when your opponent decided to attack and when they actually moved.

Agony and I were feeling each other out, neither interested in risking the kind of full commitment that would have been required to bring the fight to a quick close. Agony was content with a long, drawn-out fight because that would allow plenty of time for his power to take hold of me. He hadn't scored anything deep enough yet to be crippling, but it was only a matter of time before that happened.

He should have worried less about what he wanted and more about why I was willing to fight the kind of fight he was best at. Originally, it had been because I'd wanted my execution to make the deepest impact on the Chicago pack possible. If I was going to die then I wanted to make sure I was the most powerful symbol possible.

I still wanted that. I still hoped that my death would serve as a spark that would trigger rebellion. I'd thought in the past that it was goons like Abaddon and Marco who allowed the Coun'hij to stay in power, but I'd realized that was wrong. If the muscle that backed up the Coun'hij were to disappear tomorrow, the Coun'hij would eventually fall. Even without that, if the various pack alphas had just put their petty differences aside, then all of the Coun'hij's muscle and inconceivable power wouldn't have been enough to stand us off.

I was guilty, Ulrich was guilty, and Jaclyn was guilty, too. I hadn't been willing to abdicate my power in favor of a person, but I realized now that I would have abdicated it in favor of an ideal. It was too late for me to change my decision, but it wasn't too late to hope that Ulrich and the rest could see the truth that the Coun'hij ruled with our consent, however cleverly they'd disguised that fact.

I fought for hope, but I also fought because I wasn't ready to be parted from Adri yet. We hadn't exchanged a meaningful set of words since she'd left Sanctuary, but I almost believed that I could feel her out there at my back. She was a glowing pillar of love and strength with two equally powerful, but different, pillars on either side of her.

When you distilled my reason for fighting down to its simplest form, I was fighting for Adri, and Rachel. I was doing this for Dom and Jasmin. I was doing it for the people I loved and who loved me in return.

Agony feinted to the left, but it was the second time he'd used that move, so I took his blow on the outside of my arm where he couldn't get to anything too important and stepped in as I drove a set of talons into his right leg.

If I'd committed to the move it might have taken him to the ground, but it might have just left me open to a brutal riposte. I wasn't particularly interested in either option, so I jumped backwards and barely avoided his retaliatory slash.

We'd been going at it long enough that blood painted an irregular circle around us, but neither of us was in danger of bleeding out yet. Agony came in and then abruptly changed directions.

It earned him a long gash along the outside of my left arm just below the shoulder. On a normal hybrid it would have had a good chance of disabling the arm, but I had an extra ridge of bone that helped protect the muscle. Royal hybrids still had vulnerabilities, but unlike Brandon, Agony had only been in one other fight with a full up heir of Thanatas. He probably hadn't had a chance in the fight against my dad to realize just how different our anatomy was to what he was used to.

I let my left arm drop and hang limply at my side. The deception wasn't perfect, but Agony fell for it regardless. He came in with another slash, this one aimed at my chest, but I surprised him by slashing his arm with my *left* hand and then moved in and scored another deep wound with my talons, this time on the leg I hadn't managed to mark up yet.

Despite everything I'd decided before the fight started, I found myself pushing the tempo of the fight. A chink was starting to develop in his armor. A lot of hybrids didn't appreciate just how important their mobility was, but footwork was the core fundamental of a successful defense. If you let your opponent flank you and latch on from behind, you were finished.

If Agony's legs started giving him problems, then I had a chance of winning. It went against everything Kristin had predicted, but I couldn't just leave the chance of victory on the table without going for it. I'd already lasted longer than I'd expected to. Maybe my decision not to capitalize on one of the earlier openings had made the difference. Maybe my willingness to die for my beliefs had somehow changed the future away from what Kristin had seen.

I started working the perimeter, trying to force even more movement into the fight. It would tire us both out faster than the pace we'd settled into, me more so than him, but I pushed on regardless.

It took only another thirty seconds or so for me to decide that my new tactic was working. Agony was still fast, but occasionally I seemed faster, almost like I had an extra half step that he couldn't quite match. Blood was showing in greater and greater quantities as I managed to land blows to his arms and shoulders with increasing frequency, as he couldn't quite get around fast enough to stop all of my attacks.

With someone else I might have been tempted to step back and try to give the blood loss a chance to work on him. A few minutes might be enough to slow him down even more, but I already knew my wounds wouldn't be clotting like normal. His power would have seen to that. If I wanted to win this fight then I was going to need to finish him in the next couple of minutes before my wounds robbed me of enough strength to continue to match him.

I abruptly changed directions on him and created another opening that I used to land another slash to the side of his right leg. It felt like it was a deep one. It might be the break that I'd been looking for, but it was too soon to be sure.

I could feel myself heating up despite the cool temperature of the basement. I was pushing harder than I'd ever pushed in a fight, and the raw aggression combined with all of the blood I'd lost so far was starting to play games with my mind. I knew the fluttery feeling in my gut had to be psychosomatic, but it just served as another spur to finish Agony before it was too late.

I charged him, knocking both of his hands away as I stuck my left foot into flesh yet again and drove him to the floor. Rather than try to capitalize and go for a frontal clinch that would almost guarantee he'd have a chance to take me with him, I sprang away.

Agony used the momentum I'd just imparted to him to roll back to his feet, and there was a noticeable limp to his right leg now. A calculating, calm corner of my brain told me that the smartest thing to do would be to continue to wear him down. If he was faking then the safe thing would be to capitalize on his ruse and land some more blows. That would leave him with the choice of abandoning the ploy or risking even more damage which would eventually prove fatal.

I wanted to pursue that course, but my limbs were already starting to feel weak, and the rest of my body felt even odder than it had a second ago. I planted my left leg and changed directions yet again, but this time I was fully committed to the attack. I arrowed toward his left side and I knew the attack was good. I was going to pass by his left arm a fraction of an inch before he could get it into position to intercept me, and then I'd be behind him and the fight would be as good as over.

As it sometimes did in a critical moment of a fight, I felt time slow down. It was as though I had all the time in the world to see Agony suddenly push off with his right leg, moving with a speed that had been absent from our last several exchanges. I watched as his left arm came around much faster than I'd been expecting. He'd been faking and I'd fallen for it.

I crashed into him, but not before he sank his left hand into my chest, all four claws finding gaps between the ribs that allowed them to sink home into my lung. We hit the ground with enough force to send us both rolling, and the impact ripped Agony's hand free of my flesh.

I tried to get up. I'd suffered wounds nearly as severe in the past, but my body refused to obey my mind. Nothing would respond to my desperate commands; even my beast had gone strangely silent.

Agony pulled himself back to his feet and cautiously walked over to me. He sank the talons of one foot into my right hand and the other set into my left shoulder. As he bent down to kill me, Adri yelled and in the next instant the entire world seemed to crack.

The tiny singularity that had so steadfastly refused to heed my call for the last several months opened up wider than it ever had before. When I'd killed Brandon, my strength had been consumed to stop from being burned up by all of the energy I was drawing into myself. This time was different. This time the power that I was pulling in was going somewhere different, I couldn't have explained where it was going, but it wasn't draining me. Instead, it was energizing me.

Agony collapsed beside me. I rolled up to my feet and looked out at the gathered shape shifters. Nearly everyone in the room was on the floor. Ulrich was on the far end of the room, and he'd managed to remain upright in his chair, but I saw fear looking back at me from behind his eyes.

The only exception was Oblivion. He stood tall and proud, untouched by the pull of my ability. I reached out toward him, trying to bring him to his knees as well, but there was something inside him that was a distant cousin to the gaping hole inside me. He was like me, but different.

The singularity started to...wobble, so I tried to narrow the area of effect back down. It was like making a fist with a hand that I'd never known I had. I shrank the cyclone of power down until I was only pulling from Agony. The change seemed to have stabilized my ability, to have bought me time.

I looked out at the rest of the shape shifters in the room as they slowly pulled themselves back to their feet.

"I take no joy in what I'm about to do, but it is past time for us to stop allowing the Coun'hij to direct our aggression inward. Our natural enemies sit out there growing in strength. I will see them trimmed back, but before that can happen the Coun'hij must be brought down."

I turned back to Agony, but before I could strike he managed a scream.

"Kill him!"

Half of the Coun'hij bruisers started toward me instantly. I relaxed my grip on my power slightly and brought Agony's enforcers to the floor in two distinct groups. Those who had remained still, ignoring Agony's command, and those who'd tried to attack me. None of them had made it more than a few steps.

"We don't have a legitimate government anymore so might is the only thing that rules us now. By the might our Maker has granted me, I pronounce a sentence of death on Agony and those who were about to attack me en masse, in opposition to every tradition of challenge we've ever had as a people."

It had been me who screamed when Agony had been about to kill Alec. I'd sworn to myself that I would be strong, but when Alec had collapsed and been unable to get up, I hadn't been able to help myself. I'd cried out and squeezed both Dom and Rachel's hands.

When Alec's ability had re-manifested I'd fallen in such a way that I'd been able to see him still from my little spot on the ground. I'd watched as he'd realized that he finally had the power to protect all of us that depended on him.

The lure of that kind of power was undeniable, but when Alec looked at me I didn't see avarice in his eyes, I saw relief. More importantly, I saw hope there again.

I pulled myself to my feet along with everyone else when Alec allowed us to stand and I stopped breathing when Abaddon and the others rushed him. As Alec pronounced a death sentence on Agony and over half of his men, I saw him shrink back down to the human shape that in many ways represented what he was trying to accomplish with his speech.

I watched Alec shift his hand back to something with the claws he needed to carry out his pronouncement, and I watched as Alec ended Agony's life. It was terrible. I didn't want to be the kind of person who could watch someone die without feeling anything, but it was also justice. Agony had killed hundreds of people, and for their sakes, I refused to look away.

Alec moved from one fallen hybrid to another, killing each of them until he'd finished with the group that had tried to attack him, and then he looked over at Oblivion.

"I have no wish to fight you, Oblivion. If I let the rest of your men up will you guarantee their good conduct?"

Oblivion's nod was unmistakable, and an instant later, Alec shut off the greedy little black hole that I'd been able to feel trying to slip the bounds of his will. Oblivion waited impassively as the rest of Agony's men slowly got back to their feet. They moved like old men, like Alec had captured more than just the strength of their muscles, but maybe that shouldn't have been such a surprise. These were brutal men who'd hitched their wagons to the Coun'hij's star. It had to be a shock to see Agony fall and know they were walking out of here solely on Alec's sufferance.

Once all of the enforcers were on their feet, Oblivion led them out of the room without looking back. Alec stood in silence for several seconds while every eye in the room remained unwaveringly fixed on him.

"Ulrich, I'd like to talk to you."

"Is that a demand or a request?"

Alec sighed and pointed at the corpses he'd left scattered about the room.

"It's a request. I have no desire to kill anyone else. If you refuse me then I will take my people and leave, but I think a better course would be for you and I to talk."

Ulrich looked at Alec for several long heartbeats before he finally nodded and stood. As Alec followed Ulrich towards the stairs Vicky, Shawn and another man detached themselves from the rest of the Chicago pack to follow. James and Ash headed that direction too. I was pretty sure I wasn't supposed to be in the meeting, but I couldn't bear to let Alec out of my sight right now, so I followed along after all of the bodyguards.

Everyone moved quickly but I managed to stay only a few steps behind them. Five minutes later, Alec, Shawn and Ulrich stepped into a huge study. I tried to follow them inside but Vicki put a hand out and stopped me.

"You have no standing in either pack."

James growled and took a step forward, but Ash put a hand on his arm and shook his head. It wasn't an order, more like a bit of unsolicited advice, but James stepped back to his original position. The door wasn't shut yet so I could hear Alec's question to Ulrich.

"I know it's against protocol, but I'd like to have her in here with us if you don't mind."

It was Shawn who responded. "I'm here in an advisory capacity. It's not unreasonable for Alec to have an advisor in here with us."

Ulrich's deep rumble didn't sound happy. "Are you keeping counsel with humans now,

Alec? How can you guarantee that she can protect our secrets?"

"I can't guarantee anything of the kind, Ulrich. I have no good reason to request her presence other than the fact that I would like her here. I've...missed her."

Shawn returned to the door a second later and waved me forward. The inside of the study was only a hair short of opulent. Leather-bound books filled bookcases that reached all of the way to the twenty-foot ceilings. A massive desk dominated one side of the room, with stained-glass windows taking up that entire side of the room. I had a brief second to take in that the window seemed to be a scene with a king and four figures arranged before him, and then my attention was pulled to a group of chairs that was arranged off to one side of the room.

Alec and Ulrich were both already sitting down and Shawn was headed back towards the chair next to his father. I took the chair next to Alec and then watched while Ulrich picked up a remote that presumably turned on a privacy box.

"What do you want, Alec? I need to start damage control for the mess you just handed me."

"I want you to know that I was serious about what I said out there. Every word of it."

Ulrich snorted. "I could tell you were serious about it downstairs. You didn't need to drag me up here to tell me so in private."

"No, I didn't. I wanted to see where you stood, though, without putting you on the spot in front of your people. I won't start this out by destabilizing healthy packs. We're going to need every wolf and hybrid we can get if this is going to work."

Even I could tell that Ulrich wasn't impressed. He leaned forward and speared Alec with his gaze. "This can't work, Alec. You're one man, you can't be everywhere at once. Whoever throws in with you is going to be in constant danger of attack from the rest of the Coun'hij. You've struck a blow today but you haven't crippled them. Even if you managed to find their headquarters and wipe out every one of their enforcers, you still couldn't stand against Puppeteer. He'll bring an army of mind-controlled werewolves down upon you, and when they leave you'll all be dead."

"We're going to have to face the werewolves eventually. It's only a matter of time before they rampage through the world and destroy everything."

"I can't argue with that, but the way to kill the werewolves is a few at a time. Surround two or three of them with a couple dozen wolves and minimize our losses. That's not the way Puppeteer works. Is anybody really sure how many he can control at once? Fifty? Sixty? A hundred? Even if he has a limit to how many he can actively control, what's to stop him from staging them and bringing them in wave, after wave, after wave? Two packs can't stand against that. Hell, six packs couldn't stand against that."

Ulrich sat back in his chair, and for the first time since I'd arrived, he looked tired. Not tired like he'd just got done having Alec drain him of energy, exhausted like he was fed up with having his back to a wall, like he wished for once that he could trust someone beyond his family and his immediate lieutenants.

"Alec, I'd be lying if I said I didn't want to believe in you, but your dad and I talked all of this through more than two decades ago. Back when his pack was nearly as big as my pack, and he thought he was just months away from an alliance with Jaclyn. Even back then with more bodies than we could possibly muster right now, I still didn't believe it was possible. The other side just has too many cards in their favor. The best we can hope for is to wait Puppeteer out. Once he dies of old age, you and Shawn might have a chance."

I watched as Alec considered Ulrich's words and then shook his head. "No, there will always be a reason not to act. Between now and when Puppeteer dies, there will be more hybrids who manifest powers and join the Coun'hij. For all we know, one of the idiots that walked out the door with Oblivion is only days away from manifesting something that makes Puppeteer look positively benign. We need to act now and rely on providence to provide options for us. I will overthrow the Coun'hij no matter the cost to me personally."

Ulrich looked over at Shawn and waited for several seconds until Shawn reluctantly shook his head. I suddenly realized why Shawn was present. He was here to tell his father whether or not Alec could accomplish what he'd just promised to do. Alec needed Ulrich's support, and he wasn't going to get it.

I wasn't strong or dangerous, but Shawn's comment from back at the airport was running through my head. He seemed to think I had some kind of potential to make a difference. I didn't know if he was right or not, but I couldn't let Alec do this alone.

I reached out, took Alec's hand, and then cleared my throat. "I will do everything in my power to help Alec bring down the Coun'hij."

Shawn's head snapped towards me. It was a small movement, but it was abrupt. In someone else it would have been the equivalent of falling out of their chair.

I squeezed Alec's hand. "Promise to bring down the Coun'hij now, Alec. But remember, this isn't just about you."

Alec looked at me oddly. I knew he didn't understand what I was doing, but he nodded in trust and then turned back to Ulrich.

"I will use all of the resources at my disposal, my power and the powers and abilities of those sworn to me, those who support me in any way, to bring down the Coun'hij and usher in a new era for our people."

Shawn had gone completely still. Ulrich seemed content to wait him out, but I wasn't.

"Tell them, Shawn. Tell them exactly what you know."

Neither of the Bishop men were happy about the order, but it was Ulrich who stood up like he was going to do something about it. Alec rose to his feet a fraction of a second later and put himself between Ulrich and me, but it was Shawn who waved his father back into his seat.

"I'm the one who told Adri, Dad. She promised not to tell anyone, which she hasn't quite done yet."

Shawn looked at the three of us and then took a deep breath. "Alec, I haven't been completely honest with you. I developed a power a few years ago. I can sense whether or not someone can deliver on a threat or a promise. When you said downstairs that you were going to see the Coun'hij trimmed back, I knew you could do that, but I was surprised by the effort that was going to be required."

Shawn's eyes went distant for a moment. "You trimming back the Coun'hij will require blood and suffering on a scale I've only seen in one other potential promise. When you said just now that you'd overthrow the Coun'hij, I weighed the forces on both sides of your promise. Your commitment is pure. It is a cleansing pillar of fire that was poised to recruit powers that dwarfed your earlier promise, but it wasn't sufficient for the task you'd vowed to undertake."

For nearly a minute, Shawn looked at me in silence. "When Adri promised to help you, I felt the forces that she will somehow bring to bear, and they are only slightly less than what you were going to amass. Just now though, together, you're bringing potential power into play that makes anything else I've ever seen look like a drop in an ocean of violence. Together the two of you are truly more than the sum of your parts."

I returned Shawn's stare and then very deliberately asked the question we all wanted to know. "Is it enough? Can Alec...can we stop the Coun'hij?"

For a second I thought Shawn wouldn't respond. "It's not just the Coun'hij. I've felt the power of the Coun'hij, and they can't match what I just saw arrayed against you. There are forces at work that I don't understand, but yes. You can succeed...I think you have to succeed or there won't be anything left of the world."

Alec turned to Ulrich one last time. "Will you help me, Ulrich? Will you give our people, our world, a chance?"

Ulrich's nod was a short, simple thing, but I was realizing that it was simple things that turned the world.

"Yes. The house of Bishop will stand with you."

Chapter 21

Adriana Paige
The Bishop Compound
The Outskirts of Chicago, IL

I'd more or less moved through the rest of the day in shock. I'd tried to pay attention while Alec, Shawn and Ulrich had started planning for their war on the Coun'hij, but by that point I was so tired that it was all I could do to keep my eyes open.

Ulrich had called Vicki in and asked her to take me to the rest of the Sanctuary pack. A few minutes later I was in a different wing of the house, one that seemed to have been completely devoted to our pack's use.

Jasmin and Ben were sleeping peacefully next to each other in separate beds in one room. Donovan had judged Jasmin recovered enough now that she could be pulled out of the cage.

Knowing that she was going to fully recover took a weight off my chest, but Donovan said that Ben still hadn't shown any signs of waking up.

Rachel and Dom both looked surprisingly fragile, but I didn't wake them up, I just pulled each of their doors quietly shut and went to check on the rest of the pack. Isaac was worse off than Jasmin, but apparently Shawn's pack had a more than adequate supply of drugs to keep him from losing control of his beast. Donovan had set up an IV drip, and Jess was sitting at his bedside. She looked up as I came into the room.

"I know you from somewhere, don't I?"

"I'm Adri. We talked for a few minutes after Oblivion took away your memories."

"That's right, and then you left. Are you back now?"

That was the question. I'd just committed to help Alec, but that didn't necessarily mean he wanted me back in his life.

"I think so, but it's not entirely my decision."

Jess nodded absently; her attention was already back on Isaac. As I turned to go, she spoke again.

"I don't know what to do with Isaac. Things were going pretty well and then he blew up when I wanted to go on a trip with just my dad. Everything has been strained since he got back from New York the first time, he almost died last night, and I still don't know how I feel about him."

I wasn't qualified to give *myself* advice on matters of the heart. I was the last person who should be trying to help Jess sort out the mess that was her love life, but I found myself trying regardless.

"Don't rush things, Jess. What you and Isaac had before took years to develop. You just need to give yourself time. Eventually your heart will tell you what you want."

"How can I not love him? Everyone keeps telling me how much we were in love before. The only thing that's changed is me, so that means it's my fault if we can't get back together now."

I shook my head. "No, Jess. You're different, yes, but Isaac is different too. I can't explain it, not really, but he changed when you...went away. I don't think it's all just you. When he was in New York, he was pretty conflicted about Alec. That's different from the Isaac I remember from before."

I backed out of the room while she was still digesting that. Kristin gave me a nod as I walked by, but she obviously didn't want to talk. Donovan found me again a few minutes later.

"Miss Paige, we have a room prepared for you if you're tired."

"Thanks, Donovan. I think I'll take you up on that offer. I haven't slept in something like thirty hours."

I awoke a few hours later feeling a little better, but I still wasn't back to normal. There were six texts and a voicemail from my mom, but before I could decide what to tell her, Shawn knocked on my door.

"Hi, Adri. Can I come in for a second?"

"Sure, Shawn. What's up?"

He shut the door and turned on the white noise generator that I hadn't thought to activate before I'd gone to bed.

"You should know that I lied back there. My power didn't tell me that we can win against the Coun'hij and whatever else is going to jump in to try and keep them in power. The rest of it was true, but not that."

"So we're going to lose?"

"Would it make a difference if I told you that we were?"

"No, not for me. Not for Alec either, but I think it would for your dad."

Shawn nodded. "That's why I lied. My dad might suspect, but he won't know. You don't live in a family with so many ties to the mafia without becoming a good liar."

I took a breath and then nodded. "Okay. Thanks for telling me."

Shawn shook his head. "I'm not saying that we're going to lose, Adri. I'm saying that I don't know. I've never seen anything like it before. All of those forces arranged against each other and the decision balances on the edge of a knife. It should be impossible, but it's not. That's why I had to lie to my dad. I'm going to do whatever I can to make Alec's vision come to pass. Bringing my dad in on Alec's side is the first step."

It all made sense except for one thing.

"Why are you doing this, Shawn? What's your angle?"

He looked at me for several seconds before shrugging. "I can't ever seem to lie to you, Adri. Maybe it's because there isn't any challenge in it. I could tell you that I just want to try and avoid the devastation that will result if Alec loses, but that wouldn't be the truth, at least not all of it. I'm helping because it's a form of penance."

"What did you do?"

"Nothing. It's not what I've done; it's what I'm going to do."

Shawn left before I could ask him another question, but his words stayed with me. I was still considering them when Alec found me.

"I was hoping to be able to talk to you alone, Adri."

"Me too."

Alec walked over and sat down on the bed next to me. Someone had found him a change of clothes, and he'd taken a few minutes to get cleaned up. As I looked at him, I realized that his arms weren't injured.

"How are you healed already?"

"Honestly? I'm not sure. All I can figure is that maybe my ability was active from the start of the fight and it was stopping Agony's power from working. That or maybe all of that power that I sucked down at the end of the fight somehow reversed the effects. Even normal injuries shouldn't be healed already."

I nodded. It was another mystery that we might never have an answer for, but that was okay. The important thing was that Alec was going to be all right.

"I was worried that you wouldn't make it."

Alec's smile was full of wonder. "I went into the fight expecting to die. Kristin saw it in a vision, not just once, but twice. I knew I was going to die, but I decided I would rather die than take another step down the path that had made you leave me."

My face heated up. "I'm sorry, Alec. I've had a lot of time to think about what I did and it was a mistake."

He tilted his head slightly to the side and looked at me. "Was it a mistake? A month ago I would have said yes, but I'm not sure now."

"I should have stayed and tried to help you see what I was worried about rather than just leaving."

Alec shook his head. "I'm not sure I would have listened, not really. Look, the important thing is that you're back."

"Am I, Alec? I know I promised to help you, but that doesn't mean you have to deal with me being underfoot all of the time. I didn't...I mean, I don't want to force myself back into your life."

I couldn't bring myself to meet his eyes. I was too afraid of what I'd see in them, and after everything, I guess I was still a coward. Alec reached over to me and pulled my chin up so that I was forced to look at him.

"Adriana Paige, I want you in my life. I never wanted you to leave. I may be able to see now why you leaving was a good thing, but I never stopped loving you. Please stay with me."

It was exactly what I'd wanted to hear, but I was so choked up that I couldn't respond. Alec refused to let me look away though.

"I'm serious, Adri. I've gone back through that fight trying to figure out what changed, why Kristin's dream didn't come true, and all I can come up with is that it was you. That fight was just like every other significant moment of my life. It's always been you who has given me the strength to do the right thing, the strength to win when everything else in the world seemed arrayed against me. I'd love you for that if for no other reason, but that isn't why I love you. I love you simply for who you are. You make me a better person and I'm going to do everything I can to be worthy of you."

His voice had lost its normal smoothness as he fought back tears, but he pressed on.

"You're the most amazing person I know. You don't wear your strength on your sleeves but it's there, it's who you are. You're strong, and you're beautiful. You're kind, and you're good. You're breathtaking in ways I haven't even begun to unravel yet."

I finally managed a nod. "I love you, Alec. I was prepared to beg you to let me come back, but you don't even hate me for all of the pain I've put you through."

Alec pulled me into a kiss and for a few minutes nothing else mattered.

Author's Note

If you made it this far, then I very much hope that you enjoyed Forsaken! When I sat down to write The Greater Darkness and took my first steps into the world that Alec and Adri would come to inhabit I had some vague ideas that there were places I could go that didn't involve just Geoffrey. A couple of years after that, I sat down to write Broken and while those vague ideas hadn't become very substantial still, my plans for the Reflections world quickly expanded into something much more ambitious.

I'm thrilled with all of the six Reflections books so far. Some for one reason, some for another, but Forsaken represents a real shift for me because it's the first time that I've started really laying some of the groundwork for the more ambitious stuff that I ultimately hope to accomplish with the series. Hopefully before you picked up Forsaken you read Broken, Torn, Splintered, Intrusion, and Trapped.

If that's not the case, please consider going back and picking them up, as well as *The Greater Darkness* by Eldon Murphy. There is a lot of backstory and other bits and pieces in those stories that will become more important as the series continues.

Scent of Tears ought to be on that list as well now that I think about it. It's just a short story, but in many ways it's where everything started for Shawn, and he's going to continue to be more and more important as time goes on.

Finally, you'll be happy to know that at the time I'm writing this (December 2012) that I've already started working on Riven, the next book in the Reflections series. It's currently about 10% of the way done and I'm hoping for an June or July 2013 release. Riven is another really exciting project for me because I'm going to use it to set things up for the next several books.

Acknowledgements

All of the usual suspects need thanked and as always I'm grateful for their help and support. There a few individuals who need special mention though.

Deciding that I was going to try and get Forsaken, Trapped, Brittle Bonds, and The Greater Darkness published by Christmas 2012 meant that I had to bring in some extra help on the production side of things. Ashley Case pitched in with editing and turned Forsaken around much faster than I'd hoped. Amy Jirsa-Smith and RJ Locksley did stellar work on follow-up edits and Katie Jane did a great job on the cover for Forsaken.

Lastly, I want to express a big thank you to all of the fans out there who help spread the word on a daily basis. Thank you! I'll do everything I can to keep this journey exciting.

The Greater Darkenss

Dean writing as Eldon Murphy

Something powerful is stirring in the darkness. Something so ancient that even creatures who've been alive for hundreds of years have long since discounted this new threat as nothing more than myth.

Normal humans will be caught in the crossfire, but then that's always the way of things. Geoffrey has no memory of his past life or any idea how to survive in the violent, dangerous world in which he's trapped. Despite his best efforts, he's about to find himself in the middle of a conflict that threatens to sweep away everything, and everyone he's been fighting so hard to protect.

Frozen Prospects

The invitation to join the secretive Guadel should have been the fulfillment of dreams Va'del didn't even realize he had. When his sponsors are killed in an ambush a short time later, he instead finds his probationary status revoked, and becomes a pawn between various factions inside the Guadel ruling body.

Jain's never known any life but that of a Guadel in training. She'd thought herself reconciled to the idea of a loveless marriage for the good of her people, but meeting Va'del changes everything. Their growing attraction flies against hundreds of years of precedent, but as wide-spread attacks threaten their world, the Guadel have no choice but to use even Jain and Va'del in their fight for survival.

About the Author

Dean Murray is a prolific author with dozens of titles across multiple pen names and more than half a million copies of his work currently in circulation.

Dean started reading seriously in the second grade due to a competition and has spent most of the subsequent three decades lost in other people's worlds.

Things worsened, or improved depending on your point of view, when he first started experimenting with writing while finishing up his accounting degree.

These days Dean has a wonderful wife and two lovely daughters to keep him rather more grounded, but the idea of bringing others along with him as he meets interesting new people in universes nobody else has ever seen tends to drag him back to his computer on a fairly regular basis.

Keep up to speed on Dean's latest projects at www.DeanWrites.com.